"How dare you, Lord Stoneleigh," Charlotte began, wrapping her towel securely about her head and rising from her chair. "How dare you come into my home with neither Sir John's permission nor mine. Does your conceit know no bounds? My hair isn't even dry and you come charging into my home as though you've a right to be here—which you most certainly do not!"

Before she knew what he was about to do, he had rounded the table and dropped to his knees before her, a quick, startling movement which caused Charlotte to back away from him. "Whatever are you doing?" she cried.

"Forgive me?" he pleaded. "I came for no other reason than to offer you my humblest apologies."

When she backed away from him further yet—disturbed once more by his bizarre conduct—he followed after her on his knees.

"It was very wrong of me to press you so hard last night, Charlotte. I don't know what came over me, some sort of madness just as you said. Only I promise you I have come to realize how wrong I was, how cruel and unthinking, and need only hear you tell me you will forgive me to be restored to complete sanity."

Why did she believe him? Charlotte wondered as she looked down into his eyes. She had sat up half the night fussing and fuming over his errant misbehavior and had decided he was too flawed for her to hope he might actually be a man she could share her life with. Yet now, she did not know what to think, except that already her heart was fluttering in her breast as it always did when he was near . . .

My Lady Vixen

Valerie King

ZEBRA BOOKS
KENSINGTON PUBLISHING CORP.

ZEBRA BOOKS are published by

Kensington Publishing Corp.
475 Park Avenue South
New York, NY 10016

First Printing: November, 1993

Printed in the United States of America

But love is such a mystery,
  I cannot find it out:
For when I think I'm best resolv'd,
  I then am in most doubt.
            —*Sir John Suckling 1609-1642*

To Marguerite, a friend most excellent

One

"Stop the coach at once! Stop, I say!" Charlotte Amberley cried in vain.

Miss Fittleworth, her companion and abigail of many years, bit her lip and whispered, "I don't believe he can hear you, my dear. His appearance was most unkempt and I daresay those cabbage-leaf orifices affixed to the sides of his head are full of dirt."

Charlotte chuckled slightly then glanced up at the peeling leather of the ceiling. "I am come to think a cannon brigade would not affect this man," she responded. To the driver, she again commanded, "Sir, pray stop!"

The wheels of the salt-weathered vehicle continued to spin at full speed in ignorance of her pleas. The hackney driver, besides having the heaviest pair of hands she had ever witnessed, was proving to be as deaf as he was cow-handed. Using her parasol of dark green silk draped with summery swags of white Brussels lace, she pounded on the ceiling of the carriage and again called out, "Stop the carriage at once! *At once!*"

When the horses at last began to slow and finally drew to a complete stop near the flagways, Charlotte breathed a sigh of relief. The hackney driver dropped from his box, landing on large feet and square, stubby legs. When he opened the door, Charlotte was again surprised by the sight of his gnarled, sun-worn face and a display of teeth, brown with age and abuse. His words, when he spoke, were even less pleasing than his assorted features, "And wat dee-lightful shop was Miss wishful of seein' *this time?*" he queried sarcastically.

Charlotte lifted a brow and spoke evenly, "I'll have none of your impudence, if you please. And now, pray return to that charming little shop with all the clocks displayed in the bow window."

Gnashing his teeth for a moment, the driver responded, "And at what hour—or should I say which day—was you hoping to arrive at West Street?"

"I don't see how it can be of the least significance to you."

"It's the stopping and going and stopping again. And *stop I say,* bangin' away at me ears until I'm ready to leap off the carriage directly under me horses's hooves. The horses don't take none too kindly to waiting for this and that—and, by God, Miss, you've enough baggages and packages to last twelve lifetimes."

Charlotte refused to follow the line of his gaze, which was aimed at her knees where over two dozen bandboxes and parcels of varying shapes and sizes trapped her feet and ankles to the floor of the coach. Instead, she addressed a subject of deeper concern. "Speaking of horses, have you bruised your hacks' mouths sufficiently for one day—or should I say—*one year!* Good heavens, man, your leader's jaw must be numb by now. But I have no intention of engaging in an argument. I insist you return at once to the clock shop or I shan't pay a farthing for your services."

"Miss Amberley," Miss Fittleworth clucked. "Perhaps we ought to consider completing our

8

journey. The hour is advancing." She smiled hesitantly at the strange-looking man, who broadened his smile alarmingly at her in return.

"Oh, stuff and nonsense! I have never been to Brighton before and I intend to greet my dear friends with gifts for each of them."

"You've purchased several already," Miss Fittleworth pointed out kindly.

"But Maude adores clocks, and I haven't seen her in ages. No, my mind is firmly set—we shall return to the shop. Now, do go on, my good man. The establishment I refer to was little more than a quarter-mile back. And had you responded to my command in the first place, I would probably have made my purchases by now. As it is, it is you who have kept your horses standing."

The hackney driver pulled his stained cap off his graying, straggly hair, slapped it against his knee breeches of brown stuff, mumbled several incoherent, though undoubtedly unkind epitaphs about *The Quality*, and regained his box.

With some difficulty and a great deal of complaining, he began maneuvering his way along North Street in an effort to return to a section of shops referred to as Prince's Place, making a turn in front of a heavily laden wagon to the curses of its driver. A hot exchange ensued, followed by more complaints, but at last the coach was headed in the proper direction.

Charlotte paid no heed to the continued mutterings of the irascible man. With great pleasure, she breathed in deeply the smell of the ocean and the damp clinging moisture of the salty air. Having lived a somewhat secluded life in Bedfordshire, a county far from any beach resort, the liveliness of Brighton at the end of June, when refugees from the recent London Season were migrating to the coastal town, lifted her spirits to new heights. She had not known precisely what

9

to expect, even by all the descriptions sent to her post by her friends Maude Dunsfold and Selena Bosham. Though their letters were quite exacting in detail—the elegant Georgian terraces were precisely as described—neither lady had been able to convey in even the smallest manner, the brilliance of the sunshine, the vast number of daring equipages whisking swiftly by, nor the delightful quantity of charming shops to be found everywhere beckoning her patronage.

She tried to remind herself that her visit was not a strict holiday since she had come to Brighton on two matters of vital importance. Yet whenever she attempted to suppress the mounting exhilaration she felt at this, her introduction to the fine seaport, the more excited she became. As she watched an open landau rattle past her, carrying several young, chattering ladies squeezed into the sleek conveyance, her thoughts travelled sharply round to her purpose in leaving Bedfordshire.

Maude and Selena, so very much like the ladies in the landau, had begged her to join them for the summer, not just to partake of the pleasures of Brighton at its most glorious time of year, but in hopes she might effectually take down a peg or two a certain gentleman of their acquaintance. His name was Lord Stoneleigh, a man Charlotte had never met before nor one she knew by sight. According to her dearest friends, he was an arrogant, high-handed bachelor who had led each of them to believe he was attempting to fix his affections with them, then, at the very last moment, when all manner of well-wishing ought to have been forthcoming, instead of a proposal of marriage, he gave each a setdown.

Charlotte remembered letter after letter of wounded sensibilities and dashed hopes. First—

tall, elegant Maude had been mistreated and later—diminutive, red-haired Selena.

What a cruel man, Charlotte thought, reflecting on the tear-stained missives she had received from her childhood friends. They were hoping desperately she might be able to take revenge on Stoneleigh's impervious heart and lead him the chase he had led so many others. For herself, Charlotte was more than content to oblige Maude and Selena. She was of just such a disposition as one who not only enjoyed the prospect of showing a creature of viscount Stoneleigh's stamp the error of his ways, but as one who also held those who attached themselves to her in fierce devotion. Her loyalty knew no bounds—she would travel to the ends of the earth for those she loved. Though Brighton was not precisely the ends of the earth, she had indeed come to the busy watering-hole primarily to their aid.

She had another reason, however, for leaving her many responsibilities in Bedfordshire and journeying to Sussex, though the details of this reason had yet to be explained to her. Not a sennight earlier, Charlotte had received word from her father that he required her to attend him in Brighton where he enjoyed a close association with the Prince Regent and his wide circle of influential friends.

Sir John Amberley had written in vague terms, referring to a *singularly delicate plan* which could only be accomplished with her help. Charlotte knew so little of her father's comings and goings that she could not imagine what manner of *delicate plan* he could be devising, nonetheless one that would require her assistance. But there was just such a sense of urgency in what she could perceive was a hastily written communication that, regardless of Maude and Selena's request, she would have come to Brighton solely on his desires alone. Only, what scheme could her most beloved father possibly be concocting?

When the clock shop had been regained, and a full twenty minutes spent in deciding on which one of three ormolu clocks she meant to purchase, she realized Miss Fittleworth was right—the afternoon was advancing rapidly and a steady breeze had been increasing dramatically in strength. Through the small-paned windows of the shop, just above a horizon of ornamental clocks displayed in front of the sill, she could see a lady walking against the wind, holding her bonnet fast to her head, her violet skirts straining about her legs.

She quickly made her purchase and left the shop by the side door, heading straight toward her hackney coach. Holding her hand to her own frilly bonnet of white silk ruching and dark green ribbons in preparation for the wind which would strike her forcefully once she lost the protection of the building, she bid Miss Fittleworth to also take care against the mounting wind. With Maude's clock tucked tightly beneath her arm, she picked up the skirts of her dark green silk pelisse and ran to the facing street. Just as she would have emerged onto the adjacent sidewalk, however, a man, holding down his own beaver hat with his hand, his forehead lowered in a protective posture toward the ground, charged heavily into her. She fell backward, her head striking a hard object which proved to be quite unyielding. Her mind spun about several times, she experienced a momentary vision of a handsome face and surprised blue eyes, then drifted off to a place of wondrous peace and emptiness.

Two

When Charlotte awoke, her vision did not immediately clear, nor did she comprehend where she was nor why the strong stench of Miss Fittleworth's vinaigrette was all around her. No matter which direction she turned, the sharp aroma seemed to follow her. She squeezed her eyes shut, coughed, batted at the source of the smell with her gloved hand, and murmured, "No, no. Please, put that away, Miss Fittle! I beg you!"

Finally, the smell left her. She opened her eyes and saw not Miss Fittleworth's narrow, angular features but the considerably handsome face she had seen just before she fainted. To her surprise, the man's blue eyes were filled not with concern but with an expression which bordered on amusement.

"Are you all right, Miss Amberley?" she heard the gentleman query, his deep, resonant voice sounding strangely distant. She suspected her brain had sustained an injury and was certain of it when she became aware of a steady, pounding sensation at the back of her head.

"Of course I'm all right," she returned in a whisper.

"Oh, I can see that you are," the man whispered facetiously. "But tell me, little Beauty, is your complexion always the precise shade of freshly-fallen snow and are you wont to express your thoughts in little more than a kitten's squeak?"

"What a maddening fellow you are," she retorted, again in a whisper. She ignored the crack of laughter which erupted from him in response and pressed her hand to her forehead, wishing her vision would stop shifting about. "Where am I? Where is Miss Fittle?"

"Here I am, dearest," Miss Fittleworth said, speaking quietly and peeping into view from somewhere behind the gentleman's shoulder.

"Were you hurt?" Charlotte asked. "Did I knock you over when I fell?"

"No, you did not. I was not in the least affected. I only wish I could have prevented your falling as you did. I'm 'fraid your head struck the bricks jutting out from below the window when you toppled over. Are you feeling dizzy?"

"Just a trifle. I cannot seem to gain my bearings." Shifting her gaze back to the man, she asked, "Who are you? You don't seem in the least familiar to me."

When she struggled to right herself, only then did she realize the stranger was holding her captive in his arms, as easily as if he were holding a child—and a child she was not! "Oh, my!" she cried. "This is most improper! I beg you will put me down at once!"

"That I will not do," he responded gently, his brow furrowed slightly, the amusement leaving his eyes completely. "I fear you would fall again. And I pray you will not injure yourself further by struggling. I shan't harm you. As for who I am, I am the gentleman who knocked you over and ruined your clock. I do beg your pardon, most humbly."

Her mind still quite loose, Charlotte turned

her head and looked down at the sidewalk. "Oh, dear," she murmured at the sight of Maude's clock which was now a jumble of tiny gears, splintered wood, and coiled springs scattered over the gray stone below. "Maude will be so unhappy," she murmured.

"Maude?" the man queried. "Do you perchance refer to Maude Dunsfold, currently residing in Russell Street?"

She turned and blinked at the stranger. "Yes," she responded slowly. "A most excellent friend from childhood. I wanted her to have a gift upon my arrival. Are you acquainted with her?"

"Yes, as it happens, I am," he answered politely. Charlotte wasn't certain, but it seemed to her he disapproved of Maude. He continued, "I will see that you get another clock to replace this one. We wouldn't want Miss Dunsfold to be disappointed."

Charlotte was grateful for his consideration. "I assure you, it isn't in the least necessary, sir," she said, beginning to feel much better. "I daresay our unfortunate encounter was as much my fault as yours. I was hurrying forward and at the same time trying to warn my abigail regarding the wind. Besides, if the truth be known, I have already bought Maudie an automaton, a basket of Devonshire soaps, a packet of at least twenty ribbons, paper for her watercolors, and several other trifles I cannot seem to bring immediately to mind."

"You are quite a generous friend," the man said, his expression softening into a smile.

Charlotte chuckled. "Miss Fittle will have you believe I am not generous at all, merely dangerously impulsive. I believe her assessment the correct one—she has known me since the cradle." Smoothing back one of her dark brown curls

15

which was presently tickling her cheek, she cried, "Goodness! Where is my bonnet?"

The stranger began, "Miss, er, Fittle?" he hesitated, glancing back at Charlotte's tall companion.

"—Fittleworth," the abigail corrected softly, smiling and blushing at this careful attention to her name.

He inclined his head to her and continued, "Yes, of course," then again addressed Charlotte. "Miss Fittleworth is in possession of your bonnet. I begged her to remove it in order to determine if you had sustained an injury requiring a surgeon's immediate attention. Fortunately, you have not."

"I see," she responded. "It would seem you have taken good care of me, then." Feeling suddenly embarrassed at being held in his arms, nonetheless by the peculiarly warm sensation she was experiencing at being so close to him, she said, "You may put me down now. I am nearly recovered, I promise you."

"I don't think that would be wise," he replied firmly, his blue eyes narrowed as if he were attempting to comprehend her. "And though I am distraught at having to disoblige a lady, I feel I must support you a little longer."

Charlotte had the distinct impression he was testing her somehow. His tone held an imperative edge, one which brooked no argument, no discussion.

She was not entirely pleased. After all, she was a capable young woman who had for many years managed her father's estate to a nicety and she was quite proud of her independence of mind and spirit. Lifting her chin slightly, she regarded him with her direct gaze. "You are oversolicitous, sir," she retorted, equally as firmly, "and again I beg you will put me down. I am not such a missish young woman that I am overset at having suffered a bump on the head—not by half. Though I appreciate your concern, it is unwarranted. Besides, I fear your arms must be growing quite fatigued by now."

He looked down at her, his expression changing as quickly as a cat bats at a mouse. He smiled almost devilishly now as he regarded her intently. "You have said the wrong thing, you know, and have completely shredded any chance your reasonings might have had of persuading me to give ground to your desires. Now I must continue to hold you, if for no other reason than to prove my strength to you—a common masculine failing, I fear."

Charlotte shook her head. "That won't fadge," she countered. "For you do not strike me as the sort of man who would give a fig for such a paltry concern. Indeed, I suspect you would use it as an excuse to do precisely that which you intend to do anyway. But don't expect me to ignorantly pander to your willfulness. I am not inclined to fall prey to such an absurdity and therefore must insist you relinquish your hold on me and permit me to regain my feet."

"A pretty speech, but alas, I cannot."

Charlotte felt a blush sting her cheeks. "Sir! You are being stubborn and nonsensical. Put me down, at once! At once, I say!"

"I would only do so if I determined such a course to be a wise one, as I said before. As it happens, I do not and you will remain imprisoned in my arms."

"Have you ever been told you are exceedingly high-handed?"

For some reason, the man holding her let out another crack of laughter.

Miss Fittleworth shook her head disparagingly at Charlotte. "You oughtn't to criticize the gentleman when he is being so kind."

"He doesn't seem to be overly distressed by my observation, are you, sir?" Charlotte retorted.

"Why should I be?" he said, turning slowly toward the street. "You are not the first to accurately assess the flaws of my character."

Charlotte could not help but smile. She approved of his answer very much, but she could not resist one last attempt at being freed from his helpful embrace. "Will you not at least permit me to try walking?" she asked.

"Almost you tempt me with such a gentle query, but I must again refuse. Besides, I mean only to see you placed in your hackney."

As he stepped in the direction of the waiting carriage, Charlotte became aware suddenly that the gentleman had not been bamboozling her—he held her remarkably effortlessly in his arms. Her own arm was about his shoulders; and for the first time since reawakening from her fall, she came to realize how *intimate* their relative positions were. She had never been held by a man before—only in the rather harmless clasp of the waltz. Occasionally, her friend Harry Elstow would lift her by the waist to regain her saddle after having taken a tumble from her horse, but otherwise she was perfectly innocent. Though both Maude and Selena accused her of telling a whisker when she denied ever having been kissed, her state was worse than even they suspected for, not only was she unable to boast of having been in love, she could not even lay claim to having been afflicted by the smallest of *tendres*.

She was finding the sensation of being held in the stranger's arms quite alarming. For one thing, her nose caught the faintest bouquet of a very fine soap. Though this was hardly significant, the more profound vision of the stranger standing before a mirror and employing his shaving gear in ridding himself of his beard brought a blush to her cheeks. She could see by the darkened pattern on his considerably firm jaw that he had a heavy gracing of facial hair and, what's more, she thought it quite attractive. The hair beneath his brushed beaver hat was coal black and styled in the fashion known as *à la Brutus*—quite fitting, she thought, considering his obvious willfulness. The fabric beneath her fingers was a high-quality blue superfine and fitted his shoulders to perfection—shoulders which she could easily ascertain were quite broad and manly.

When he reached the hackney, he chanced to glance down at her; and, in an objective manner, she scrutinized his features. His brows were as dark as his hair, thick and becomingly arched. His cheeks were high and pronounced; his nose was straight and quite attractive; and his lips were moderate with a distinct tendency to twitch when he was amused, which apparently he was now.

"Your verdict, Miss?" he queried.

Charlotte Amberley had never been a young woman to simper and fawn over a man. Her opinions she held forth in an open, direct manner which for the past few of her four and twenty years she was convinced had kept every eligible man of her acquaintance at bay. Maude and Selena had both warned her that if she hoped to master Lord Stoneleigh's heart, she would be required to take on the more usual artifices associated with the talent of flirtation. It did not occur to her in this moment, however, to be other than the young woman she was and so she responded, "You are quite the most handsome man I have ever met."

He appeared stunned, his color first paling a trifle then rising in a shade she perceived as pleasure. He smiled quite warmly, the wind buffeting his hat as he passed the protective side of the building and moved close to the hackney. "You have confounded me," he said at last.

Drawing his gaze away from her with some effort, he called loudly to the hackney driver who was staring into the sky and scratching his head. "You there! Will you not open the door for these ladies?"

The driver, apparently oblivious to all that had gone forward, leaped down from his box and immediately began his assessment of the situation. "By all that's wonderful," he cried sarcastically. "Did *Miss* suffer a fit o' the vapors from all her tiresome shoppin'? I could a told you 'ow it would be if—I—that is—" He cleared his throat, and Charlotte watched in amazement as the color on his cheeks turned to a profound crimson.

Before she turned to look at the stranger holding her in his arms, she could sense the purpose of his thoughts by the hard flexing of the muscles in his arms, chest, and shoulder. He was displeased, and his displeasure had easily communicated itself to other parts of his anatomy. When she regarded his face, the coldness of his expression as he eyed the impudent driver gave little doubt as to his opinion of the man's manners and worth.

Charlotte was not surprised that the hackney driver immediately began bowing, scraping, and stumbling over his quickly doffed hat in an effort to make his apologies. His mortification was so thorough that Charlotte found herself admiring her champion's abilities. He had said nothing to the obnoxious driver, words clearly being unnecessary in the light of his controlled, silent rebuff.

The driver obsequiously opened the door and handed Miss Fittleworth into the carriage. As the abigail began pushing aside the mound of packages obscuring the floorboards of the coach,

Charlotte murmured a faint, approving, "Well done," into the stranger's ear.

He turned to look at her steadily for a long moment. He smiled in return finally. This time, the warmth upon his lips travelled all the way to his wondrously blue eyes as he responded in a whisper, "Thank you."

She blinked twice at him, feeling that an unspoken understanding was passing between them. Who was this man and why did the mere looking into his eyes cause a rather distinct warmth to surround her heart? Her chest felt suddenly tight, and she was finding it surprisingly difficult to breathe. His gaze was no longer fixed to her eyes but travelled in a questioning manner over her brow and her cheeks, to settle finally upon her lips. Though the hackney driver was holding the door for her, the stranger remained where he was, staring down at her, his eyes refusing to stray from her lips. Her heart began pounding in her breast with the sure knowledge that, had they been alone, this man would have taken a kiss from her. The sudden and shocking knowledge that not only would he have done so but that she would have delighted in permitting him so scandalous a liberty caused her to murmur, "Oh, my."

Goodness! What was happening to her?

When he at last withdrew his gaze from her lips, she decided to tease him a little, hoping to ease the remarkable tensions between them. "You know, you ought to take better care to look where you are going from now on. It wouldn't do to be knocking down young ladies all over Brighton."

She watched his lips twitch as he gently set her on her feet. "You are right of course," he responded. "And I shall most certainly heed your advice. However, might I suggest that the next time you hope to gain a gentleman's attention, you try asking for an introduction in a ballroom?

You could have been more seriously injured than you were in this particular instance."

Charlotte was stunned. She blinked at him several times but could not form an appropriate retort in her brain. Did he actually believe she had purposed ramming into him, that she had meant to fall backward, to strike her head on the bricks, to drop unconscious upon the stone sidewalk? Truly, it was the height of arrogance, of conceit, if he believed what he said!

When she did not respond but remained staring at him in mute disbelief, he smiled knowingly, "Then I was not mistaken?" The disapproval she had heard earlier in his voice when he had spoken of her friend Maude replaced the former warmth in his blue eyes. She thought in this moment he seemed very unfriendly, so different from the creature who had almost kissed her not a few seconds earlier.

Whatever good opinion had been forming while he had held her in his arms now took a sharp downward turn. "You were entirely mistaken, sir!" she cried, at last finding her voice. "I would never engage in what I believe you are describing. It is the very lowest of feminine devices."

The guilt-laden thought however occurred to her suddenly that just such a scheme was precisely the tactic she meant to employ in her forthcoming pursuit of Lord Stoneleigh. But then, such a creature as Stoneleigh deserved to be mistreated.

"Never?" the stranger queried lightly.

She did not like him, she decided. He might have held her gently in support of her injured head; she might even have wished for the barest moment that he would kiss her—but his character had been revealed to her, and most certainly she did not like him. He clearly believed every female who ever chanced to lay eyes upon him immediately set her cap for him. Really, such extreme self-consequence was not to be borne! In fact, he was behaving very much in the manner she would expect Lord Stoneleigh to behave.

"I have never treated the gentlemen of my acquaintance with such *manœuvres* and absurd schemes," she returned, eying him with considerable hostility. "I have too much respect for them."

His smile was all disbelief as he responded, "Then you are to be congratulated, and obviously I must beg forgiveness for having mistaken your intentions." He bowed stiffly to her, then withdrew a card from the pocket of his waistcoat. "I am fixed in Brighton for the summer. If during that time you require a physician's attention, pray refer his bill to me."

"You are too kind," Charlotte answered with mock sweetness, taking his card and curtsying ever so slightly. "Good day, and I thank you again for your assistance."

As Charlotte settled herself on the squabs next to Miss Fittleworth, she could see from the corner of her eye that the gentleman remained standing dutifully on the sidewalk. She wished he had not done so, particularly when she chanced to glance down at his card. How her cheeks burned with shock and surprise as she read the inscription: *Stoneleigh!*

Lord Stoneleigh watched the hackney pull away from the flagway, nothing short of confusion running rampant in his head. He would have wagered his last groat that this lady—previously unknown to him save that he was acquainted with her father—had charged into him to a purpose. Yet the final expression of astonishment on her

23

face as she read his card as well as her heated assertions she would never stoop to such wiles as he had suggested caused him to reconsider his opinion.

He did not know what to think. She was, after all, Charlotte Amberley, as her abigail had proudly informed him while he was holding the beautiful, unconscious young woman in his arms. She was the daughter of a baronet, of Sir John Amberley of Bedfordshire.

That was the rub. Amberley, whom he had never valued above half anyway, had become his enemy some four years earlier under circumstances of the most heinous. He had for some time intended to ruin the baronet if he could. Yet it seemed the oddest quirk of Fate that he had not needed to lift a finger to bring it about— Amberley had succeeded in the task all by himself. He had gone down a most troublesome path, like so many others before him, embracing the ignoble pastimes of *rouge et noir*, faro, and hazard until he had brought his entire fortune trembling on the precipice of complete disaster. The smallest gust of Fate at this point in his unsteady career would surely topple him over and set his estates to wrack and ruin.

Stoneleigh remembered seeing all the parcels on the floor of Miss Amberley's hackney. She had even spoken of her own *impulses*. A familial vice, perhaps—the indulgence of impulses.

But what had brought Miss Amberley to Brighton?

Was there mischief brewing?

His instincts shouted to him that all was not as it should be and that he would do well to avoid any furthering of his acquaintance with the daughter of his avowed enemy.

Now why the devil, he wondered as her hired coach disappeared in front of a Tilbury and pair, did he hope more than life itself that Fate would force their paths to cross again? And the sooner the better!

Three

Charlotte blinked at her father then began pulling slowly on the green silk ribbons of her bonnet, ribbons that could no longer bear close scrutiny since each was smudged with dirt from her recent accident. She was standing in the entrance hall of her father's town house in West Street and had received unsettling news from her parent.

Her gaze drifted away from her father's imploring eyes to fall on the four fobs and a seal which dangled habitually at his waist. She was struck in an odd way by the sight of the familiar articles. She had always thought her father impeccably groomed. And so he was, to a large degree, for Weston fashioned his clothing and, in the tradition of Beau Brummell, even his gloves were fit to the peculiarities of each digit.

However, the number of seals and the fob now seemed quite extraneous, a judgment she had never before applied to her papa. As her gaze drifted upwards to the scarlet waistcoat and the buckram-padded shoulders of his snug-fitting blue coat, she had the distinct impression her parent was dressed in vanity. Though she was reluctant to admit the origin of her deduction, she knew at once she was comparing him to the initial impression she had had of Stoneleigh—no need for buckram wadding there! But her diverging opinion was based not so much upon the artificial enhancement of the size and shape of her father's shoulders but in the overall impression that, while her father sought notice, Stoneleigh appeared to strive for anonymity.

Each aspect of her scrutiny whirled brightly about her brain like gulls swooping down upon the sea. She was left feeling unsettled, wondering why she had not noticed the dandified appearance of Sir John's costume before.

The more urgent matter at hand, however, ignored her disquieting thoughts and rose to her lips.

"How badly are you dipped, Papa?" she asked quietly.

She had a brief glimpse of large, handsome blue eyes before Sir John shifted his gaze away from her and turned bodily to face the staircase. She could see he was consternated by her question, and she did not immediately press him for an answer. He placed a glossy, booted foot upon the bottom step and leaned his elbow on the curved banister. Charlotte's gaze fell to the finely crafted Hessians. Who had once said her father followed Brummell's lead and used champagne in his blacking in order to achieve the shine on the strong leather? And where was Brummell now? Living in poverty and exile in Calais, a ruined gamester.

Charlotte experienced a strange sensation that she did not even know the man before her. Merciful heavens, he was wearing pale yellow pantaloons! Perhaps she had never known him. Her gaze moved upward to his silver hair. He wore his locks cut in a youthful style known as *à la cherubim*, his loose curls graced lightly with Macassar oil drawn from trees in the East Indies.

The oil was not popular with more fastidious hostesses since it tended to mark their fine silk-damask furniture where droopy heads might loll at a late-night ball. She could not, however, picture her father snoring gently in a forgotten antechamber—as many older gentlemen were wont to do—while the younger men were wearing their ball-slippers thin through exertion on the dance floor.

No, not this man. He might be five and fifty, gray-haired, with a small tendency to the gout, but he still possessed the energy of a man half his age.

Over the years, since her mother's death, Charlotte had heard fragments of gossip regarding Sir John's liaisons with various ladies of rank. As a baronet and as a man of wealth and property, Sir John Amberley enjoyed an *entrée* into the most select circles—Prinney's obvious and long-standing affection for him would always assure his success. Glancing at his handsome profile as he stroked his chin nervously with his hand, Charlotte could readily believe the gossip she had heard—that he was a man who enjoyed the company of the fairer sex.

She felt as if she were standing thirty feet away from her father in this moment, instead of three. It was inevitable, she supposed, that as his daughter, she would one day have to see him as a mere mortal, as a man she had known in only a limited sense as her father. But why must it be today, when she had but just arrived in Brighton—her first notable excursion from Bedfordshire? This new perception of him, which had all the markings of separation, did nothing to diminish the anxiety she was experiencing by what he had just told her.

She took a step forward, wanting to ease the sudden pain which seized her heart. She fondled the sleeve of his coat as she had done since she was a child.

"How badly, Papa?" she queried again, taking a deep breath, readying herself to hear his answer. If it were two or three thousand pounds—or even five—she knew she could reassure him that the estate would prosper in spite of the many curtailments such a debt would naturally demand. Seven would cause a severe strain, and anything more was unthinkable. The thought he might have behaved irresponsibly at Brook's or Watier's and lost ten thousand pounds she dismissed with an inward laugh.

Sir John would never have squandered his fortune so absurdly—especially when his own young son, his darling little Henry, would one day inherit his title and estate. A man might be less conscientious for a distant cousin or a disliked nephew. But with Henry showing every promise of breaking out of the nursery quite soon with a strong, happy disposition, Sir John had been given every reason in the world to keep a steady eye to his fortune.

No, ten thousand was unthinkable, and her thoughts renewed her sense of confidence that though her father had begun the conversation with the daunting proclamation that he was in debt to the moneylenders, the sum was probably manageable. Ten would be such foolishness and would require he sell off some of his acreage or sell partially out of the funds. Her father might be many things, but he certainly was not a fool!

"The size of my debts is no concern of yours," he responded at last. "But since I know the turn of your mind, that like your mother you will pursue the matter until I am hounded into a tree, I will tell you anyway." He glanced toward the door, craning his neck to see if the footman was nearby before giving answer. "Twenty thousand," was his quiet, shattering response.

Had he slapped her hard across the face, he could not have stunned Charlotte more. She gasped, felt the blood rush from her face and took a step backward. She could hardly breathe. Her thoughts ran rapidly together. "Papa, no! How is this possible?"

She turned around slightly, pressing her hand to her cheek, and stared horrified at the mound of packages littering the floor. Of a practical mind, she cried, "I shall return everything at once. I shouldn't have—Papa, why did you not tell me? How long have—how could you have—how did you possibly lose twenty thousand?" Without thinking, she whirled around to face him, closed the distance between them, and roughly took the lapels of his coat in both her hands. "Papa! Pray tell me! Have you become a—a gamester?"

Four

Sir John pulled Charlotte's hands off his coat and released them with a toss as if he were dropping something hot. He seemed disgusted and annoyed as he straightened his lapels in quick little jerks. "For heaven's sake, Charlie, of course I have not! A gamester, indeed! And I hasten to remind you that I am not the first to have had a run of bad luck. Besides, it is not as if—oh, the devil take it, will you please close your mouth, and do stop gaping at me as though I've sprouted horns. I wish now I hadn't mentioned the matter to you at all. If I'd known you would become missish just when I have need of you most, I wouldn't have asked you to come to Brighton in the first place. As it is, I'm of a mind to send you, and Henry, back to Amberley this very night! A gamester, indeed!"

Charlotte repressed an urge to apologize to him. She knew she had provoked his temper, but it seemed to her not only was he impenitent but the size of his debts seemed to be of little consequence to him as well. If he were not a gamester, then how could he have lost twenty thousand pounds?

Twenty thousand. She weaved on her feet at the mere thought of so horrendous a loss!

The appearance of the footman, staggering beneath a load of more of Charlotte's recent purchases, his formal wig askew, brought the unpromising discussion to an abrupt halt.

"Good God!" Sir John cried with a laugh. "How could you stand there so brazenly and take me to task for wasting the ready when I daresay there is probably not a shop remaining in Brighton which you have not yet patronized? And you, only just arrived! Silly chit!"

Charlotte was completely unable to concoct a sensible rejoinder to his accusing sally. She knew there was a difference between purchasing a mound of trumpery for the first time in a year—and that by spending monies she had saved from her housekeeping accounts—and her father having amassed an unexplained debt of twenty thousand pounds. Her senses, however, were still considerably disordered from her fall; her head ached dully, and she could bring no reasonable argument to mind. She therefore permitted him to pinch her chin and to call her a spendthrift without defending herself and acquiesced to being led upstairs.

"We shall forget our joint indiscretions," he said in a whisper as they mounted the stairs, arm in arm, "and shall turn our attentions instead to the future, for I wish to make known to you several particulars of the scheme I mentioned to you in my letters—a scheme which will restore our losses." Looking over his shoulder, he waited until the footman had disappeared outdoors before continuing. "My plan is simple, really. I have need of a favor from His Royal Highness, the Prince Regent, which I am most certain he will grant if I am able to speak with him for a few minutes privately. If I can have his promise to use his influence with Parliament in the coming months, I will be able to set everything to rights—I'm sure of it. There is only one hindrance to speak of, but with your help I know it can be overcome." He looked down at her, scrutinizing her face intently. "You are certainly become a pretty young woman, which I've little doubt will aid our cause, only do tell me if you have left off that truly wretched habit of yours of arguing with every man you see?"

Charlotte blinked at her father several times. She was completely lost, not comprehending one whit what either her propensity to give voice to her opinions or the configuration of her features had to do with why he required her presence in Brighton. She supposed he would explain his meaning, but as they crossed the threshold of the drawing room, Charlotte's attention was entirely diverted from the subject at hand. "Oh, my! How very lovely! I have never seen such an exquisite chamber. Papa, you are to be congratulated!"

The windows of the drawing room had been thrown wide, permitting a fresh breeze to roll round the room. The vibrant sea air gave a decided lift to her drooping spirits and seemed to ease the ever-present ache at the back of her head.

Delicate muslin curtains billowed and danced with each ebb and flow of the breeze like graceful ballet dancers in the finest gossamer costumes. Each drape was kept from flying away completely by heavier dark blue silk damask curtains draped diagonally across the muslin and tied back upon large, elegant, gilt rosettes. The striking blue fabric adorned every wall, stretched smoothly between carved, wooden borders painted a glossy white. The ceiling was decorated in intricate patterns of white stucco. Upon the floor was a blue-and-gold Aubusson carpet.

Charlotte felt as if she had entered another world, an ancient world evoked by the feminine caryatids supporting a fine table of zebra wood, by the gilt fish shapes framing a pair of exquisite Grecian couches in gold and white silk, by the Empire chairs in black lacquer and gilt, also dressed in the dark-blue silk damask, and by the numerous vases, whether painted *à la Chinoise* or bearing Egyptian figures. A rosewood pianoforte, placed in a dominant position in the chamber, opposite the fireplace, completed a portrait of a classical age of beauty, of intelligence, of accomplishment. A full length portrait of Sir John above the mantel, astride his favorite black horse, with several hunting dogs gathered about the gelding's hooves, first jarred then softened in a charming manner the formality of the chamber. Charlotte wasn't certain whether she wished the painting gone or felt grateful that imperfection had a place in her father's drawing room.

Setting her bonnet on a pedestal table inlaid with brass, she exclaimed, "Magnificent. I did not do half as well at Amberley."

"You do not like Reynold's portrait, though, do you?" Sir John asked with a laugh. "Now, don't deny it. Everyone tells me to consign it to the attics or to my hunting lodge, but I cannot." He gazed fondly at the picture of himself astride the horse and, after a very long pause, murmured. "I was better in those days."

Charlotte wondered if she had misunderstood him, but there was just such an expression of melancholy on his face that she was reluctant to repeat what he had said. He appeared to give himself a mental shake, his brow lightening. He turned and slipped his arm about her shoulder, giving her a squeeze. "I am glad you approve of this room. I took great pains to make certain everything was to your liking. The pianoforte is quite excellent. I trust you brought your music with you?" When she nodded, he cleared his voice and added, "Charlie, I am very glad you've come."

Charlotte glanced up at her father's face, warmed with a familiar smile of affection, and she felt unexpected tears start to her eyes. "I am, too." She touched his hand gently and sighed, realizing how much she loved him.

Sir John returned her gaze for a time until a frown, in stages, marred his brow. Clearing his throat again, he moved away from her and seemed lost for words.

Charlotte broached the former subject. "Papa, could you tell me more of your plans?"

"Ah," he said brightly. "Well, here it is. I need a Charter to form a joint-stock company for a certain business scheme I have in mind. Prinny can help see that I am given the Charter, which only Parliament can grant. I am persuaded, for the sake of the friendship he and I have shared these many years and more, that he will be inclined to extend his hand to me. Unfortunately, a certain nobleman keeps guard over the Prince— a peer whose own ambitions are evident in his courting of Prinny's good graces at every conceivable turn!—and I need you to distract him that I might share a private word with the Prince."

Charlotte was not certain she had heard her father correctly. *"Distract* this nobleman?" she queried, gazing intently into her father's blue eyes.

"Yes," Sir John responded impatiently. "You know, talk with him, flirt with him—or have you grown so spinsterish living all these years in Amberley's restricted society that you have forgotten how to encourage a man's interest?"

Again Charlotte felt knocked out of stride by her father. "A man's interest?" she repeated blankly.

She watched her father's cheeks turn a dark, choleric pink. He pinched his lips together and blew a frustrated puff of air through his nose. "I have failed you, haven't I?" he cried, exasperated. "I have let you have your way, permitted you full reign over Amberley Park, and you have buried yourself in the stuffy details of managing an estate to the point of becoming an ape-leader! How old are you, anyway? Good God, you must be four and twenty if you are a day! Well, let me inform you, those days are gone and your education hereby commences. A man's *interest* involves his desire to engage you in conversation, his fervent hope you might give the next two dances to him and not to the nodcock standing beside him, his obsession to search out your particular face among a multitude of damsels, even if the rest are prettier, wealthier, and more fashionable than you, his constant worry that you will think him less handsome than his brother, or uncle, or the blacksmith in the village. That is a man's interest. Can you do as much? Good God! It never occurred to me you might not be up to snuff. Let me have a look at you! Take off your pelisse and let me see if you know how to direct your needle-women."

"Papa, there is no need, I assure you! Though I may have immersed myself in the care of your properties, I have attended the Bedfordshire assemblies quite regularly; and, though I have not been to London, I devour *Ackmermann's Repository* and *La Belle Assemblée* whenever I am able. But more to the point—"

"—off, I say!" he cried imperiously.

Charlotte began to unbutton her silk pelisse. "I have become crumpled from travelling, Papa. But again I say, more to the point, how can you ask me to intentionally attempt to win the attentions of a man I don't know and for so—so questionable a reason as this?"

"I have asked only that you flirt with him, not

that you engage in a clandestine assignation. And I don't comprehend why you should consider my desire to speak with the Prince Regent privately a *questionable reason*. Damme, I knew I ought to have insisted you join me in London this year. Charlie, I don't like to mention it, but you've grown abominably stuffy!"

Charlotte stopped attempting to explain that she disliked the notion of engaging a man's attention that someone else might profit from it and concentrated instead on her buttons. If he could see nothing wrong with it, she was unlikely to change his opinions. Besides, it seemed so little to ask, after all, particularly when the restoration of twenty thousand pounds was at stake.

When she removed her pelisse, she began smoothing out the white silk skirts of her fashionable gown. She fluffed the short, puffed sleeves and lifted the gathered lace adorning the bodice with feathery movements of her fingers. Red cherries and green leaves—the latter just the shade to match her parasol!—had been embroidered in two long rows down the front of her skirts and circled the hem just above three flounces of red silk ruffles.

"Charming!" was her father's response, his face breaking into a smile. "A trifle crushed, as you have said, but otherwise, I give you credit for possessing a proper amount of good taste. But whatever is the matter with your hair? It looks torn to pieces."

Charlotte felt a slight blush creep up her cheeks as she patted the many unruly strands escaping the ribbons tying back her hair. She had not wanted to mention the accident to her father or the fact that she had met Lord Stoneleigh—a gentleman with whom she knew her father to be acquainted—under such unpropitious circumstances, but it seemed there was nothing for it now. "I'm afraid I took a tumble outside the last shop I visited."

"Mm," was his only response as he continued to scrutinize her general appearance.

Charlotte did not know whether to be offended or relieved. She had not wanted to explain the nature of the accident to him at the same time his obvious indifference to her ordeal disturbed her. She was about to ask him whether he wished to know the particulars, when a familiar voice intruded.

"Charlie! You will never guess what Nurse and I saw in London! Lions!"

Five

"Henry, my little darling," Charlotte returned, opening her arms wide to him. She knelt at the same time that she might take her young brother in her arms and give him a hug. When he was held fast in her embrace, she noticed Nurse standing by the door, smiling her approval at the familial scene, waiting for her charge to welcome Charlotte to Brighton.

The aging woman, who had been Charlotte's nurse in infancy as well, had travelled with Henry to London in order to show him several sights before completing the trip to Brighton. A full sennight had separated Charlotte from her brother. She released him only enough to keep him securely in the crook of her arm, to look into his face, and to gently pinch each cheek. "And were the lions very fierce?" she asked seriously.

Henry's small face wrinkled in disgust. "They were all asleep and would only roar when poked with a long, sharp stick. Even then it was more like a growl. But Astley's Amphitheatre was marvelous! Oh, Charlie, when we leave the ocean, we must return to London so that you can see the horses and riders for yourself. They have a battle and even fire off cannons until everyone is choking from the smoke! The lady next to me fell

39

over as if she were dead, and I was sure she was killed until Nurse held her little silver box under the lady's nose. Then she cast up her accounts—not Nurse, of course—but the fat lady that swooned. Really, Charlie, you should have been with us. It was such fun!"

Charlotte bit her lip and tried not to laugh, for she could see that Henry was deeply in earnest. That she was content not to have witnessed such an unhappy spectacle as the swooning lady she left unsaid. Henry clearly thought it a famous excursion and nothing else mattered. She then asked how he had enjoyed the remainder of his journey. When he began to recount each exchange of horses—beginning with the lively pair at the Swan with Two Necks and giving every indication he meant to enumerate the points and failings of each new pair all along the way—her hearing dimmed as she gazed down at him fondly.

She was always surprised at how much he resembled his father. His hair was blond and curly as Sir John's had been in his youth and his nose was already showing signs of aquiline definition, though it would be ten years at least before all the childish features dropped away and the young man emerged. But most significantly, there could be no mistaking the large blue Amberley eyes. She, herself, had taken after her mother, who had had fine brown eyes, and so had not been blessed with the prettiest of the Amberley features. But not Henry. His eyes were so blue you were certain the sun shone just above them, causing them to glint and sparkle like sunbeams on a brook. A miniature of Sir John at age five, forming part of an ancestral collection in the entrance hall of Amberley Park, had already been mistaken for Henry at least a dozen times.

She loved him so. Every small bit of him.

Watching the excitement glittering in his eyes, Charlotte felt a profound rush of affection for her brother. Since the death of their mother, who succumbed to a fever shortly after giving birth to Henry, Charlotte had rarely been separated from her sibling. She needed his companionship as much as he surely needed her steady presence, particularly with Sir John away from the Park so much of the time. The loss of a beloved mother had left a terrible breach in Charlotte's life which only the caring of little Henry seemed to fill.

Sir John had been sympathetic, of course, but he had been unable to comfort her. His concerns had always been much broader than her own. She, along with her mother, had been content in Bedfordshire, while Sir John moved about the country with each shift of season. After Christmas, he travelled to London, where politics and the Season dominated his life. June took him to Brighton for much of the summer. In late August, he would return to Amberley Park, where he spent a few mornings discussing his estate with both Charlotte and his bailiff, only to fall asleep over a glass of wine and the rentrolls one afternoon out of two. Autumn brought another change, and the hunt was on. His lodge saw more of him than the Park, until the ground froze hard and a first snow dampened his enthusiasm. By early December, he was again settled at Amberley, only not settled, since a pervasive restlessness clung to every word he spoke, to every fidgety movement of his tall, lithe frame as he moved about the Park and pretended to be content, to every sigh issuing unawares from his dissatisfied soul. Home was not in Sir John.

However much Charlotte loved the Yuletide holidays and her father, she always found herself grateful when Sir John—so much more comfortable among his friends and busier drawing rooms than Amberley Park could provide—returned to London once again.

Her father's voice brought her abruptly out of her reverie, cutting off Henry's description of a fourgon that had lost a wheel on the downs just outside of Brighton. "Henry," he began sternly. "You'll have every morning hereafter to regale your sister of your adventures, but right now you will have to excuse her." He chewed for a moment upon the inside of his lip before finally addressing Charlotte. "I know how much you prefer to be informed of every detail in advance, Charlie; but as it happens, I've accepted an invitation for this evening which I doubt will please you. We are to go to the Pavilion at Prinny's request. Eight o'clock and not a minute later."

Charlotte did not immediately respond, for one thing she could not credit her ears. "What?" she asked, stunned. "The Pavilion? Tonight? You cannot be serious." He could not have surprised her more if he had tossed a cup of iced champagne in her face. She released Henry from the circle of her arm and rose to her feet. "Papa, do you tell me we are to go to the Royal Pavilion in a matter of two hours? I cannot possibly be ready to meet the Prince in so short a time. Two hours to attend to my toilette! You should have written and told me. Had I known, I would have planned on being here yesterday."

Sir John pinched his lips together and scowled. "Had you been here at the appointed hour of one o'clock, you would have had seven hours with which to make your preparations," he responded. "But the truth be known, I secured the invitation only two days ago, having exerted every influence to achieve it. So don't come the crab over me, I beg you."

"My hair is crushed beyond repair," she stated

disjointedly. "Oh, dear! I wish I had known. Papa, I can't go. I can't! I will disgrace you!"

Sir John took his daughter's hands in his own and pressed them firmly. "You must and you will go! I—I am under some pressure to secure the matter we've already discussed. I need your help tonight—*tonight,* I tell you!"

"Charlie," Henry exclaimed, tugging on her hand. "Will you take me sea-bathing tomorrow? Remember you promised. I want to go to the beach and collect shells and walk on the pebbles and look for fishhooks. Oh, and ride in one of the bathing-machines Nurse told me about!"

Charlotte blinked several times, trying to gather her senses about her yet again. She had scarcely been in Brighton but a few hours and already it seemed her world was spinning every which way in quick stages. She looked down at Henry and said, "Of course we will go." Turning him bodily about, she gave him a gentle push in the direction of the door. "Now, there's a darling. Go to Nurse. It would seem I am to meet a prince tonight, and I must hurry and ready myself."

Satisfied that Charlotte intended to see to his desires, Henry skipped back to Nurse, where he demanded to know if Cook had something other than boiled fish and artichokes to offer for dinner.

Charlotte took a deep breath, a feeling very much like panic scattering her thoughts. She watched Henry disappear into the hall, and a strong presentiment came to her that more was amiss than her father had yet explained. A quick shiver of fright raced down her spine. Was little Henry's inheritance in jeopardy? If so, then she had every reason to do as her father bid her.

But surely her father's affairs had not come to such a desperate pass that she must concern herself about Henry's future? Surely not!

Something of her fears must have played upon her face, for her father patted her shoulder gently. "Don't fret yourself, child," he said. "I have already instructed my housekeeper, Mrs. Glover, to see that *Fiddle* makes ready your best gown. I've little doubt she's set one of the maids to smoothing out the wrinkles even as we speak and a pair of curling tongs will set your hair to rights soon enough. Now, off with you and be quick about it."

"Yes, Papa," Charlotte responded quietly. She could do little more than acquiesce after all. She crossed the elegant chamber, picked up her white bonnet from the table of inlaid brass, and, letting it dangle at the end of its green ribbons, turned to query, "Papa, you never told me the name of the gentleman I am to, er, *distract*?"

"You don't know him, of course, but I imagine you've heard his name before. Stoneleigh of Sussex. Viscount Stoneleigh. A handsome fellow but as shrewd as they come. Now, do hurry, child. I'll want to arrive beforetimes. It won't do to keep a prince waiting."

Six

"Oh, dear," Miss Fittleworth murmured in sympathetic accents. "It is no wonder then that your checks are as dark as ripe figs. But are you certain he said *Stoneleigh*, for Mrs. Glover was telling me of a Lord Donnelly who is a frequent visitor to Brighton?"

"There can be no mistake," Charlotte sighed. She was sitting in a mahogany Empire chair by the window, her legs drawn up to her chest in a most childlike manner, her chin resting on her knees. She wore only her thin muslin shift, waiting for one of the maids to finish pressing the wrinkles from her gown. She touched her fingers lightly to her forehead for a brief moment. Her head still ached—though not sufficiently, she supposed, to cause her any real concern, especially in light of her father's pressing need for her help. *"Stoneleigh of Sussex, quite a handsome fellow but as shrewd as they come!* That is what Papa said. Fittle, however am I to attach such a man to my side? His arrogance and his belief I had actually tried to injure myself in order to gain his attention all speak of a gentleman who cannot be *distracted* as my father wishes. Whatever am I to do?"

Miss Fittleworth knelt before the fireplace, where a glow of coals washed her profile in warm

45

light. She was heating the curling tongs and so did not look at Charlotte as she responded, "Though I am not a woman of great experience, as you very well know, it still seemed to me you had little difficulty, er, *distracting* his lordship this afternoon."

"How difficult can it be to divert a man's attention when he is carrying you in his arms?"

"With another woman, I expect it could have been quite another matter," Miss Fittleworth stated. "And most certainly an impossibility if she didn't please him generally." She then glanced back at Charlotte, her eyes visible just above the light-blue counterpane on the four-poster bed, and smiled. "I hadn't thought to mention it before, Miss Charlotte, but Lord Stoneleigh was quite struck with your beauty of person—a halfwit could have seen as much—and what's more, your conversation amused him. He actually threw back his head and laughed when you called him a *maddening fellow*. Mrs. Glover says that he is one of those poor, unfortunate gentlemen who are bored by nearly everything and everyone—so rich he is. If I may say so, he did not appear so very bored in your company. In fact, for a moment I thought he meant to steal a kiss from you."

Charlotte felt her cheeks grow warm as Miss Fittleworth held her gaze. A smile slowly overtook her abigail's thin face, and Charlotte could not keep from smiling in return. "He did seem to wish for it, didn't he?"

Miss Fittleworth nodded and returned her attention to the task at hand.

Charlotte drew her thin shift tightly about her ankles, clasping her hands together around her legs, and turned to gaze out the window. He had wanted to kiss her. Fittle had not been mistaken in that, she was sure of it. How very intent his expression had become for those few seconds, his blue eyes almost devouring her every feature. And how very much she had desired to feel his lips upon hers as well. It was all so inexplicable, so sudden, so strong. Then it had passed, like a gust of cool wind on a warm day, leaving one to wonder if it had really happened yet knowing full well it had.

She peered through the slatted shades adorning the window and watched the last rays of the sun dance brilliantly upon the ocean. The golden shimmering on the water never stopped but dazzled and dazzled until she felt mesmerized by the sight of it. The faint sounds of gulls reached her ears along with the shouting of fishermen at their nets and the squeals of children still at play. How different from Bedfordshire, she thought for the hundredth time since arriving at the coast. And how wonderful!

Brighton was an ancient town. A heritage that had known the march of Roman soldiers, the presence of William the Conqueror, and now the social rule of the Prince of Wales. Still occasionally called Brighthelmstone, the original, old fishing village and all its cottages had long since been swallowed up by the sea to be replaced by permanent dwellings on higher ground. There was talk already of building a seawall to keep the devastating tides from taking more of the town away from its loyal inhabitants and more island away from England. For the present, the cliffs of chalky limestone held the encroaching water at bay, a long, rolling wall of land that met each storm with a dare and a chuckle.

Bright Brighton. Blue skies, white gulls, the dance of light on water.

Charlotte found herself charmed as she continued to look through the slats at the view beyond. And everywhere, the sea air was a balm, drawing the dust of the roads deep into the earth and making each breath a pleasure.

Brighton was a place of pleasure, where a prince who loved pleasure came to partake of it to the full. Charlotte wondered if she would know pleasure here. Probably not, she mused with a half-smile, not when Maude and Selena were expecting her to vanquish Stoneleigh's heart, not when her father needed her to distract the same, immovable gentleman for his own purposes, not when her limbs trembled at the mere thought of meeting the man again who had, with only one vibrant look, caused her to long to be kissed.

Oh, lord, what would happen next to further cut up her peace and stay pleasure for another day?

Seven

From the moment Charlotte stepped down from her father's travelling chariot beneath the protective stone *porte-cochère* on the west front of the Pavilion, she sensed her life, her comfortable ideas formed at Amberley Park, would never be the same. Her first day in Brighton climbed to this height, a musicale at the Royal Pavilion and an introduction to His Royal Highness, the Prince of Wales. What would happen, she wondered, once she passed through the portals of what was, by all accounts, a classical wonderland overlaid with a myriad of Chinese and Indian influences?

The outside of the royal residence was undergoing a transformation which would not be complete for at least three years, her father had said. He had seen John Nash's drawings and said that India had come to conquer Brighton, for several domes in the shapes of onions would soon top Holland's original designs.

As she stepped through the glass doors entering the outer entrance hall, she was struck at once by the beauty of its octagonal shape. At the same time, she was surprised by the simplicity of the decor, which consisted of a few hall chairs and a mahogany side-table set against pink walls, with only a glistening brass fireplace to embellish the modest chamber.

Aware vaguely that she was clutching her father's arm tightly and that he was murmuring something about a monstrous dragon being crafted for the banqueting hall, she crossed the threshold to the inner entrance hall. Here, just a hint of the world she had heard so much about began, for the length of the room was decorated in panels of imitation green and pink marble, colors at odds with the usual genteel chambers trimmed in reds or golds or blues.

"Prepare to be amazed, if not disgusted," her father whispered in her ear with a chuckle.

She heard him as through a mist and, though she wanted to tell him not to be absurd, she was unable to open her mouth and utter the words. She caught glimpses of the exotic scenery beyond the entrance hall peeping at her through the doorway opening onto the long corridor—pink-papered walls covered with a grove of bamboo and cheerful blue birds. Reaching the threshold to the corridor, her heart simply stopped as her white, silk-slippered feet touched the red-and-gold geometric carpet. Though at least two score of ladies and gentlemen filled the extraordinary hall that ran the entire length behind the principal receiving rooms of the Pavilion, the exotic effect of the decor was not in the least dimmed but met her senses like a quick, welcome breeze. She wasn't disgusted at all, as apparently her father was, by the oriental spell of the corridor, but charmed. Deeply and euphorically charmed. She could not say why, but every nuance was like a dream she had once had but never remembered, save strong sensations of delight and pleasure.

Chinese lanterns, red-tasseled and flowered, lit the gathering assemblage in a soft glow. Her father was already acknowledging acquaintances and only vaguely did she realize she was bowing and curtsying to people she had met once or twice before at Amberley. Her attention could not remain fixed quite yet on anyone, for her gaze drifted in continuing anticipation from real Chinese bamboo chairs to the life-sized Mandarin figures occupying niches along the wall to the three imitation bamboo chimney pieces. Overhead was the most startling feature of all, a skylight which must have been twenty feet long, colorfully painted with dragons, flowers, and an image of what was undoubtedly a Chinese deity of some sort.

"The God of Thunder," her father whispered to her, aware of her fascination. "But do close your mouth, Charlie. You are staring agape and causing a great deal of whispering."

Charlotte clamped her mouth shut, though not in the least disconcerted that her behavior might seem odd to those about her. She was enraptured and enjoying herself hugely. "I am amazed, Papa, just as you said I would be. There is pure fantasy all about me—everything so different from our Bedfordshire homes—and I am thrilled more than I can say. The walls just below the skylight are so intricately painted. I wish I might be here one afternoon when the sun is overhead and light pours through the glass. It must be astonishing!"

Sir John grunted amiably, a soft sound Charlotte recognized as disinterest. His attention was not easily caught by his offspring and so she was neither offended nor surprised when she found her father ogling a pretty young lady toward the north end of the corridor. Her gaze flew quickly past the object of her father's interest, being led onward by the sight of the imitation-bamboo double staircase at the terminus of the corridor.

"Did you not tell me it is worked entirely in

51

iron? But it is the image of bamboo! Really, it is incredible."

"Indeed, quite remarkable," Sir John responded enthusiastically.

Charlotte did not think his comment in keeping with the unhappy opinions he had already expressed to her regarding the Prince's taste in decor. When she glanced up at him, she realized his quizzing glass was now fixed solidly to his eye and he was enjoying the sight of the same young lady's ankles exposed below a jaunty row of white point lace at the hem of her gown. She rapped his arm sharply. "Papa!" she cried with a laugh. "You are incorrigible. I only wonder that the young lady—"

"Miss Kemp."

"—I only wonder that Miss Kemp is not blushing at your quite indelicate attentions to her."

"They never do blush, my dear," he said, taking her by the elbow and leading her away from Miss Kemp. "Make your best curtsy now. Here is a woman I admire prodigiously. Ah, Lady Purcell! How do you go on?" To the older, quite stolid gentleman supporting her ladyship's arm, he bowed and added respectfully, "My lord. May I present my daughter, Miss Amberley."

"Very charming," Lady Purcell said brightly in response to Charlotte's curtsy. His lordship murmured an acknowledgement of her presence but neither smiled nor met her gaze. Lady Purcell continued, "You must bring your daughter to the Steyne tomorrow evening that we might become better acquainted."

Charlotte had a glimpse of large, flirtatious green eyes which never once left her father's face, eyes adorned by lashes which fluttered behind a fan painted prettily in bluebells. Before her father could respond to her ladyship's suggestion, Lord Purcell urged his wife onward, saying that Lady

Hertford was nodding to her. "You must excuse us," Lady Purcell said sweetly and was gone.

"Pity," her father muttered. She would have asked what he meant, but catching sight of his expression, she knew she needn't inquire. He was watching Lady Purcell move away, her elegant demi-train of blue silk sighing across the carpet, his own eyes hungry as he stroked the shirtpoint of his collar lightly with the tip of his finger. "Damned fine woman."

Lady Purcell was easily twenty years his junior. Charlotte felt as if she had been privy to the inner, secret workings of his mind and appetites and wished it had been otherwise.

She looked away from him and her attention was soon caught by yet another female who nodded to her and smiled then pointedly looked at her father. "Papa," she whispered, holding up her own fan of white lace and pearls in order to mask her speech, "there is a woman with bright red hair not far distant who seems quite anxious to gain your notice."

His attention was diverted on the instant. When he caught sight of the lady in question, his expression softened into a smile. "Eugenia," he breathed with a sigh.

Immediately he took Charlotte again by the elbow and guided her toward the lady, who was soon introduced as one Mrs. Wyndham, and beside her a tall lady, Mrs. Knight. The latter had dark brown hair, nearly the shade of Charlotte's, and nodded somewhat stiffly to Charlotte's greeting and slight curtsy.

"So you are Sir John's daughter!" Mrs. Wyndham exclaimed. "Isn't she pretty, Jane?"

"Very pretty," Mrs. Knight agreed blandly. "I daresay she will break a dozen hearts while she remains in Brighton." To Charlotte, she said, "Be advised, Miss Amberley, that there are a score of fortune hunters ready to pluck the unwary. I recommend you be wise in the choice of your acquaintance. Do you intend to remain the entire summer?"

"Yes," Charlotte responded, not liking Mrs. Knight's cold manners nor her haughty demeanor. She was tall and at one time would have been accounted a beauty, but the years seemed to have stiffened her pretty features, hardening them, as it were. She had all the warmth of a statue. Disliking the impertinence of her advice and the manner in which she stared at her, she smiled sweetly and continued, "I intend to partake of all the pleasures of Brighton for the summer, I hope, or until my father has grown *bored* with society-by-the-sea and decides to return to Amberley."

Mrs. Wyndham hid her smiles behind her fan. Mrs. Knight pressed her lips tightly together.

Sir John cleared his throat and, with expressed hopes of calling upon both ladies quite soon, he drew his daughter away. "You quite took the wind out of her eye, my dear."

"I am sorry," she said quietly, though without penitence. "But she was so unkind! Do you know her well?"

Sir John nodded to yet another acquaintance before replying. "Not as well as Mrs. Wyndham. You must forgive Mrs. Knight. Both her friends, Lady Purcell and Mrs. Wyndham, married above her. And she, being the daughter of a viscount, has been less than gracious in adjusting to her diminished station, particularly since for a considerable time she had been expected to snabble a viscount herself!"

"I see," Charlotte responded.

Mrs. Knight's sentiments were hardly new under the sun. Even in the restricted confines of the neighborhood surrounding Amberley Park, such jealousies and disappointments abounded, not less so because the daughters of each genteel household had little more to occupy their minds than whatever matrimonial prospects chanced to appear. She might easily have made such an object the focus of her own daily activities and concerns had not the untimely death of her mother forced her to undertake the management of Amberley Park. Amberley had kept her busy, indeed!

Sir John interrupted the course of her thoughts by pinching her arm and saying quite urgently, "Now remember, my dear, you must attract Lord Stoneleigh's notice as quickly as possible, though I doubt you will be able to achieve a great deal initially. However, once the orchestra strikes the last note, I want you to be prepared to distract him immediately afterward. I shall have only a moment or two with which to gain Prinny's ear. Do you understand?"

"Yes, father," she whispered in return. Somehow the birds cavorting on the wallpaper no longer seemed as cheerful as they were before and the lotus lights mounted in elegant Chinese vases had entirely lost their enchantment. Even the carpet beneath her slippers felt hard and unfriendly, each footstep toward the future a reminder that she was no longer merely a guest in the Regent's marine Pavilion, but a young woman with a questionable purpose.

"Good God!" Sir John cried.

She wondered what had overset him until she turned to glance in the direction of his gaze and saw Maude and Selena hurrying toward them.

He continued, "We are about to be trampled upon by your friends. Since I cannot abide the squeals of young females, I will leave you to greet them alone."

Charlotte let her father go without regret. She knew he wished to speak privately with more than

one female he had already acknowledged and, if
the truth be known, she cherished the interrup-
tion since it would divert her mind from the
forthcoming trial, if but for a time.

Eight

Maude Dunsfold and Selena Bosham had been situated at the southern end of the corridor. Having caught sight of Charlotte, they were hurriedly—if not literally—running to greet her, their demi-trains billowing out behind them, their ankles in full view from hastily gathered-up skirts, their faces alight with smiles.

Her father was wrong about one thing—neither Maude nor Selena would disgrace themselves by squealing, for that would be unforgivably unladylike. But it seemed to Charlotte, who had not seen her friends since February, that the squeals of delight and excitement emerged in spite of their gentle breeding—in the silent bounces of glee as they circled round her, the dancing joy in their eyes, the fluttering of their fans, and the charming bob of Maude's black ringlets and Selena's charming red curls.

"How do you go on?" Maude cried.

"What a pretty gown!" Selena's childlike exclamation overlapped her friend's question. "Did you design it yourself? Of course you did, as you always do! I suppose you hired the seamstresses in the village to sew for you—always thinking of the poor. Oh, my dearest Charlotte! How glad I am to see you, for now justice will prevail in Brighton. You shall set all to rights!"

Maude interrupted. "Are those new eardrops? What lovely pearls. But then you wear pearls to such perfection!"

"Have you seen Stoneleigh?" Selena interjected.

"How can she have *seen* Stoneleigh," Maude chided, "when she has never even met him before? And though we described him in our letters, I imagine there must be a dozen gentlemen present who could answer to a description presented in a neat paragraph. Oh, but do let me have a look at you. Oh, yes, very fashionable! You shall do! Indeed, you shall!" Lowering her voice, an amused smile on her lips, she cried, "Only do tell me what you think of our Prince's Pavilion?"

Charlotte found herself laughing in spite of herself. She was exceedingly happy to see her friends—even if they were quick to remind her of her duty where Stoneleigh was concerned. Wouldn't they be surprised when she told them she had already met his lordship? As for the Pavilion, she fanned her warm cheeks and said, "I have never seen anything so—so unusual, so striking! The colors are wondrous! I feel as if I have been transported to another world, another time! I vow I am utterly enchanted!"

"You admire the Pavilion?" Maude whispered, apparently stunned. Her entire demeanor became quite serious as she continued, "I think the whole of it is a monstrosity. How can you speak of these atrocious patterns and designs as *wondrous?* And as for another world, I believe you have the right of it—one without a sense of taste or appropriateness of line or architectural symmetry."

Charlotte was a little surprised as she looked up at her tall friend. There was just such a censorious note in Maude's voice, so at odds with the young lady who had once stolen peaches with her from Mr. Robson's orchard, that for a moment Charlotte did not recognize her friend from childhood. Maude had become quite elegant and fashionable over the years, she realized, not more so than tonight, wearing a single white ostrich feather in her black curls and diamond drops upon each ear. She appeared to great advantage in a patterned silk gown of pale blue adorned by an orange-blossom shawl draped elegantly over her thin, graceful arms. She was in every respect a modish young lady, from the several rows of carefully hemmed ruffles on each of her puffed sleeves to her exquisitely fitted white silk gloves to her matching white slippers embroidered in silver thread. Charlotte could not help but approve of the decorous manner in which Maude moved and spoke, in distinct contrast to her memory of a younger Maudie, her walking dress muddied at the knees from having tumbled from the low branch of a peach tree. Still, she had the feeling that something had been lost in the transition of schoolgirl to young lady.

She tilted her head, imploring her. "You cannot mean you think the Pavilion a monstrosity. Surely! I agree that it is quite bizarre in the uniqueness of its decor, but I rather find the oriental ambience exhilarating."

Maude smiled sweetly. "I shan't argue with you on your first evening in Brighton, though you may soon find your opinion is not shared by many."

"I share her opinion," Selena countered in her girlish voice. She was a diminutive young lady with sparkling blue eyes, a delicately pale skin attractively arrayed with freckles, a pert nose, and a wealth of pretty red curls which she wore drawn up into a knot atop her head. "Well, perhaps not entirely, but I do think all the bamboo furniture and railings to be quite cleverly done."

"Very kindly said," Charlotte responded with an approving nod of her head.

She wondered if Maude would continue the argument. Indeed, Maude appeared as if she wished to do so, but her expression underwent a sudden change as she drew in a small gasp and bit her lower lip. Her gaze had gone past Charlotte's shoulder to light upon some object or other down the hall in the direction of the inner entrance hall.

"I cannot believe he has *her* on his arm," was her only remark as she lifted a single, disapproving brow.

Charlotte turned slightly in order to discern to whom Maude was referring. For some reason, she was not expecting to see Lord Stoneleigh and so she was caught completely unawares by the sight of him.

Maude was on her right and Selena, her left. As though responding to some signal between them, they each leaned near to Charlotte and intoned solemnly, *"Stoneleigh."*

"Indeed, it is," Charlotte responded in a hushed voice.

Nine

Both Selena and Maude began speaking to one another at once in hushed whispers behind their fans, the object of their conversation not Stoneleigh but the lady he was escorting. Charlotte, however, seemed unable to attend to their excited chatter. The moment her gaze fell upon Stoneleigh, she lost all sense of her surroundings, as if the spell of the Pavilion had become concentrated in the lean lines of his tall frame and the warm, inviting smile he wore as he conversed easily with the lady whose arm he supported so gently.

In the soft light of the Chinese lanterns, standing beneath the God of Thunder painted boldly on the skylight above, he appeared exalted, not less so than by the fact that the moment he began strolling down the hallway in her direction, scarcely a one was not excited by his appearance, straining to gain his notice. He was polite in his nods of acknowledgement, but he kept his attention fixed civilly upon the lady he was with, a mode of conduct Charlotte found herself approving heartily.

He even laughed at something the lady said, the warmth of his smile suffusing his whole face as he then responded in kind and brought a warm smile to her lips. She was obviously charmed, but then what lady would not be at such complete attention and devotion to her pleasure?

Charlotte found herself scrutinizing his entire appearance, wondering why he seemed better dressed than any other man present. Save for the white of his moderate but well-starched shirt-points, the white of his neckcloth and shirt, he was dressed entirely in black—coat, waistcoat, black slippers, pantaloons that fit his muscular legs to perfection and which were held in place with straps looped beneath his feet. A diamond pin glittered in the intricate folds of his neck-cloth. Several gentlemen lifted their quizzing glasses, carefully examining the arrangement of his neckcloth, perhaps in hopes of one day being able to imitate it.

Had she known nothing of the man advancing steadily toward her, she would have believed she had met her ideal. But remembering how he had accused her of orchestrating the accident outside the clock shop, she was reminded that his char-acter was not all that it should be. The more she had considered his arrogance in attaching the worst possible motives to their encounter, the more she had become convinced Maude and Se-lena had not exaggerated in their descriptions of him but had spoken the truth. She ought, there-fore, to have felt indifferent to his presence; in-stead her heart seemed to flutter about wildly in her breast.

Maude's voice intruded sharply. "I believe he is in love with Mrs. Hastings," she whispered. "Every-one speaks of it—that he has loved her for years."

Charlotte felt a wave of dread rush from her heart and suffuse her face with heat. Does he love this woman? Could he be in love with the wife of another man? For reasons she could not explain, she did not want it to be true.

Selena clicked her tongue. "And with the Colonel away, who is to intervene on his behalf should Stoneleigh desire to sway her affections away from her husband?" She gave her red ringlets a disapproving shake, her blue eyes opening wide.

"No one, of course," was Maude's cold response.

Without thinking, Charlotte cried, "He would never do so. Indeed, he would not! I'm sure of it!"

Her words had been spoken during one of those curious moments which occur at odd times in a crowded chamber when, as one, the entire gathering takes a breath and leaves the air vacant—ostensibly for the sole purpose of providing a stage for just such an intriguing pronouncement as Charlotte had made. More than two dozen heads snapped in her direction, and her cheeks grew hot. "Oh, my," she murmured, quickly wafting her fan over her face. Not wishing to do so but finding it impossible to do otherwise, she looked at Stoneleigh.

His expression was first one of mild surprise which softened quickly to a quiet smile. He was still some twenty feet from her, yet he bowed to her, a gesture of recognition which caused a gentle whispering to rise up quickly all around her and to begin filling the silence her words had created.

Charlotte curtsied in response as his gaze drifted over her hair and her gown. What would he think of her, she wondered, her heart again beginning to make itself known in its flutterings. A final nod of his head, and he returned his attention to the lady beside him.

"One would think he was already acquainted with you!" Maude whispered, incredulous.

Selena interjected, "And you curtsied in return. Is it possible you know Lord Stoneleigh? Is that why when we first saw him you said, *indeed, it is,* as if you recognized him?"

"As it happens, I have met him," she answered quietly, her gaze still directed toward the viscount. He was speaking to Mrs. Hastings, probably informing his companion of her identity. The intriguing pair appeared desirous of joining Charlotte and her friends but, taking a step in their direction, they were suddenly hailed from behind by Lady Hertford, their intentions cut off.

Charlotte did not know whether relief or disappointment held sway in her mind, but she rather thought it was the former. She did not yet feel equal to the task of meeting Stoneleigh again. For one thing, though she was reluctant to admit it, her head still hurt her and occasionally a mild dizziness assailed her. And for another, the thought of being required to pounce upon Stoneleigh in order to aid her father in speaking privately with the Prince appeared an insurmountable chore.

To Maude and Selena's intense queries as to where and how she had become acquainted with his lordship, she responded, "I had meant to tell you, indeed, I had, but I could not find a breach in the conversation broad enough to utter even one word, nonetheless the number required to inform you of my misadventure this afternoon."

"This afternoon!" they cried as one.

Charlotte quickly regaled her friends regarding the tumble she had taken outside the clock shop and how Stoneleigh had actually held her in his arms for several minutes until he placed her in the hackney, even refusing to return her to her feet when begged to do so.

Maude eyed her curiously, her slanting, green eyes suddenly seeming quite distant. "You appear to have bewitched him already, Charlie. How clever of you. Why, the way he looked at you just now—I don't know, it was so welcoming. I knew you were going to succeed with our schemes, but never would I have thought so quickly or so well. It almost seems as if the Fates have destined you to be Stoneleigh's Nemesis; unless, of course, you have yourself decided upon a different object entirely."

Charlotte looked at Maude and smiled uneasily, "I don't know what you mean, but as for succeeding, I'm afraid it is no such thing. If he has shown me any civility at this moment, I don't think I can explain it, since I fear I quarreled with him upon climbing into the hackney. For some reason, he was convinced I had intentionally bumped into him for the strict purpose of gaining his notice. Have you ever heard anything so absurd?"

Charlotte watched Maude's gaze slide away from her own and an odd suspicion entered her brain that her friend had once stooped to using such a device. She felt a strong impulse to discover whether or not it was true, but Selena's giggles prevented her as she cried, "Oh, never mind that, Charlie. Do but look. It is *Sir Florid.*"

The light, sarcastic tone of Selena's remark was not lost on Charlotte. She had spoken so very fashionably, so worldly wise that, for the first time since her coming-out ball nearly six years earlier, Charlotte felt uncomfortably countrified. She supposed Selena was referring to some coxcomb or other who had grown high in the flesh and paraded himself about in a silly manner; but when she followed the direction of Selena's gaze, she was dumbfounded.

"But is that not the Prince?" she queried in a startled whisper.

Maude rapped her arm gently with her folded fan and in a low voice said, "Don't pay the least heed to Selena, dearest Charlie. She is still annoyed that His Royal Highness suggested she cease wearing pink since it does not complement her red hair, and you know how very much Selena favors pink."

Charlotte blinked twice as she glanced at Selena. She bit her lip, for it came to her that there was scarcely anything Selena was wearing which was not either completely or partially pink, from the pink ribbons wound throughout her red curls atop her head to her ivory broach dangling upon a pink ribbon to her balldress of pink silk to her pink slippers. Even her fan was painted with pink roses.

Selena sniffed. "The Prince is wrong."

Charlotte did not agree with her but saw no reason to say as much to her friend. Besides, it made no difference to her whether Selena wore pink or green or an ugly brown. She would always be her dear friend—nothing would change that. What more could possibly signify?

Selena glanced toward the southern end of the corridor and said, "Mama is waving her fan at me. She will want us to be with her now, Maude, since the Prince has arrived and will be greeting each of us. Charlotte, pray join us that we might sit together during the *musicale.*" Mrs. Bosham had charge of both young ladies during their holiday in Brighton.

Charlotte, however, begged to be excused knowing that her father would need to choose their seats with care and would want her to be prepared to *distract* Lord Stoneleigh. When Sir John returned to Charlotte, Maude and Selena scurried away, but not before Selena whispered, "Remember—take Stoneleigh down a peg or two, Charlie! We are depending on you to revenge our poor hearts!"

Ten

A few moments later, Charlotte found herself curtsying deeply, her head bowed. Her heart was nearly bursting. For all of Maude and Selena's flippant indifference to His Royal Highness, she could not be anything but awed. She was not so hardened by the exigencies of life among the *haut ton* as her friends, and she believed her visit to the Royal Pavilion would live forever in her mind as one of the finest evenings of her life.

"You have a beautiful daughter, Amberley," she heard the Prince say. Only then did she rise from her curtsy and dare to look up into his face. She was pleased to find that his expression was entirely affable, as if designed purposely to set her at ease. He smiled at her, a friendly, gracious smile that further gave her courage and strengthened her trembling knees. When Sir John thanked His Royal Highness for his compliment, the Prince narrowed his eyes slightly at Charlotte and said, "So tell me what you think of my Pavilion. No nonsense now, the truth!"

Charlotte let her gaze drift past his shoulder to the imposing Mandarin figure housed in a niche in the wall, to the blue bamboo grove floating across the pink sky nearby, to the lotus lamps sitting jauntily atop the Chinese vases. "I believe you have quite thoroughly reached into my dreams and built a world to make me happy, if for just one night. I am enchanted beyond words."

An expression of surprise and delight shone in his eyes. He seemed nonplussed for a moment, then laughed rather gleefully. Glancing from Charlotte to Sir John, then back to Charlotte as if he could not credit his ears, he finally exclaimed, "You understand, don't you? It is very rare, you know, particularly in one so young. But I must warn you, if my corridor has charmed you, my music room will likely cause you to swoon. I suggest you fortify yourself, therefore, with a vinaigrette, as you ladies are extremely fond of doing."

Charlotte laughed. "I'm certain it won't be necessary. I'm not such a poor creature even if I thought it were true. But I confess I am now all impatience to see your music room."

"You shan't have long to wait," he responded, again smiling happily. Turning to Lady Hertford, whom Charlotte understood to be his constant companion, he reiterated. "She understands what I have been trying to achieve. So little do, isn't that correct?" Lady Hertford nodded and smiled politely in agreement, fanning herself with long, elegant sweeps of a white, befeathered fan.

Returning his attention to Charlotte, he bowed his quite famous bow and said, "You have made me very happy, Miss Amberley. If there is ever anything I can do for you, you have but to ask, you have my word on it. And that is my solemn promise as your future Sovereign."

When he moved on, Charlotte again curtsied deeply, aware of the great honor he had conferred upon her—a favor from the Prince just for the asking! She watched him go, her heart beating joyfully in her breast. Though his advancing age and general corpulence hid the handsome youth he must once have been, she could only think he was a great host and a good man. She paid no heed to the curious looks she received nor to the buzzing of gossip which flew past her several times, her name borne on its busy wings, but contented herself by following the Prince of Wales' progression as he proceeded in the direction of the music room, greeting everyone by name.

"I congratulate you, my dear," Sir John whispered, giving her arm a squeeze. "And how very clever of you to placate his vanity so completely. I only wonder I didn't recommend such a course to you in the first place, but then you always were a clever child."

Charlotte looked up into his smiling face, "But Papa, you speak as if I purposed to compliment him and I did no such thing. I offered my opinion, my true opinion. Nothing more."

"Indeed?" Sir John queried, startled. "Do you tell me you really do admire the Pavilion?"

"Yes, I do," Charlotte returned, strolling slowly down the corridor along with the other guests. She watched the multitude in front of her moving steadily onward, the soft light of the Chinese lanterns overhead illuminating a gentle bobbing of ostrich feathers, jewels, ribbons, and carefully brushed and pomaded hair as the *beau monde* prepared to be entertained.

The Prince Regent would be playing his cello, followed by a performance of his unusual woodwind band made up of the finest musicians, many of whom were German. Charlotte continued, "I might not wish to have Mr. Nash transform Amberley Park into an exotic home reminiscent of the Orient, but I can surely value and appreciate His Royal Highness' vision."

Sir John grunted his familiar grunt. Charlotte glanced quickly up at him and noticed he was yet again observing Miss Kemp's well-turned ankle. When a quite inconsiderate gentleman stepped between Miss Kemp and the baronet's view of her limbs, he bethought himself and whispered, "Remember, Charlie! Do what you must to distract Lord Stoneleigh. I shall do the rest."

"Papa, wouldn't it be best, since the Prince has granted me a favor, that I ask him for the Charter? It would be a much simpler course; and he has, after all, made his solemn promise to me."

Sir John laughed at her apparent naïveté. "Do but think, Charlie. His Royal Highness has been exceedingly polite, but I sincerely doubt he expects you to come to him on the morrow and request a Charter for a joint-stock company. It would be more in keeping with the general tone of his gracious vow that should you request a Haydn sonata, for example, he would feel compelled to honor your request because of his promise to you. No, no, you would trespass on his sense of propriety were you to make such a demand. Having known the Prince for such a long time, I can assure you he sets a great store by such things."

There was nothing more to be said, and Charlotte fell silent as the doorway to the music room came into view.

Eleven

Once inside the music room, Charlotte forgot completely about her mission and about Stoneleigh. The magnificence of the large, domed chamber could not be easily assimilated, and she began to wonder whether the Prince had had the right of it after all when a giddiness caused her to feel quite dizzy. Would she fall into a swoon? Whether she would or not hardly mattered, since she was beginning to enjoy the sensation that extended itself to her slippered feet—were they really touching the blue-gold carpet as she crossed the room?

Her father led her to a chair at some distance from the band, seating himself beside Lady Hertford. Charlotte was surprised by the distance until he leaned toward her and explained, "The band plays brilliantly but loudly."

After this one brief comment, he seemed to forget entirely about his daughter and concentrated all his drawing room abilities upon her ladyship.

Charlotte scarcely noticed her father's inattention for the beauty around her. Her gaze slid, as it had at least a dozen times since entering the chamber, toward the lofty, intricately worked ceiling. She had heard someone comparing the Pavilion to the enchanted palaces of the *Arabian Nights*, but only now did she realize why. No fewer than nine enormous *lustres* were suspended from the ceiling, dazzling the company below with an abundance of light. The interior of the dome was a blue cove, embellished with bullrushes on a gilded trellis. Smaller and smaller scalloped shells in green and gold climbed upward meeting large triangles arranged in a circle around the perimeter of the dome. The largest *lustre* hung from the center of the dome and was composed—as were the remaining *lustres*—of a hemisphere of translucent glass in the shape of several joined lotus leaves painted with either flowers or Chinese figures.

Charlotte could not credit the clever manner in which the round dome transitioned to a rectangular chamber. A red, octagonal canopy—just a few inches in width—extended in geometric precision around the widest base of the dome. More decorated ceiling stretched, completing the transition, from the octagonal canopy to each of four walls. Beautifully worked Chinese landscapes dominated these walls, depicting palaces, palm trees, lakes, pagodas, egrets, and fishermen—all painted in gold on panels of a deep red background. The landscapes seemed to create an illusion that the vista was unlimited, taking Charlotte's eye beyond the room itself to an endless oriental horizon. Colorful, blue dragons and gilded serpents bordered each red panel like a frame around an exquisite work of art.

On the window wall, blue-and-crimson satin draperies, fringed with gold tassels, were supported by huge silvered dragons and serpents and adorned each window. Pagodas, some as tall as twelve feet, flanked the room in blue and gold; and on the floor, drawing the chamber together, was an Axminster carpet, also of deep-blue and gold.

Charlotte did not know when the music actually started, only that the welcome, haunting sound of the cello now filled the chamber. She felt deeply satiated, both by sight and sound, her spirits uplifted in the presence of a beautiful room and by the beautiful music.

The Prince was performing. Who had once said he was *the most accomplished gentleman in Europe?*

Lord Stoneleigh sat across from Charlotte, some twenty feet away. The chairs had been arranged in a semi-circle which faced the Prince, the band, and the enormous Lincoln organ beyond. Stoneleigh had been to the Pavilion countless times, having owned a house in Brighton for some ten years, journeying to the sea resort every summer following the London Season. But in all these years, he could not remember ever having enjoyed a newcomer's introduction to the Prince's marine residence as much as he had Charlotte Amberley's. Her brown eyes had been opened wide and childlike from the moment she entered the music room, her attention riveted intensely not to the august assemblage of peers and peeresses about her but to the fantasy-come-to-life in every inch of the sixty-foot chamber and in the person of the Prince Regent.

To Stoneleigh, a frequent guest and steady friend to the Prince, the Pavilion in its many stages of transformation had become a familiar but incidental setting. He had forgotten until this moment that the surroundings were indeed magnificent besides speaking of a generous heart, one that was forever encouraging the arts.

Charlotte's delightful daze had reminded him of these facts, and he found himself grateful to her since he could renew his own appreciation of the Pavilion through her eyes. If he soon found his gaze riveted to her instead of to the dragons or the pagodas or the Prince's quavering fingers as he plied the long, vibrating strings of the cello, he supposed it was because, like the Pavilion, she was something of a mystery—and a beautiful one, at that.

She was an exquisitely gowned lady, too, though he understood from Emily, who sat beside him, that the death of her mother and later a beloved aunt had prevented a traditional introduction at the Queen's court. Where then had she gained so obvious a polish and the serene manners she displayed which most young ladies acquired only in the course of a half-dozen spring pilgrimages?

His gaze passed to Sir John on her right. A beloved wife's death had not prevented the baronet from continuing his usual round of pleasures.

Stoneleigh had no love for Sir John; indeed for some time he had believed they would come to cuffs, perhaps even a duel, though he shuddered at the thought. Theirs was a long-standing rivalry, and not even a pretty, young daughter would serve to ease the dreaded tensions between them. He had done all he could to hint the Prince away from his association with the baronet—and therefore whatever scheme Amberley was brewing— since he strongly suspected that Sir John had fallen into the clutches of the Marquis of Thaxted. The marquis was a man who had befriended *duplicity* and *cunning*.

Thank God Thaxted was not here.

And Charlotte Amberley was. Lord, but she was a Grecian goddess come to life, dressed in a delicate white, silk gown, embroidered in gold acanthus leaves from the right shoulder across a full, inviting décolletage to glide at an angle down the

74

front of the bodice and travel the full length of the skirt. About the hem were several rows of white silk ruffles. She was a pure, white rose amongst the *ton*.

In her brown hair, dressed in a gentle array of curls which draped in soft ringlets down her neck, she wore a crown of gold acanthus leaves, accented with pearls. A necklet of pearls and pearl-drops upon her ears were her only adornments. Tight-fitting long white gloves, not quite meeting her short puffed sleeves, white silk slippers, and white silk stockings completed a toilette greatly appealing in its simplicity. He approved very much of her choices and thought that whatever her motives might have been in bumping into him earlier that afternoon, he could forgive her all because of the perfection of her appearance.

Mrs. Hastings touched his wrist gently with her painted fan. "Are you aware you are staring at Miss Amberley?" she queried softly through the powerful strains of the woodwind band as it performed a Beethoven symphony.

He turned to look down at his friend of many years and saw the delightful turn of her lips which meant she was teasing him. "Yes," he whispered back. "And I shall do so until my eyes are reddened and sore, so long as it pleases me."

"Am I to wish you joy?" she queried, feigning astonishment.

He chuckled lightly. "Only from you would I tolerate such an impertinent remark, but I know you too well to believe you anything but facetious. Now, do attend to the music before Lady Hertford begins staring us down."

Mrs. Hastings most properly turned her attention back to the band, but not before she gave his arm a solid pinch.

Stoneleigh knew only a handful of people he

was willing to call true friends. Two of them were Emily Hastings and her husband Colonel Hastings. The latter was in London on business but would be returning shortly to join his wife and their two small sons for the remainder of the summer. It was a great irony in his life that Emily Hastings was niece to the Marquis of Thaxted and her eldest son, his heir. If Sir John Amberley were his enemy, Thaxted was his Nemesis.

As his gaze fixed itself yet again upon Charlotte, whose eyes were at the moment closed, lending her face an expression bordering on rapture, the loose thought presented itself in his mind— why was she here, now, after so many years? Why had she come to Brighton?

The devil take it, he thought. Had he been involved in the Prince's affairs for so long that he must see stratagems and evil designs upon every unlooked-for event? Not tonight, he decided. Tonight, he would allow Charlotte Amberley to be simply a beautiful woman whom he felt compelled to know better.

And she was beautiful, possessing delicately arched, dark brows, a snowy complexion, high, rosy cheeks, a slightly retroussé nose, cherry lips, and a soft, rounded chin.

Why on earth was she not yet married?

He bethought himself of how quiet she had been in his arms when awakening but then how quickly and forcefully her vigor had returned—as if she had never even suffered a blow to the head—how straightforward she had been in expressing her opinions, how she had even taken him to task for his own stubbornness—and he had his answer. For all her beauty, refined manners, and general air of fragility, Charlotte Amberley was made of stern stuff and would not easily tolerate the absurdities of a halfling spouting poems at the moon, not when she thought his lines full of stuff and nonsense.

No. She remained unwed because none of the less hardy bucks about Sir John's manor house would have her.

But then, her friends were not married either. Perhaps more than a certain wilfulness flawed Charlotte's character. Perhaps Maude Dunsfold and Selena Bosham were a reflection of Charlotte Amberley. If so, he thought tight-lipped, he would soon know and would not hesitate to dismiss her as indifferently as he had both her *dearest* friends.

Thoughts of these two ladies, both of whom had set their caps for him—or more aptly, for his title—during the course of the last two seasons, caused him to seek each out. What he discovered when he found pretty Selena startled him, for she was watching him with a sad, mooncalf expression.

Good God, did the chit really believe she was in love with him?

He shifted his gaze to Maude, sitting beside Selena. She was also watching him and held her fan to her lips, then smiled and nodded to him. An invitation if there was one!

He found himself annoyed, the pleasure of the evening dimmed perceptibly. He was fatigued with the whole business of his bachelordom— wishing he had married Emily before the Colonel had swept her away with his charm and humor.

He realized it was odd how his thoughts seemed to travel all of their own in a careful circle. He glanced down at the fine eyes and noble chin and quite ordinary features of the lady beside him. She had told him forthrightly that she did not love him and never could—that she was very much in love with Colonel Hastings. After the first jolt of her rejection and her subsequent marriage to the Colonel, he had come to realize he had never loved her either. Not truly, but had welcomed her as a buffer between himself and a dozen match-making mamas, a relationship which had worked wondrously well so long as he paid her court and excited the belief amongst the *haut ton* that he would one day wed her.

Seven years had gone by since her wedding day. He had lost his buffer from that day forward and had been unprotected the entire time from the pursuit of a score of avaricious females.

Again his gaze was drawn to Charlotte.

Was she one of these ladies who had come to Brighton for the sole purpose of trying her charms on his coarsened heart? After all, she could easily effect a perfect solution to Amberley's considerable financial woes if she were to win his love and his fortune.

Only as this last, truly unfortunate thought overtook his mind did Stoneleigh finally turn his attention to the woodwind band. Several times he felt compelled to glance in Charlotte's direction but always quickly afterward reverted his gaze to the music until the last notes had been struck.

As if driven by a force beyond his comprehension or power, he again turned to watch her. Only this time, he saw Sir John whisper something in her ear which, even from a distance, he could see took the rosy color from her cheeks. She then lowered her gaze and clasped her pretty, gloved hands tightly together on her lap.

What the devil, he murmured to himself, as Charlotte sought to compose herself. The guests began to rise from their seats. He continued to watch her through a maze of bodies as the *beau monde* began moving slowly from the music room. He could see she was suffering some acute anxiety, her hands clenching and unclenching as she remained seated. Then suddenly her chin rose and she stared straight ahead, as if mesmerized by something, some inward thought.

To his astonishment, she jumped from her seat and all but ran from the chamber, weaving her way erratically through the crush, ignoring her father and friends completely.

A mystery, indeed!

Twelve

Once in the corridor, where the air was cooler and fresher than in the music room, Charlotte slowed down as much to catch her worried breath as to avoid attracting notice. She had scurried from the music room, like a hare released unexpectedly from a woodland snare, wanting only to be quiet with her thoughts, if but for a moment. She had enjoyed the music so very much, but her euphoria had lasted only as long as it had taken her father to whisper, "See to Stoneleigh!" The knowledge that both Maude and Selena were expecting her to do the same somehow flooded her with panic.

Up she had jumped, her feet turning her abruptly in the direction of the doors, her heart pounding furiously in her chest and hard in her head.

She couldn't do it. She couldn't entrap a man by her wiles. What wiles? She was a fledgling in society for all her four and twenty years. What did she truly know of enslaving a man's heart? The truth was she was far more comfortable with estate ledgers and housekeeping keys than with drawing room intrigues.

No, she couldn't do it. Even if she had pos-

80

sessed the dubious feminine skills required, she couldn't do it.

But whatever was her father to do? Would Maude and Selena ever comprehend her unwillingness?

She felt disloyal and dismally inadequate.

She left the crowds behind her as they swept into the Red Saloon, where a supper of sandwiches and wine would be passed around. She walked on, uncertain to what end, until she came to the last chamber opening onto the corridor. She moved past the darkened threshold, this chamber even cooler than the corridor.

She found herself alone in what proved to be the banqueting room. Two candelabra on the long table cast large, grotesque shadows on the domed ceiling and walls but did little to properly illumine the chamber. The panic which had originally set her feet flying from the music room dissipated in quick stages, her hot face cooled by the empty, fireless room. Once alone, she discovered that her head was pounding fiercely, a latent result no doubt of her misadventure of the afternoon. She fanned her face with her lace fan, staring at the flickering candles. She did not feel well at all, in fact, rather queasy.

"How curious that I should find you here and alone, but this was your purpose, wasn't it? Or am I entirely mistaken that something ignoble is afoot?"

Charlotte turned slowly around. She knew Stoneleigh was not eight feet from her, but how his voice did wiggle and the words he spoke were still swimming disjointedly about her head. She was trying to make sense of what he had said, but the chamber began shifting about strangely.

"How very vexatious," she murmured. She then took a step toward him not even able to bring his

81

lovely blue eyes into focus. "Pray inform Papa I must, I must . . ."

How much time passed Charlotte did not know. Time, blackness, and the soft butterfly playing on her cheeks and eyelids and upon her ears. She tried to move away from it, particularly when it touched her neck and sent a chill all down her side. Still the butterfly persisted.

What was wrong with her? She could scarcely move her hand. It was so heavy that when she lifted it up slightly, it flopped back against her stomach. She couldn't open her eyes either, but then the butterfly would touch her lids and she began to like it very much, so feathery soft and warm.

Words began reaching her ears. She gave a chuckle. How could a butterfly speak? Oh, she must be dreaming, but how real, yet how misty did the butterfly and the words seem. But where was she? Was she in bed? What of the Pavilion?

The wings batted the line of her cheek, all the way to her ear. But what nonsense was this?

"Tell me, Charlotte," the butterfly whispered. "Did you come to Brighton to make me tumble in love with you?"

Love a butterfly?

She giggled. "No, silly," she breathed.

The wings moved over her forehead, over her eyelids, down her nose. "I could have loved you, I think," the butterfly whispered back.

Again she murmured, "Silly."

"Oh, yes, very much, I think. Only tell me why you've come."

The butterfly's wings began barely touching her lips, a wondrous sensation that brought a sigh pouring from deep within her soul. "I wish I might be kissed as sweetly," she murmured into the wings. "I should like that, I think, very much."

"Then you shall be kissed," the butterfly responded, sounding very familiar and not very different from someone she knew. But whom? Why was she so confused?

As if some unspoken desire were being fulfilled, the butterfly transformed and she felt the kiss upon her lips she had just requested, but this was a man's kiss. Responding to the touch of his lips, so dreamlike, so unreal, yet real, she gave herself thoroughly to the experience, accepting the kiss as if it were the most natural occurrence in the world. How sensual and moist the kiss was, covering her lips in pleasure and delight, drawing nectar-sweet desire up into her mind, obliterating rational thoughts, leaving only a longing for the touch to continue forever.

At what point she realized she was being kissed in truth, and that quite thoroughly, Charlotte did not know, except that a certain urgency seemed to flood the man's touch, frightening her.

"No," she whispered, only to find a hand holding her neck firmly so that she could not pull away. She felt so weak, so helpless. "No," she repeated again.

"But you wanted a kiss," he responded. "You said so."

Only then did she know she was caught in Stoneleigh's embrace. "My lord," she whispered. "Whatever are you doing? I must be ill, I didn't even know—"

"You did not seem ill a moment ago. You were even giggling, Miss Amberley. No more whiskers, if you please!"

Charlotte was able now, though with some effort, to place her hand on his chest and push him away from her. "I thought I was dreaming," she breathed, her throat dry.

"Dreams of being kissed, then?"

"No—yes! I don't know. My poor head."

She placed the back of her hand on her forehead and leaned against his shoulder.

"Cut the theatrics!" he snapped as he scooted her off his lap and summarily set her flatly upon a chair.

She weaved there, staring up at him, trying to focus on his face but finding the task impossible. He was standing in front of her and she saw him reach into the pocket of his coat. Searching for snuff, no doubt, she thought, aimlessly.

She held onto the armless dining chair, gripping the front edge of the seat with her hands and holding on as if her life depended upon it.. She was so abominably dizzy, and now her head was pounding fiercely again.

"Pray fetch my father, I beg you," she again whispered. "I am not well, I tell you. I think the accident this afternoon—"

"I congratulate you, my dear. You are by far the most accomplished actress I have ever known. Certainly you excel all the *ladies* of my acquaintance, but it ends here." His voice had a familiar hard edge to it. "Whatever you and your *dear friends* were attempting, it won't fadge, not by half."

"No," she whispered, her head reeling. "You are mistaken, sir. I am ill. Pray—pray, will you not—" She could not finish the sentence and only had the smallest knowledge she was falling.

Stoneleigh watched Charlotte's pretty dark curls slide down the front of his shins as she toppled forward off the seat and landed finally face down on his slippers.

"Good God," he muttered.

For the first time since having followed her into the banqueting room, he began to wonder if she truly were ill.

"Miss Amberley?" he called to her. She had fallen onto the tops of his slippers, pinning his feet to the floor; and for that reason, he was in some danger of losing his balance. He tugged his right foot backward and was able to pull it out from under her head. He leaned down sideways in order to better see her and noted that her cheek was squished against his other foot, her mouth open, her complexion a chalky white. She looked so disheveled and not in the least as one who was doing everything she could in an attempt to fix his affections that he could only conclude she was not playacting as he had first supposed.

"Oh, good Lord in heaven!" he murmured as he scooped her up again quickly in his arms and carried her to the doorway. There he met Emily, who had apparently been looking for him.

"I kissed her and caused her to faint and all because I would not believe she was ill," he cried, cradling Charlotte's head against his shoulder. "Oh, Emily, have I become a complete coxcomb?"

Emily touched Charlotte's cheek then her forehead, her expression one of great concern. "Yes," she answered baldly. "But at least you have a strong provocation for behaving so abominably."

"You do not give me the least comfort, you know," he responded, permitting her to take charge of the situation as she commanded him to follow her up the bamboo staircase.

Thirteen

"But you were remarkable!" Sir John cried, gesticulating excitedly with both arms as he paced in front of the window at the foot of Charlotte's bed.

"It is not so, Papa," Charlotte answered with a sigh. "It was only by accident he came upon me." She was lying in her bed, barely able to concentrate on her father's words. It was late morning but felt more like late afternoon, so fatigued was she. Her gaze kept shifting lazily from the light-blue counterpane on her bed to the zebra-wood chest of drawers on the wall nearest the door to the delicate yellow-and-gleaming-white woodwork of the walls to the several delightful landscapes by an obscure artist named Constable to land finally upon the airy muslin drapes billowing in a light morning breeze, a breeze which filled her bedchamber with healing sea-air.

"Nonsense! You were merely using the Amberley instincts. And how right you were! A man of Stoneleigh's stamp can only be won by giving him a taste of the hunt. To think I was ready to box your ears when I saw you run from the music room! I should've known better. You have never disappointed me. And oh, my dear, I shall have the Charter for my company and to spare, for

Prinny spoke of sending a letter along to the Rothschilds if we need investors from that quarter! I shall have all the ready I need, and then we shall see! We shall see, indeed! Our fortunes are all but repaired!"

Charlotte could protest no longer, about anything, as she slumped into her pillow and slipped a hand beneath her cheek. She had not expected Stoneleigh to follow after her, but it was clear she could never convince her father of that.

The doctor had put her to bed the night before, informing her that to rise before the sun had set twice would do serious injury to her brain. She believed him—first, because her head had not stopped throbbing from the moment she had fainted a second time at Stoneleigh's feet and, also, because all she seemed to want to do was sleep and sleep again.

"Yes, Papa," she murmured, closing her eyes.

"Ah, yes," he said, clapping his hands together softly. "You must rest, clever girl. Imagine, pretending to faint three times! What a daughter I have bred!"

"Indeed," Charlotte again murmured. She heard him leave and drifted off again, wondering why butterflies filled her dreams.

The next time she awoke, Maude and Selena were sitting in her chamber talking in low tones, appearing like colorful birds against the yellow-and-light-blue stillness of her bedchamber. She saw them through a mist of muslin that hung in sheer, diaphanous folds from the cornice of her cherrywood bed. Maude was dressed in a deep-blue silk morning gown, with lace standing up high about her white throat, and Selena wore a pelisse of rose-silk embroidered with white butterflies on the collar. All around her, the smell of the sea-air kept her spirits content.

"Darlings," she called to them in little more than a whisper.

They rustled and bobbed toward her, cooing the entire distance from the Empire chairs by the bright window to stand beside her bed.

"Are you feeling better?" Maude queried.

"But you are grown so pale," Selena's girlish voice sympathized.

"We didn't mean to disturb you."

"Dearest, cleverest Charlie!"

Both young ladies leaned down to place gentle kisses on her cheek and, after expressing hopes her recovery would be quick, Maude whispered, "You cannot imagine what is travelling through every drawing room in Brighton. It is too wondrous to be believed. It is rumored Stoneleigh kissed you! Can it be true?"

Charlotte glanced at Maude wondering where she had got such a notion. "No, of course he did not!" she returned, giggling. "Whoever heard of such an absurdity. He was kind to me when I was ill. That's all."

Selena, her impish tone low and conspiratorial, said, "But it is spoken of everywhere. It is said he carried you out of the darkened banqueting room and told Mrs. Hastings that he had caused you to faint—that he had kissed you and made you quite unwell!"

Charlotte strained to remember all that had transpired, but her memories of events in the banqueting room were unaccountably dim and confused. Without thinking, she responded again with a giggle, "A butterfly kissed me, I remember that much! All over my face, my cheek, even my ear. What a delightful butterfly."

The young ladies, whose heads had been bent together as they spoke with Charlotte, turned to look at each other and blinked at the same time.

"A butterfly?" they queried in unison, turning back to her.

"Oh, my dear, we will leave you now," Maude said quietly, giving her shoulder a gentle squeeze. "You must have suffered a great deal more than any of us suspected—a fever of the brain, perhaps. We shall depart now; but remember, the moment the doctor says you are able, we shall all take a promenade on the Steyne—very fashionable, if you must know! Now do be a dear and mend yourself ever so quickly."

Charlotte sighed. "I will," she said in a voice that did not sound quite like her own.

She again slipped her hand between her cheek and her pillow, closed her eyes, and fell fast asleep to dream of butterflies and Stoneleigh and kisses as sweet as honey from the comb.

Fourteen

"I suppose it will have to do," Charlotte said skeptically as she flared the heavy sea-bathing gown at the sides with both hands. "But won't it be quite heavy in the water, once it is wet?"

Waves lapped at the wheels of the large, square bathing machines, which had been drawn into the water by the sturdy female dippers. "Come, Miss," the dipper said, ignoring Charlotte's concern and bidding her descend the steps of the machine into the ocean. "Bring the boy with you and hold 'im tight about the hand—or under the arms is better yet."

Charlotte took a deep breath and did as she was bid. She turned to Henry and said, "Are you ready then?"

Henry pursed his lips together. He was wearing an old pair of nankeens and a shirt. Putting his hands on his hips, he said, "Charlie, if you will please move out of the way, I can have a nice swim. You needn't worry. I'm very strong, and I've been holding my breath under water for this year and more!"

"I know," Charlotte returned and held out her hand to him.

"I don't need to hold your hand. Nurse has brought me out five times already, once each day you were abed. Follow me. I'll show you how it is done!"

With that, he pushed past her and literally bounded from the top step of the bathing machine and flung himself into the ocean, avoiding the dipper's great arms. Charlotte stood there laughing as she watched Henry surface, sputtering and smiling and splashing water into the dipper's face. Slowly she descended the steps herself, easing herself into the cold water and flinching the whole time.

After five days in bed, she felt completely recovered. Her head had not bothered her for the past three days, and the day before had seen her so anxious to be moving about and partaking of Brighton society that there was nothing for it but to ignore the doctor's orders to remain abed for a fortnight, to put her illness behind her, and to begin again.

Sea-bathing was her first excursion.

When she was finally submerged to her neck, she began to enjoy the tugging sensation of the currents as they pulled back and forth on her heavy, weighted gown. The machines were pulled out into the water only far enough for the bathers to stand thigh-deep where they could float delightfully or swim without the smallest danger of drowning. Charlotte did so, permitting the dipper to keep guard over Henry, who was matching the robust woman stroke for stroke as they swam to the next bathing machine and back.

The ocean became heavenly as her body adjusted to the cold water, her gooseflesh disappearing entirely. The sun was warm on her face, the gulls sounding a jaunty cry that played like a persistent clarinet against the symphony of the continuous, rolling waves. She could hear the ever-present fishermen calling to one another, sometimes laughing sometimes cursing, proof that

91

hers was a privileged life and that Brighton was as much a place of work and industry as it was a pleasure haunt to those who courted the Prince Regent.

"I thought that might be you," a woman's voice intruded. "Perhaps I am being presumptuous, Miss Amberley; but I am Mrs. Hastings, and it was my coach which saw you home so many days ago. I am glad to see your health so delightfully renewed."

Charlotte stood up in the water and met the direct gaze of Emily Hastings' fine, hazel eyes. "How do you do?" she responded immediately. "I am so very much in your debt. Did you receive my letter?"

"Indeed, yes, but only this morning. I have been to London and back since you were abed and have only returned last night. Here are my boys. Permit me to introduce them." She turned, encouraging her sons to step forward. "William and George, please make your best bows to Miss Amberley."

The boys giggled at meeting someone new and that in the water. They were fine lads, nearer to seven and eight, Charlotte supposed, a little older than Henry. Wearing impish smiles, each bowed to Charlotte as their mother bid them, only instead of lifting their heads as they were supposed to, they dove beneath the water.

"Incorrigible," Mrs. Hastings murmured, glancing mischievously at Charlotte.

Charlotte burst out laughing, especially when the young gentlemen surfaced near her, beaming bright smiles and thinking themselves monstrously clever.

"Oh, yes, you're both very precocious, aren't you?" she cried facetiously then rapped each upon the head once lightly with her knuckles. They found it necessary to feign having received

92

death-blows and disappeared once more below the water.

"I love Brighton," Mrs. Hastings said. "Every summer we have such fun here." She then lowered herself to her neck and began paddling about gently. Charlotte could see the lady took her sons sea-bathing often, for her nose was quite pink as well as her cheeks and her chin and underneath was a fine browning from the sun.

She seems so at ease, Charlotte thought, wondering if she would ever be so comfortable with herself or with her surroundings. She supposed she gave the same appearance when she was at Amberley. But Mrs. Hastings had a serenity she knew she did not possess, at least not yet. Perhaps if she were one day a happily married woman, with children of her own, and mistress of her own house, she might, too, know such peace and contentment. She hoped so.

But then, perhaps it was love, she mused, her heart feeling as though it had just been pricked by a pin. *He loves her, you know,* Selena's voice rang in her head. Did Stoneleigh love this woman?

"Who is that little man calling to you, Miss Amberley?"

Charlotte had been so wrapped up in her thoughts all other sounds had completely disappeared. She looked in the direction of Mrs. Hastings' gaze and saw Henry standing at the top step of the nearest bathing machine. He was calling out to her over and over and waving his hands madly.

"That is my son," she said, not thinking.

"Your son?" Mrs. Hastings exclaimed, her hazel eyes opening wide.

"No, not my son," Charlotte replied, laughing, wondering why on earth she had said something so odd. "My brother. I suppose I have come to think of him as my son because I have cared for him since he was a babe. Our mother died when he was born, you see."

"Of course," Mrs. Hastings responded, with a quick nod of understanding. She told her boys to swim over to the next bathing machine and fetch Miss Amberley's brother back, a task which appealed readily to the high spirits of the young men.

By the time the boys were swimming between the ladies, they were all famous friends and planning to meet again on the morrow.

"I hope you will go sea-bathing frequently," Mrs. Hastings said, her kind eyes resting lightly upon Charlotte. "I should be honored to know you better."

Charlotte was pleased, though had anyone told her five days prior she would be chatting amiably with the woman suspected of being the object of Stoneleigh's particular interest, she would have laughed outright. At the same time, she began to discount Maude and Selena's conjectures. She strongly suspected that Mrs. Hastings, from the way she spoke of her husband, was very much in love with him and that she was a friend to Stoneleigh but nothing more. She responded, "I'm certain if Henry were to have his way, we should spend each entire day here at the beach. For myself, I confess I find the water and the sun and wind exhilarating and will not find it difficult to oblige my brother. You have been very kind to me, a stranger to Brighton, Mrs. Hastings. Tomorrow, then?"

"Tomorrow," her new friend agreed, gathering her boys with gentle tugs upon their ears as they swam away to their bathing machine several yards away.

Fifteen

Over the next three days, Charlotte fell easily into the habit of spending a delightful hour each morning at the sea-bathing machines with Henry, Mrs. Hastings, and her two exuberant boys. By the third day, any constraint on her part was entirely gone, and she swam with them all and played in the surf and felt as she had not since childhood—free, unhindered, at ease.

After sea-bathing, Charlotte would bid goodbye to her friend and take Henry to the Castle Inn, ostensibly to partake of breakfast. But this morning proved to be no different from the last two. She might enjoy her repast, but Henry could barely swallow a crumb of fresh-baked bread. He was far too enraptured by the activities of the inn's narrow arched drive leading to the stables to be in the least concerned about eating. Life apparently held no greater pleasure for him—except perhaps playing in the water—than watching the coaches arrive and depart—some for Lewes, some for London.

"I want to be a coach-driver, Charlie, when I am grown up! Do but look at those fine-steppers and how the coachman holds the reins in his hands. He has them looped just so over each finger." He was a very intense young man, staring in wild fascination at the magnificent maroon-and-black coach beginning to roll forward to the cries of the driver. His hair was still damp from his morning exertions, the saltwater drying on his neck in a fine dust. His breath spread out in a warm mist on the window against which his nose was pressed flat. *Ohhhhh,* he breathed in deep satisfaction.

Charlotte chuckled. "Eat your eggs, darling, or you'll never grow up strong enough to manage such a team."

"I am strong already!" he countered, flexing his arms. "This is how the prizefighters do it! William showed me."

A man's deep voice resounded across the table, startling Charlotte. "That wouldn't be William Hastings, now, would it, young man?"

"Wh—why, yes, sir!" Henry responded, baffled, his cheeks red with surprise. "But how did you know?"

Charlotte glanced up and saw two men standing next to her table. One was dressed in uniform and the other in a blue coat, scarlet waistcoat, and buff breeches. "Lord Stoneleigh," Charlotte cried. "How do you do?" She looked from him to the man who had spoken and who was now bowing to her quite deeply—in penance for his intrusion, she thought.

"Very well, but may I present my singularly ill-mannered friend, Colonel Hastings?"

"Indeed you may," Charlotte responded, the mystery solved instantly.

Lord Stoneleigh turned to the colonel and said, "Miss Amberley of Amberley Park."

"Very pleased to make your acquaintance, Miss Amberley," Colonel Hastings said.

"How do you do, sir? And may I present my brother, Henry?" Charlotte tugged on the sleeve of his velvet coat and dragged his attention away from the window where a Stanhope suddenly whirled by. At the hint that he might make his best bow for the gentlemen, Henry scrambled down from his chair. "Yes, of course!" he cried, standing next to the chair and offering each man a careful, polite bow.

He was rewarded when both the Colonel and Stoneleigh bowed gravely in return. When, with an impish smile, he started to bow again, Charlotte clicked her tongue, "That will do, jack-a-napes. Up again and no more foolishness."

"Yes, Charlie," he answered meekly, taking his place in his chair, his head turning with a will of its own to scrutinize for the hundredth time the view through the window.

"I am acquainted with your wife," Charlotte said, addressing the Colonel with a smile. "We have enjoyed a little sea-bathing together with the boys, only this morning as it happens."

"I thought as much. Your nose is as pink as I imagine hers must be by now. The sea is wonderfully bracing, though, isn't it?"

"Yes, very. Delightfully so. But won't you join us? We are partaking of a little breakfast, at least I am. Henry has other, more important, matters consuming his attention." Since Henry was whistling low at the sight of a high-perch Phaeton, whose wheels stood over five-feet tall, the gentlemen quickly discerned her meaning.

Lord Stoneleigh slapped his fine beaver hat against his thigh. "Thank you for your kind invitation, Miss Amberley, but I'm sure Colonel Hastings is anxious to return to his family. He is but just arrived from London and we were attending to a matter of business when I saw you seated here. I wished to present Emily's husband to you. It would seem she has found a friend in you."

So Mrs. Hastings has spoken of me already, Charlotte thought. Aloud she said, "I am delighted with her company. We made great fools of ourselves among the fish this morning."

"Indeed," Stoneleigh remarked, a wondering light in his eye. "Only tell me now that you are fully recovered from our mishap and I shall be content."

"By Jove, that's right!" Colonel Hastings cried, turning to look at the viscount askance, though not without a twinkle in his gray eyes. He was a fine-looking man, Charlotte thought, though neither as tall nor as handsome as Stoneleigh. His sandy-colored hair was already peppered with gray, and his eyes had fine, crinkled lines beside them. She understood from Mrs. Hastings that he had seen considerable action in the Peninsula, serving with Wellington many years ago, but that an injury had prevented further service. "Emily told me you had nearly killed some poor female by running her down by a clock shop." To Charlotte he said, "Bless you, child. I shouldn't like to be rammed by such a lout as Stoneleigh myself. It is only a wonder you've survived to tell the tale."

Stoneleigh rolled his eyes slightly, ignoring the Colonel's jesting. To Charlotte's surprise, he twisted nervously the brim of his hat as he again stated his question. "Are you well? Are you very certain you are recovered?"

She had received several bouquets from the viscount during the course of her recovery—red roses and ferns, irises, daffodils, and a posy of violets. He had also sent a letter of apology. "I am more than well," she assured him. "Perhaps it is the medicinal effects of the sea-bathing, but I truly cannot remember having felt so energetic in years. You needn't fear for my health a moment longer, if that is your concern."

He smiled, a certain tension easing from his

shoulders. "That has been the whole of my concern these many days and more. Seeing you and hearing your assurances quite convince me my worst fears were unfounded. Good day to you."

"Goodbye, Miss Amberley," the Colonel echoed. "I have every confidence we shall be meeting again quite soon."

The gentlemen bowed to her, and she would have insisted Henry say a proper goodbye; but since a heavily laden waggon was lumbering into the drive, Stoneleigh laughed and said, "Don't disturb his pleasure. The day I become more interesting a figure to him than any conveyance upon wheels, you must rush him to the surgeon immediately!"

With that, the gentlemen moved away, their heads quickly bent together in conversation. Charlotte watched them go noting the tall, straight form of Stoneleigh and the Colonel's slight limp that caused her heart to stretch toward him in friendship and compassion—and wished they had been able to stay for a few minutes.

She realized she had enjoyed the light banter of the two men immensely, as much as she had taken delight in Mrs. Hastings' company earlier. She did not know it until this very moment, but she was lonely for rational company. During her recovery, Maude and Selena had visited her frequently, with the surprising result that Charlotte came to understand how different her interests were from her friends'. It was always gossip with the young ladies and an enumeration of the matrimonial prospects of each unattached gentleman who might have chanced to arrive in Brighton the night before.

A little gossip could be very amusing, but a large dose scraped Charlotte's nerves. Getting a husband was most naturally on every unwed lady's mind, but it seemed to her that Maude and Selena were obsessed with it. When she tried to shift the subject to which play was being rehearsed at the Brighton Theatre Royal, the conversation quickly metamorphosed into a recital of which officers of the Tenth Light Dragoons had been present at a recent performance and whether or not it was true, as one of the officers had informed her, that the Marquis of Thaxted was indeed intent upon coming to Brighton for the summer.

"For you must know," Selena giggled, "his lordship is quite the most eligible matrimonial prize on the Marriage Mart."

Charlotte had soon ceased attempting to turn the subjects of their discourse into more profitable channels and permitted them to ramble at will though, if pressed, she could not recount a tithe of what was said to her.

As for her father, she scarcely ever saw him, much to her great disappointment. She realized now that part of her desire to come to Brighton was not just to help him but to join his world that she might become better acquainted with it. That their paths showed few signs of crossing during the course of any given day was a blow to her hopes Brighton might be different from Amberley. He rose late in the day—and that generally bleary-eyed—to play billiards in the afternoon at one of the subscription rooms. He would then return to his home for dinner only to depart quickly afterward, his destination unknown.

The whole process was painfully familiar to her, for his days at Amberley Park were spent in a similar manner. Only now, as she watched the comradery of the Colonel and Stoneleigh as they departed the inn, did she put a name to what she felt and it was loneliness, pure and simple.

But she wasn't lonely at Amberley!

She wasn't.

But then, she had a thousand duties to perform

100

day in and day out to keep her from becoming blue-devilled.

As she sipped her tea, she had the sensation that Brighton was changing her life in ways she had never expected it to. What would she do, she wondered, when the summer drew to a close? Would she even want to return to her life at Amberley Park?

She wished she hadn't come to Brighton at all, she thought in despair. Brighton was changing everything, and she didn't like it one whit.

Sixteen

On the following morning, after Charlotte returned Henry to Nurse in West Street, she donned a lacy cap over which she placed a straw poke bonnet trimmed with blue silk ribbons. Within fifteen minutes, she was on the Steyne; and a few minutes more saw her standing on the threshold of Fisher's Lending Library, where she immediately recognized Maude's voice. Discovering her whereabouts, she noticed that both her good friends were exclaiming anxiously over something or other.

"Selena, do but look!" Maude cried. "Lady Purcell's name is registered in this subscription book as well!"

"No," Selena breathed, leaning her head so close to Maude's that black curls intermingled with red as the two ladies scrutinized the ledger bearing the names of those gentlemen and women who subscribed to Fisher's Circulating Library.

Charlotte watched them with great fondness, seeing neither the modish-print silk gown draped about Maude's tall, elegant figure nor the pink muslin in summery ruffles all about the hem of Selena's walking dress—goodness, one, two, three, four, five, six, seven . . . yes, seven . . . rows of ruffles about the hem of Selena's gown—but rather two incorrigible ladies who had once scattered the ducks from one end of Amberley to the other. She could still hear their squeals and envision the sight of the gardener emerging from the yew shrubs flapping his fat arms at the girls, causing them to laugh and scream louder and the ducks to scatter further in short bursts of flight across the terraced lawns.

"We should go immediately back to Thomas'," Maude cried. "And insist your mama subscribe there as well! And what of Walker's? Do you think Lady Purcell has put her name down there? It wouldn't do to be seen falling behind the current mode!"

"No, indeed," Selena agreed. Their eyes met in a sort of panic which Charlotte found amusing.

"You cannot be serious!" Charlotte cried, approaching her friends and slipping an arm about each small waist.

"Charlie!" the girls intoned together. Hugs and gentle kisses were delivered all around.

"You did not tell us you were recovered! Naughty girl!" Selena chided, pressing Charlotte's hands. "But you do look marvelous and so pretty in your blue muslin and bonnet and—oh, my, is that sea-water dampening the lace ruffle of your cap?"

Charlotte giggled. "Of course it is. Henry splashed me so thoroughly that my hair got completely wet. But I was determined to visit the lending libraries today. I must have a new book to read. I understand Miss Austen's books may be found here and Fanny Burney's as well."

Maude took her by the arm and directed her toward the authors she had named but whispered, "You oughtn't to make so public an exclamation of your morning's activities. I don't know if Lady Purcell sea-bathes; and really, she is so very *ton-*

nish! If you hope to succeed in Brighton, nonetheless impress Stoneleigh with your air of gentility, you would do well to follow her lead. Hers or Mrs. Wyndham's. I would add Mrs. Knight, but I really cannot abide her."

Charlotte came to a conclusion which had been forming in her brain from the moment she first embraced Maude and Selena at the Pavilion nearly ten days earlier. "You have been going about in society so long, Maudie, that you have forgotten how to enjoy yourself—much to your detriment, I think."

Charlotte picked up a thin, calf-bound volume of *Sense and Sensibility* and fondled it gently. "A little more *sense*, if you please, Maude Dunsfold. There is no reason to *drop your blunt*—as Henry would say—at two booksellers, when one will do nicely and both are considered respectable. Don't eat me, now. Instead, join me day-after-tomorrow for a little sea-bathing—you, too, Selena. Henry will be with me. And Maude, you used to be the finest swimmer of us all and you may show us the way."

Maude pressed a hand to her breast and looked all about the bookshop, frightened lest anyone heard the truth that she was a young woman of physical abilities which could far outshine most of the young men she knew. "I wouldn't think of it! You are being quite absurd."

Selena leaned in closely and sniffed. "I don't want to get my hair wet. You know what it is once water gets at it. It will be sticking out in all directions like a Bedlamite."

"Pooh!" Charlotte cried. "Pooh, the pair of you! I refuse to accept your refusals. You will join me or—or I shan't continue to *enslave* Stoneleigh's heart!"

"Hush!" Maude cried. "There is Mrs. Knight, and I vow she heard you."

"Then I shall say it louder still. What's more, I shall happen to tell Papa's housekeeper that you once carried a pile of horse-manure from your stables to the church barely an hour before services!"

Maude gasped, clasping her hand to her mouth. "What a dreadful vixen you've become, Charlotte Amberley! I vow I scarcely know you anymore."

"And what a prude you are! But I don't mean to argue, only to have your solemn promise that you will go sea-bathing with me day-after-tomorrow!"

"I suppose I must now, since you are being so cattish!"

"That's better," Charlotte smiled triumphantly. "And you, Selena?"

"I won't go—and don't get that look in your eye like you mean to tell everyone that I helped Maude, for I did not. I would never do anything so unladylike. Manure in the church, indeed!"

Maude pinched her lips together and fairly hissed beneath her breath. "You little hypocrite! What about the time you put cherry stones in the cake you had your cook bake for Mrs. Plimstock when her husband died."

"But everyone hated her! She was so mean to the poor, never giving a farthing to those in need—and she so wealthy!"

Charlotte bit her lip. "Oh, my! Stones in the cake? Did you know she had to have a tooth drawn because she cracked it eating your cake!"

Selena's eyes grew wide with horror. "I didn't know. I knew she had had a tooth removed, but I thought it had become rotten just like her miserly old soul."

"I had it from the parson a year later," Charlotte said. "When you and Maudie were in London."

Selena bit her lip. "I wish I had known she would suffer," she said quietly, her expression mockingly penitent. A squeak of laughter sneaked out of her as she added, "Because if I had known, I would have put a pound of pits in her wretched cake!"

This was too much for all the young ladies, who immediately fell into stitches from which they did not recover—even under Mrs. Knight's disapproving eye—for some few minutes.

When Charlotte had wiped her eyes dry, she purchased her novel and begged the young ladies to sit with her on the piazza for a few minutes. "If you must know," she whispered, "Mrs. Hastings said that at this hour, all the handsome young men are likely to be returning from their angling and hunting adventures." As though to prove the Colonel's wife correct, a pair of handsome, if not dirt-laden, young gentlemen trotted by, their coats covered with pockets designed to facilitate their sport. It was clear they had been out hunting.

"Oh," Maudie whispered as one of the men tipped his hat to Charlotte, whereupon recognition dawned on his face and he reined in his horse. "By all that's wonderful! Charlie! I—I didn't know you was in Brighton!"

Charlotte moved forward to greet him. "And I didn't recognize you for all your dirt, Mr. Elstow."

"Don't play off your formal airs with me, *Miss Amberley*. It will be *Harry* to you, or I promise I shan't acknowledge your acquaintance while I am here."

Charlotte laughed. "Simpleton," she chided, then introduced him to Maude and Selena. "How are improvements progressing at Pavenham Priory?" The Priory was an ancient farmhouse which had been acquired by Mr. Elstow, Harry's father, who was a wealthy man of trade and who was currently engaged in the difficult transition between businessman and gentleman. He was deep in the troubles and turmoil of seeing the priory restored to some of its former beauty.

Harry and his brothers had been reared and educated as thoroughly as any gentleman's son in England. He had been schooled first at Eton and then at Oxford, so that his connections were expansive. He was acutely aware of his awkward position in society and at the same time fighting-proud of his father and of his family.

"I had a letter from Papa only yesterday. It would seem that several of the floors are quite rotten and will require twice as long to repair, not to mention twice the expense. You know what my father is. He cannot bear such unknowns, though I suggested to him that when a building is over four-hundred-years old, it has a right to have rotten flooring if it wishes. He saw no amusement in it at all."

"He's a good man, Harry. One of the best. I adore him."

Harry smiled broadly. "He feels the same about you and still asks me when we are to be married."

It was an old joke between them since, though they were the dearest of friends and had been so for years, love had not been part of their course. Together, they had worked to see that the brick-works were reopened in order to ease the unemployment of soldiers returning from Waterloo. They had also bettered the conditions of the farms around Amberley and in the environs of the Priory during the horrendous years of the Corn Laws, helping many smaller farms to survive during trying times when so many farmers lost everything.

"How is it I never tumbled in love with you?" Charlotte whispered.

Harry only smiled and shook his head, apparently as mystified as she was. He then bethought himself and introduced his companion, Mr. Brown, a budding intellectual and admitted Pantisocrat.

"A Pantisocrat!" Charlotte cried. "You believe then that, given a much simpler, purer environment, we would all exemplify perfection?"

"Oh, yes, indeed," Mr. Brown cried, a warm friendly smile revealing crooked teeth. "Coleridge certainly thinks so and Southey has been a proponent for years. As for myself, I—"

"Enough, Brown," Harry said, cutting him off with a teasing laugh. "We will keep Charlotte standing too long in the sun if we embark on that pilgrimage."

A shadow fell across Charlotte's face and, looking up, she saw Stoneleigh seated astride his horse and bowing to her. "Good day to you, Miss Amberley, Miss Dunsfold, Miss Bosham."

"And to you, Lord Stoneleigh," Maude and Selena chimed from under the shelter of the piazza.

Charlotte merely smiled and extended a hand to him. To her surprise, instead of shaking it, he took her gloved hand in his firm clasp and placed a gentle kiss on her wrist. "Are you well?" he inquired solicitously, not releasing her hand immediately.

Charlotte felt strangely breathless as she looked up into his concerned blue eyes. She spoke in scarcely more than a whisper as she responded archly, "Not less so than when you inquired yesterday."

"You will have to forgive me if I am oversolicitous; but as long as I live, I shall never forget the sight of you crumpled at my feet."

Stoneleigh then released her hand and turned his attention to the two men, greeting each by name. "Hallo, Mr. Brown, Harry," he said, smiling. To the latter he asked, "Is your father apoplectic yet about news of his floors?"

Harry laughed, "Almost! But I believe your letter did him some good. He has not complained quite so much about the cost since then."

"Excellent. Well, I have an appointment, but I wished to bid you all good day." He appeared ready to move on, but stayed the reins of his horse for a moment and narrowed his eyes slightly at Charlotte. "I didn't know you were acquainted with Mr. Elstow."

Harry spoke for her, quite enthusiastically. "Yes, indeed, sir. We've seen a great deal of mischief together. Haven't we, Charlie?"

"I shan't say anything lest Lord Stoneleigh get the oddest notion of me."

Stoneleigh smiled. "Miss Amberley, I already have the oddest notion of you."

"How's this?" Harry queried.

Charlotte replied, "Stoneleigh believes me to be the sort of female who has nothing better to do than swoon at his feet."

"So that is the meaning of his lordship's most cryptic remark, *crumpled at my feet*. But I can't credit it. You, Charlie? Falling into a swoon? Never."

"I'm 'fraid so, Harry. I know I've disappointed your opinion of me, but there it is—and not once, but thrice. Poor Stoneleigh has had his hands full with me, quite literally I fear."

Stoneleigh merely laughed and, after tipping his hat to all the ladies, gave his horse a solid kick and was soon trotting down the Steyne.

"He is the greatest swell!" Harry exclaimed, watching Stoneleigh depart, admiration shining in his eyes. "If you knew half of what he's done, his generosity in all quarters—my father can't say enough fine things about him—you've no idea!

But never mind that! How long are you fixed in Brighton?"

"For the summer, I think. Henry is with me, and I am completely at my father's disposal. You know what Papa is; he will not consider returning to Amberley Park until summer's end."

The shine slowly dimmed in Harry's eyes as he watched Charlotte's face. "Tell me," he said quietly. "How is Sir John? Is everything well?"

"Of course," Charlotte responded, a strange tight sensation grabbing at her chest. "Should anything be wrong?"

Harry shook his head. "No, I suppose not. One hears rumors, but you know what gossip is." He chanced to look past Charlotte's shoulder, and his expression changed suddenly, softening, warming.

When Charlotte turned around slightly, she saw the cause of his shift in demeanor. He was looking at Maude as if he had never seen a young woman before, taking in her animated face as she sat chatting happily with Selena under the covering of the piazza.

Maude, perhaps becoming aware of his scrutiny, glanced toward him and, seeing his interest, smiled sweetly, almost shyly, an expression Charlotte had not seen in a long, long time on her friend's pretty face—the Maudie she knew! She heard Harry utter a sigh.

What would Maude think of him once she knew his connection to Trade. Charlotte felt for a moment as if the sun had just crept behind a cloud. Maude would despise Harry of course, quite freely, as she did anyone without exalted connections.

Her heart ached for Harry suddenly. She loved him, as a beloved brother, and did not want him to suffer at Maude's sharp, fashionable claws. Should she speak with Maude? She didn't know what to do. All she knew was that she did not want Harry to be hurt but she saw no means of preventing it since he was obviously smitten by the mere sight of her.

To Harry, she said firmly, "I shan't detain you, but pray call upon me in West Street. I know my father will want to see you again, too."

He seemed a little surprised but bowed to her and said he would do so very soon. With one backward glance toward a now-blushing Maude Dunsfold, he and Mr. Brown were soon trotting away from the Steyne.

Once he was gone, Maude leapt to her feet and queried, "Who is he, Charlie? What a dashing young man, and he was on such familiar terms with Stoneleigh! Why didn't you introduce us? He was so very handsome. His hair is nearly the shade of yours and what fine, large brown eyes he has. He is the very image of Bryon, only a shade more beautiful. Who are his parents? You seem to know him so well!"

Charlotte felt her heart sink. "His father made a fortune in Trade," was all she said.

Maude gasped as though she had been struck hard in the stomach. She fell backward into her chair, her complexion paling so completely that Charlotte was convinced had Maude been standing it would have been her turn to swoon.

Charlotte was so angry suddenly she found it impossible for a long moment to do more than glare at her friend. When she finally spoke, her words were clipped. "Whatever has happened to you, Maude? I don't even recognize the generous-hearted creature I knew so many years ago."

"I don't know what you mean!" she retorted, lifting her chin, tears brimming in her eyes.

"You know precisely what I mean. Oh, the devil take it, I am out of reason cross and, before I begin saying a dozen things I will regret, I shall take my leave of you. I will only say this, if you do one thing to encourage Harry then break his heart, I shall never speak to you again!"

With that, she left both her friends staring at her agape as she turned in the direction of a waiting hackney.

Seventeen

On the following evening, just as the sun was dipping low in the west, Charlotte accepted Lord Stoneleigh's arm. They followed behind Colonel Hastings and Emily as the foursome progressed along the Steyne at the fashionably late hour of dusk.

"So tell me, Miss Amberley, why did you run from the music room?" Stoneleigh queried in a low voice. "I have been considering the events of that most wretched of nights over and over and cannot conceive of an answer that satisfies me."

Charlotte tucked her paisley silk shawl up about her neck against the encroaching mist. The air cooled quickly in the evening as it swept across the graying ocean, scattering among the fishermen's nets stretched out on the field beside the Steyne to finally nip at her sunburnt cheeks and neck.

"I'm not certain, precisely," she responded, wondering if the shiver which raced down her neck were due to the sea air or if it were because her arm was wrapped about Stoneleigh's. His face was quite near her own as he listened to her. "I was very confused at the time, I think. In fact, my recollections are disjointed and almost useless.

I was ill. I suppose that is the only rational answer I can give you."

He fell silent, apparently satisfied with her response, keeping a gentle pace with her lady's stroll.

The Steyne was a large grassy field which ran parallel to the Prince's Pavilion. For nearly half a century, it had been the fashionable, evening Promenade of the *beau monde,* at least during the summer months when the Prince resided in Brighton.

Every few feet Charlotte travelled afforded her the opportunity of nodding to an acquaintance here and another there, many of whom were passing them by in hopes of gaining the best views of the illumination which was scheduled to take place shortly at Fisher's Circulating Library.

She had originally arrived at the Steyne with her father; but the moment Emily—who was no longer a formal Mrs. Hastings to her—engaged her in conversation, her father simply begged to be excused and disappeared. Colonel Hastings made some laughing remark about *rouge et noir* at one of the lending libraries, but it seemed unlikely to Charlotte that Brighton would offer a forbidden form of gaming. On the other hand, if cards or dice did not call to Sir John, then what did?

She was deeply chagrined at first, feeling that her father in abandoning her had imposed on Colonel and Mrs. Hastings, but Emily immediately reassured her. "Now we will have an excuse to take you up in our new coach, which I am terribly anxious for you to see. The Colonel had it brought down from London—it arrived this morning while you and I were being *dipped.* It is the most delightful barouche, well-appointed and a charming burgundy in color." She then drew her onto the Promenade. "The Prince's band

114

plays every night between eight o'clock and ten—
unless, of course, he is giving a musical evening
at the Pavilion. Only tell me, after we parted from
the beach this morning, did you return to the
Castle Inn as Henry insisted you do?"

"I'm afraid it has become a ritual of sorts.
Henry is *aux anges* with the coaches and carriages
arriving and departing and I admit even I find
the mail coach an awe-inspiring sight as it de-
parts—so glossy and jumbled up with legs, arms,
and faces, packages, and thick, carpeted baggage.
Afterward, I returned him to Nurse and then
spent a half-hour or so at one of the lending
libraries. I am still overwhelmed by how magical
Brighton is, supplying so many amusements every
day. And the air is so restorative. It must be the
salt—as the doctors insist."

They had walked together some distance, conversing easily, until Emily vowed she had grown
quite fatigued and needed her husband's support.

Charlotte had, therefore, been consigned, not
unhappily, to Lord Stoneleigh, who had immediately possessed himself of her arm.

After a time, Stoneleigh addressed a subject
which had clearly been weighing on his mind. "I
have been wanting to apologize to you for some
time, Miss Amberley. It would seem I judged you
harshly that evening at the Pavilion, attributing
your flight to a most unwarranted design upon
my affections."

Charlotte was surprised by his candor. She
glanced up at him, the fading evening light casting his face in long, warm shadows. His eyes were
still visibly blue, she noted, even in the dimness
of the hour as he caught her gaze and smiled
faintly. A breeze buffeted his black hat, catching
wisps of his black hair and sweeping it to the line
of his sharp cheekbone. She knew a profound desire to tell him the truth, that she had been en-

couraged by her friends and by her father to lead
him a merry dance that evening but that she had
fled the music room because she couldn't bring
herself to bow to their wishes. But how could she
say as much without doing a great deal of harm
to persons not present to defend themselves? Instead, she whispered, "There is something I
would like to know. Once within the banqueting
room, my memory seems to have succumbed to
my illness and my recollections are hazy at best.
But later, I was told that—well, did you—"

She could not complete her query. She was
grateful that the sun had disappeared at last and
that her embarrassment was hidden in the dark.
She was certain her cheeks were the color of
flames leaping up from a crackling log fire.

She chewed upon her lip and shifted her gaze
to the brick path in front of her.

"May I guess the remainder of your question?"

"It's nothing to signify, I'm sure. Pray forget
that I spoke of it."

"The answer is, yes," he responded. "I kissed
you, though you mustn't think I have not suffered
from having taken such extreme advantage of
you—you cannot imagine how lowering it has been
to my pride, to my self-consequence, to my discernment when I realized my kisses had caused
you to swoon. I was only afraid I had done mortal
damage and forced you into a decline."

Through the mist of the damp sea-air and the
happy gloom of the fading light, she saw his lips
twitch, but in his eyes was real chagrin.

"Oh, but you are the most absurd man I have
ever known," she cried. "You know very well your
kisses did not cause me to faint. The accident at
the clock shop earlier performed that feat."

He stopped her in their leisurely progression
down the length of the Steyne and drew her near
the railing which separated the fishermen's turf

from the Promenade path. He did not speak for a moment as he permitted the last of the promenaders to pass by. Once out of earshot, he began quietly, "You must know that, however much I might speak lightly of the matter, I am indeed very sorry for my improper conduct on that evening and I do beg your pardon for . . . for everything."

Charlotte looked up at him and blinked. He was standing very close to her, his face cast in darkness except for a faint illumination of his left cheekbone, a small reflection on his straight nose, and another line of light the length of his firm jaw. She could not be comfortable, either with the nearness of him or with the contrition in his voice. She had the oddest sensation of being completely surrounded—bathed, as it were, by his closeness. Again, the breathlessness which frequently assailed her in his company afflicted her in the most extraordinary manner. She did not know how to account for it precisely, but the feeling carried with it a sudden and intense desire to throw her arms about his neck, to press her cheek against his own, to feel his lips upon hers as she had before.

Then, quite miraculously, her memory returned to her with a vengeance. She remembered in vivid detail everything that happened between herself and Stoneleigh in the banqueting room.

"Oh, my goodness," she murmured, dumbfounded. "How very odd, but I suddenly am able to recall everything to mind. Stoneleigh, you wretched creature! You kissed me not once, but a hundred times." She touched her cheek and her ear, staring at him in astonishment. She looked at his lips, remembering the extraordinarily sensuous warmth of his kiss as he had placed his lips upon hers. A shiver went down her neck. "I do believe you are quite the wickedest man I

117

have ever known." She then covered her face with her gloved hands and laughed. "Do you know, I was so disoriented I thought I was being kissed by a butterfly and afterward I could remember nothing? Only Maude told me it was being rumored you had kissed me and, until now, I simply couldn't remember—save some absurdity about a butterfly!"

An odd expression came over his face, a tautness in the line of his jaw as he leaned toward her. "So why did you come to Brighton, Miss Amberley?" he whispered intently. "Do you effect your charms to a purpose? Tell me! By God, if we were alone, I'd kiss you all over again, if for no other reason than to force the truth from you."

"If I told you the truth, you would be very angry with me and with others. You might never speak to me again—and that I couldn't bear. I don't know how it is, Stoneleigh, but I am growing to depend on you for at least some of my happiness. I will only say, it is not as you think."

"Then what is it?" he whispered, leaning down to her, his lips not far from hers.

"I wish you would kiss me," she said brazenly, not knowing why. For the longest moment, as he leaned nearer to her still, she felt certain he would oblige her and longed for him to do so.

Oh, lord, she thought. Why was she behaving in so hoydenish a fashion and why with Stoneleigh? And why did she want so very much to feel his lips upon hers again?

"There you are!" the Colonel's booming voice cut through the misty gloom. "Could hardly see the pair of you what with the ridiculous hour of the Promenade and not one lamp to show the way. Emily says the Prince's band is about to play "God Save the King." Oh, I say, have I cast a rub in it?"

118

"Of course not," Charlotte replied quickly. "We were merely having a friendly argument about—about butterflies!"

She glanced mischievously up at Stoneleigh, who again offered his arm to her.

"I wish to know more about this butterfly," he whispered as they fell in step beside the Colonel. When the band broke into a vibrant version of the promised anthem, Stoneleigh leaned down and in her ear said, "And one day I shall grant your wish and kiss you properly. Then we shall see!"

"Oh, I am trembling just to think of it," she retorted playfully, disbelieving she was speaking to him in such a daring manner.

"Vixen," he murmured in response.

The illumination spelled out the words *Long Live the Prince* to the delight of the crowd. Charlotte searched the faces surrounding the front of the shop. The light played jauntily off foreheads, noses and chins, off the round visage of the Prince himself as he acknowledged the appreciation of his well-wishers.

But in all those cheering faces, in not one could she discover her father's familiar features as the band struck up "God Save the King."

Eighteen

Selena's flannel cap had come off her head early in their sea-bathing adventure on the next day. True to her prophecy, her hair was sticking out wildly in every direction imaginable. She looked as if she belonged to the sea and to Poseidon, her red hair reflecting shards of sunlight as the morning sun danced on the waters. She was laughing and splashing Henry thoroughly and giggling as if she had just discovered she had the ability to laugh.

Maude was floating flat on her back in the water, letting the waves gently rock her to-and-fro. The large woman who had *dipped* them all stood by, entranced by her abilities. Maude had already swum to the nearest bathing machine and back six times and was now resting from her exertions by floating as easily in the surf as if she were a sea lion.

"La! But she's the finest swimmer I've evuh seen!" the dipper cried. "Duck me twice if she ain't!"

Charlotte watched Maude, her friend's expression relaxed in a manner she had not witnessed since her arrival in Brighton. She was grateful now she had pressed both her friends to sea-bathe with her, for they were clearly enjoying themselves prodigiously. The harsh words she had spoken to Maude regarding Harry two days earlier had been addressed by Maude herself, who only this morning had tearfully begged Charlotte not to think too unkindly of her. "If I seem a trifle high-in-the-instep," she had said, dabbing at her cheeks with a lace kerchief, "it is because both Mama and Papa have taught me to consider my family's consequence first along with the future of the younger children. I would be doing a disservice to those who depend upon me to contract an acceptable alliance were I to encourage one who is unacceptable to my parents."

"But what of love?" Charlotte queried. "Harry certainly seemed struck with you and, if I am not mistaken, the smile you gave him was probably the most genuine expression I have seen you don since my arrival."

"You are cruel," Maude said, crushed.

"I am speaking the truth from my heart."

"I know you are. I always despised this part of you. We were all so comfortable before you arrived in Brighton!"

Charlotte put an arm about Maude's shoulders and kissed her cheek. "But not very happy."

Maude shook her head, more tears coursing down her cheeks. "No, not nearly so happy. Well, you may worry your head no more about your precious Harry Elstow. I won't pay the least heed to him if that is what you wish."

"That is not what I wish," Charlotte retorted. "I said I only wanted you to be sure not to break his heart."

"I won't break his heart then," she said finally.

Charlotte suspected that Maude had spent at least one sleepless night considering Harry's large brown eyes and regretting infinitely his poor connections. The violet-colored circles beneath her pretty green eyes bespoke the torn state of her heart.

Charlotte straightened the lacy half-veil which came down almost to her nose, a piece of apparel she was sporting in hopes of preventing the sun from doing further damage to her tender skin. Her nose was already the shade of a ripening tomato, and she was determined to take greater care with her complexion lest she be required the remainder of her days to apply crushed strawberries to her skin—as many young ladies with defects of complexion found it necessary to do.

It was all Henry's fault, of course. He pestered her every day to make the trek to the sea. She laughed to herself, knowing full well he did not have to work very hard to persuade her. If the truth be known, she wasn't certain who enjoyed the sea more—herself or Henry.

"Charlie," a masculine voice whispered to her over the sound of the waves.

"Who is that?" Charlotte cried, startled since men were not permitted to come near the ladies' machines. She stood just outside the dipper's view and turned around to see if she could discover who was calling to her. She dropped quickly to her neck, below the level of the waves, to hide her wet, clinging flannel gown.

"Charlie, 'tis I," the voice called again.

"Harry?" she whispered back.

When she caught sight of him, she saw that he was only some fifteen feet away, buried up to his nose in the water. "What are you doing here?" she cried. "You must go away! Indeed, you must! It is most unseemly, and you will surely ruin my reputation if you are found here."

"Where is Maude?" he whispered, keeping his head low in the surf and easing toward her.

"On the other side of the machine. But it will

do you no good to try to flirt with her here. She is—she is not for you!"

"I saw the way she looked at me the other morning."

"She has certain unyielding notions about the sort of marriage she must contract—her parents would never forgive her for aligning herself with a man of Trade. I do not speak to give you offence, only to explain that your attentions are not welcome. Do go away, simpleton."

"No," he countered firmly. "And as for her parents, she is of an age and I have a fortune. Besides, I only want to race her to the next bathing machine, not ask for her hand in marriage."

"Race her to the next machine! Are you serious?"

"Completely. Now, fetch her at once. I saw her swim. She was magnificent, and I'll not leave until I've raced her!"

"I shan't permit you to even speak with her," Charlotte retorted, preparing to swim away from him.

"You had better do so at once," he barked. "Or I shall raise a hue and cry such as you have never heard before. Now, fetch her!"

She knew Harry well enough to believe him capable of doing precisely as he said. He was a stubborn man, in some ways very much like Lord Stoneleigh. When he opened his mouth as if to yell, she shook her finger at him and, in the end, did as he wished her to.

When Charlotte had made certain the dipper was fully engaged with Selena and Henry, she drew Maude away from the bathing machine and in her ear whispered, "You must do as I say or all shall be lost. Harry is here."

"What?" she exclaimed.

"Hush! You mustn't alert the dipper or we shall all be in the basket. Harry is here, and he insists upon racing you to the next bathing machine. Apparently he has been watching you swim for some time now."

"How—how impertinent, and I most certainly will not race him."

"You must," Charlotte responded. "Or he has promised to rain fire down from heaven."

"Then let him do so. And—and remember, Charlie, you were the one who told me not to encourage him or to break his heart."

"Yes, I know. And I tried to hint him away, indeed I did. But this is a desperate matter! You have only to swim a short distance, and then he has promised to leave us alone."

She watched Maude carefully and saw an odd light come into her eye, very much like the time she said she was going to haul manure into the church the day that mealy-mouthed *clerk* had promised to return and bore the entire congregation yet again.

"Very well," she said with a cool lift of her arched, black brow. "But did you tell him I don't take kindly to losing?"

"No, but I suspect he knows as much," Charlotte responded. "And Maude, Harry doesn't like to lose either."

Charlotte watched Maude paddle easily away from the bathing machine toward deeper water. Approaching Harry, she laid herself straight out in the water, stroking her lean, strong arms through the uneven waves with the ease of a born sea-creature. She watched Harry fall into stride beside her, not once speaking or otherwise making himself known to her. They reached the first machine, and Charlotte saw Maude lift her head ever so slightly in his direction and, without a pause, continue on.

She was about to return to the machine when Selena appeared beside her. "Where is Maude?"

she queried, brushing her moppish red hair out of her eyes.

When Charlotte had silenced her with an expressive glance toward the dipper, she then directed the large, burly woman to take charge of Henry and, if she wouldn't mind, to throw him from the top step into the water, which was currently his favorite form of water-sport.

Henry gave a cry of delight as the dipper tossed him into the water. She responded amiably, "I like the children to enjoy the water and to learn to swim properly. We prevent them from drowning, we do."

Charlotte then told Selena in a quiet voice, her words disappearing into the noisy ocean all about them, where Maude had gone and with whom.

Selena clapped a hand over her mouth, her blue eyes growing large and round. "She didn't! Our Maudie? Whatever was she thinking?"

"I believe she wanted to teach Harry a lesson. I only fear it is she who will be made to suffer."

"How do you mean?"

Charlotte would have explained, but at that moment, she noticed an odd sight. A large woman in flannels began approaching Charlotte's bathing machine slowly through the water. She didn't think much of it until the woman's face gradually became clearer to her. She was so startled she let out a strong gasp.

"What is it now?" Selena cried.

Charlotte looked at her and didn't at first know what to say. After a moment, she said quietly, "Do you remember the reason you and Maude wished for me to come to Brighton?"

Selena nodded, apparently mystified. "Yes, to overset Stoneleigh's heart if you could."

"Well, do not make even the smallest move to look toward the fishing boats but return to the dipper and engage her attention more fully if you please, for it would seem Stoneleigh is approaching. No, don't look, but rather move slowly back to Henry."

Selena murmured excitedly. "But he can't be! It's forbidden! Oh, Charlie, he must really be enamored of you. But how marvelous and how easily you seem to have intrigued him! Yes, yes, I will go! What fun!"

Selena, who was not a great swimmer, scurried away as quickly as one is able, dressed in a weighted flannel gown and moving at thigh depth through the ponderous ocean currents.

Charlotte tried to keep her face expressionless as she turned to move toward Stoneleigh and, therefore, away from the eyes of the dipper. But she thought the whole of it absurd, that he was gowned like a lady with a silly flannel cap on, so that the closer she got to him, the harder it became to remain impassive until she simply fell into stitches, stumbled, and a wave tumbled her over. She rose from the water, sputtering but still laughing, only now her fine veil was drenched and clinging to her eyes. She had to lean her neck well back in order to even see Stoneleigh.

What a sight she must have appeared in that moment.

When she had reached him, dropping almost to her knees—as he apparently was—in the water, she attempted to peel the veil away from her face and, in a low, laughing voice, asked, "Whatever are you doing? Were you following Harry's lead?"

In a hopeless attempt at achieving a feminine tone, Lord Stoneleigh took his voice into his falsetto and squeaked, "I'm afraid he dared me to do it and, though I don't usually succumb to such wagers, I was rather intrigued with the notion. Now I don't know what has caused you to fall into a fit of the hysterics, my dear—"

"Oh, not hysterics," she cried, laughing all the

more. "Oh, dear! Oh dear! Do stop speaking or I shan't regain my breath, ever! Only what has possessed you to such madness, a wager or no? And do you know how absurd you look in that cap?"

"Yes, I think so," he said, continuing to talk in a high voice. "But not more so than you, if you don't mind my giving you a little hint, with your lace sticking to your eyelashes." He clicked his tongue, "Most unbecoming."

"I beg you won't say another word," she cried, laughing harder still and attempting in vain to press the lace backwards against her forehead. But she only succeeded in bending the veiling forward so that it stuck straight out from her forehead at a right angle.

This time he laughed but quickly dipped lower in the water lest his masculine chortle had been heard. Charlotte turned around and saw that her dipper was eying her companion suspiciously.

"You must go," Charlotte hissed.

"Only if you will accompany me to the next machine."

"I shan't," she replied. "I am no great swimmer as Maudie is, so I must refuse. Besides, however much I am enjoying your little joke, really, Stoneleigh, I don't think it proper. Oh, dear, here comes Henry. Pray take your leave. Please."

Stoneleigh had but to see for himself that Henry was rapidly approaching his sister, and he dove into the waves and was gone.

"Who was that, Charlie?" Henry queried. "Do but look how well she swims, better than Maude!"

"Miss, er, Stoneman," she responded. "I believe her time at her machine was almost up and she had to leave. Speaking of which, if we do not hurry, we shall miss the departure of the morning mail coach at the Castle Inn."

"Right!" Henry squealed and quickly returned to the machine.

"What did he say?" Selena queried once the dipper was engaged in helping Henry up the steps. "Why did he come here?"

"It was a silly wager between Harry and him." Selena could ask no more questions since they were too near the dipper to say more.

When Maude arrived, exhilarated and breathless, not a minute later, Charlotte packed both ladies into the machine and afterward joined them. When the wheels began to move and Henry was forced to turn away from them that they might exchange their flannel bathing gowns for proper clothing, only then did she consider the morning's adventure.

She glanced at Maude and saw that her color was high and her green eyes sparkling as they had not sparkled in a long time. What her thoughts were she couldn't know, but she rather suspected that had Harry been otherwise connected, she would have seen her friend married by summer's end.

She couldn't help but wonder what would happen to Maude or even to herself. For Stoneleigh to have ventured near her bathing machine, so absurdly begowned, filled her heart with a warmth that caused a spattering of gooseflesh to cover her arms.

"You are cold," Selena said. "Do you need another towel?"

"No, it is nothing," she reassured her friend.

"But you've been ill. You ought to take great care lest you succumb to a brain fever or the like."

"Truly I am not ill, just a little frightened perhaps. Lord Stoneleigh was not at all what I expected him to be."

Both Maude and Selena looked at her carefully

128

at these words, pausing in their awkward attempts to dress themselves in the small confines of the swaying machine.

"Oh, dear," Selena murmured. "Are you losing your heart to him? I hadn't counted on that, for you were always the most sensible among us."

Maude appeared considerably distressed as she said, "Pray take care, Charlotte. You've given me ample warning, now let me warn you. He has broken more hearts than he has hairs on his head. Pray take care."

Charlotte nodded in agreement. "I know and I will," she promised, another shiver traveling in rapid movement over her skin again, giving rise to a second wave of gooseflesh.

Nineteen

"But why on earth did you do it?" Charlotte asked, holding her fan in front of her lips in order to hide her smiles from the rest of the company in the red saloon. She stood facing Lord Stoneleigh near the long windows of the Royal Pavilion's most elegant drawing room and spoke to him in low tones. "I vow I shall never forget the sight of your face beneath that drooping flannel cap. You have amazed me! You have an extraordinary reputation, as you very well know, for everything that is proper and respectable, and then you disguise yourself as a lady and accost me. I should have called for assistance and had you publicly flogged for your roguish misconduct!"

"It was Harry's fault, if you must know. It would seem he was struck with Cupid's arrow the moment he laid eyes on your friend, Miss Dunsfold, and promptly wagered me that not only would I be unable to persuade you to swim with me but that he could convince Miss Dunsfold to do so without kicking up the smallest dust or ripple of water as it were. He won the wager quite easily, of course. Even had I been able to persuade you to accompany me, he still would have won. Miss Dunsfold accompanied him past three bathing machines. I don't mean to disparage your abilities, but I know few men who could do as much and so quickly."

"Maude is quite athletic, though she does not like it generally known."

He regarded her wonderingly for a moment, his blue eyes sporting a rather quizzical expression. "Do you know that since your arrival in Brighton, I have seen aspects of Miss Dunsfold I had not believed existed? You seem to have an ability to cause those about you to enjoy life a bit more. I was surprised she had even agreed to go down to the sea."

Charlotte laughed. "It did require some coaxing on my part. But you must remember, I grew up with Maude and Selena, and fashionable society does not always permit young ladies to exert themselves as much as they might wish to."

"Save in the inexhaustible pursuit of getting a husband."

"You have said so, my lord, not I."

Charlotte thought of Maude's tear-stained letters and bitter disappointment that Lord Stoneleigh's initial interest in her, indeed his strong pursuit of her, had come to nought. And worse, that in the end, he had given her a setdown by way of leaving her standing alone on a ballroom floor. Maude had been utterly devastated.

She looked away from Stoneleigh and reminded herself that whatever warmth she might be feeling toward him needed to be tempered. He might have been fulfilling a playful wager when he flirted with her at the sea-bathing machines, but he was also capable of wounding deeply.

It seemed an age since her arrival in Brighton nearly a fortnight ago. So much had transpired, yet so little, really. Her friends' hopes that she might break Stoneleigh's heart seemed both a distant memory yet oddly enough a distinct possibility. She was not unaware that he was singling her out. Was this how he had treated both Maude and Selena, each for a Season?

"Now what have I said," he queried, "to have brought that guarded look to your pretty brown eyes?"

"I have enjoyed your company very much and the attentions you pay me, but you must know your reputation precedes you, sir."

She was surprised by the look of shock which overtook his features.

"My—reputation?"

Charlotte closed her fan slowly, realizing she had unwittingly erred. "I see that I have distressed you, and that was not my intention. Naturally, I presumed that you were conversant with how you are viewed by others—"

"You mean, by your friends."

"Yes, by my friends. But I daresay were you to inquire of many with whom I can claim only a passing acquaintance, I believe you might find my friends' opinions to be shared."

He was clearly displeased, his nostrils flaring slightly. "If I have been maligned, I wish you might tell me in what way that I might defend myself."

"You are not only stubborn," she said, keeping her tone light, "but you are proud as well. Pray do not come the crab over me. I do not wish to argue with you about your character, and I certainly don't intend to begin repeating to you what has been said about you."

"But I resent being disliked because of mere gossip."

"Mere gossip?" Charlotte queried. "I wish it were true. But can you deny that you hurt both Maude and Selena terribly and made it easy for their London acquaintance to despise them and all because you had decided each, in turn, was unworthy of your hand?" Charlotte did not know why she had chosen just this moment to address so prickly a subject.

He grew very quiet as he looked at her, weighing her words. "If it seemed so to your friends, then I clearly have injured each of them, which is no compliment to me. You must believe me that I had no intention of laying them open to painful repercussions when I chose to discontinue my advances. But you must understand how it is from my perspective. How am I able to become acquainted with a female unless I make her to some degree an object of interest and, in doing so, can you understand that I cannot always control what occurs afterward?"

Charlotte heard her father's voice coming from somewhere in the center of her brain, saying to her, *Do tell me you have left off that truly wretched habit of arguing with every man you see.* He had been warning her that she would likely perish a spinster if she did not take greater care with her opinions.

And here she was arguing with Stoneleigh.

There was nothing for it, however. She was in the middle before she realized she had begun. "You may not be able to *control* how a flirtation will end, but perhaps if you exercised a little more discretion when you made a lady your object, you would not wound her so deeply when your interest waned." She paused, frowning slightly. "I did not mean to take you to task for something of which I truly have no immediate knowledge. Pray forget what I have said."

He ignored her last comment. "You trust me so little, then?" he queried.

She thought for a moment before answering. "It would be more accurate to say that I have concerns which are not easily dismissed. But let

133

me ask you—do you trust me, completely? After all, we hardly know one another."

He, too, paused before giving answer, his blue eyes searching hers intently. After a moment, he shook his head. "No, I suppose I do not. But it is no fault of your own, I assure you."

She laughed. "How can it be no fault of my own? What absurdity is this?"

"Would I offend you terribly, Miss Amberley, if I told you it was because of your nearest relation?"

Charlotte felt her complexion pale, felt the blood rush from her face, felt her heart turn over painfully in her breast. She was not offended, just very hurt. And not so much because he had spoken, but because what he had spoken was true.

"I can see I have offended you."

"No," she assured him, touching his arm lightly with her gloved hand. "No, you have not. Indeed, you have not. From your perspective, given the animosity between you and my father, you cannot be entirely unjustified."

"Still, I should have kept silent," he said.

Charlotte looked up at him, and a sense of the absurd suddenly rose through all her painful thoughts. "It would seem, then, that we share the same fault, perhaps. Neither of us appears capable of discretion, for I most assuredly should not have rebuked you for your past mistakes."

He smiled crookedly and sighed. "I still don't think your reproof was entirely deserved, however."

"You alone must determine that."

"Again, I see the guarded look in your eyes. Miss Amberley, I promise you I am not the callous, unfeeling creature you think me to be."

"Pray let us not brangle further. We have both agreed that neither of us should have spoken. Forget then, everything I said to you."

"Will you do the same?"

"How can I?" she queried. When she heard her father call to her, she moved away from him, her heart deeply unsettled. She looked up at her father and wondered whether he had ever considered how much his own conduct reflected upon his children. Knowing him as she did, she could only conclude that he undoubtedly had never given the matter a moment's thought.

Lord Stoneleigh was left standing beside the crimson draperies with so many thoughts and strong emotions running rampant through his head that he did not at first move away from the window. Instead, he let his gaze drift about the chamber as if he were examining the room for the first time.

The rectangular receiving room was supported by several columns decorated to appear like brightly colored palm trees. On the walls of the chamber were twenty-six Chinese oil paintings pasted onto a wallpaper covered with dragons and framed with mock bamboo borders. The beautiful chimney piece was of white marble.

He turned away from the beauty of the chamber, finding that the decor distracted him from the task of bringing his thoughts to order.

How could Miss Amberley have criticized him so harshly? Was he at fault? He took a deep breath, then another. Had he become so lacking in sensibility that he could not see the pain he inflicted? He had always prided himself on his discreet, decorous conduct where the objects of his pursuit were concerned? Had he been so blind, then?

Miss Amberley seemed to think so, and that was the rub. For some reason, which he was loth to explain, he trusted her opinion almost as much as he trusted Emily's.

He felt a touch upon his sleeve and, thinking it was Miss Amberley, he turned around at once, hoping she had returned to retract her opinions and to soothe his wounded pride.

Instead, he found Emily looking at him in that penetrating manner of hers which she favored only when she had something to say to him he had rather not hear.

"Good God, what is it now?" he exclaimed.

"Blue-devilled?" she queried, teasing him.

"Amberley-devilled," he countered.

"What is the matter, Edward," she began facetiously. "Did she not tell you how charming you are and how pleased she is with every word which proceeds from your mouth or how you are the example which every man ought to follow?"

He smiled ruefully. "We quarreled."

"Yes?" she queried, hopefully.

"Regarding my character."

"This is most promising. I am intrigued. Pray continue."

"It would seem she has gained an impression I am a rather hardhearted fellow and have ill-used the ladies of my acquaintance rather badly."

"Have you?" she asked, taking his arm and guiding him toward the doorway. The Prince Regent had arrived and, taking Lady Hertford's arm, was preparing to lead his guests to the banqueting room.

"Of course not," he retorted.

"Not even a little?"

"You agree with her then?"

"To some extent," she replied. "Charlotte, of course, is not fully aware of the exigencies of being one of London's prized marital objects, so she cannot know with what assiduousness some ladies are wont to pursue you."

"Still, you think I am to blame."

"Yes, you are," she said, but not unkindly. "But I can't fault you entirely. You cannot always, year after year, guard your actions with complete care. But it has come to my notice in the past two, possibly three, seasons that your patience has worn a trifle thin."

"You refer to the time I left Miss Dunsfold standing on the ballroom floor at Mrs. Knight's home."

"Miss Dunsfold may have been unhappily unwise in expressing her love to you in the middle of a waltz; but, Edward, you destroyed her womanly pride."

He sighed heavily. "Do you know how fatigued I am of it all? Wearied to the bone, I think. Do me a favor, Emily, find a wife for me, one with your sweetness of temper and kindness of heart. All you have to say is *marry her,* and I will drag her to the altar then and there."

"Be careful," Emily retorted. "If you remember, I have a *cousin,* a most delightful lady of advancing years, who is very *sweet* and who possesses the *kindest* heart I have ever known and who would make you a most admirable wife—"

"—and who is buttertoothed, platterfaced, older than I am, and an avowed bluestocking. No, I thank you. Perhaps I oughtn't to give you so much power, after all—clearly you would abuse it."

"Clearly."

Lady Purcell sat in a settee adjacent to the windows, her gaze fixed to the tips of her lace gloves.

Her neck had begun to ache in that peculiar way it did whenever a female set her cap for Stoneleigh. She lifted her chin in a delicate attempt to relieve the fuzzy yet pinched feeling that afflicted the nerves just beside her spine at such a moment as this. But to little avail. The ache persisted and ran its usual course to the center of her heart.

She had seen *that* particular expression on Stoneleigh's face a dozen times since she had accepted Purcell's hand in marriage some seven years ago. She was now four and thirty, with a brood of children whom she adored residing at home attended to by a bevy of nurses and nannies, and a tutor for the two oldest boys.

Her husband, fifth baron, Lord Purcell, was a doting husband and father. He professed his love for her every day—in words, in kindnesses, in trumpery gifts which never failed to please. She glanced at him now and watched him walking toward her. She smiled at him, hoping in doing so that his answering smile of affection would cause that pinched feeling near her spine to depart and so spare her a period of misery as familiar as it was persistent.

"Are you feeling well?" he queried as he reached her. He offered his arm to her. She rose and placed her own arm gently within the circle of his.

"I—I have something of the headache," she replied.

"Oh, dear, and a lengthy dinner to endure, unless you wish me to beg the Prince to excuse us."

"No," she responded hastily. The pain was already rising upward from her neck and would soon reach her head. Her ability to see in her right eye would diminish considerably and successive bouts of nausea would afflict her. But not for the world would she decline the opportunity of watching either Miss Amberley as she set about attempting to win Stoneleigh's heart or the viscount himself to see how he would respond to her quite clever tactics.

Imagine, giving him a setdown at the Royal Pavilion.

She had never been so clever and so had wed Purcell when she had failed to bring Lord Stoneleigh up to scratch. The viscount had tested her and she had failed, but even to this day, she did not comprehend in what way she had disappointed him.

Where did I fail? her mind cried for the thousandth time, her head beginning to stretch and tighten and stretch again.

She knew Stoneleigh had been putting her through her paces, as he had a dozen others before her and a dozen since, but where had she failed?

For one thing, Emily Hastings had approved of her and befriended her for a time, just as she was befriending Miss Amberley.

For another, Prinny had delighted in her company, she could not have been mistaken in that.

In addition, she had danced well in Stoneleigh's arms and when he had drilled her on her accomplishments, who could have found her lacking when she had mastered French and Italian and was considered to excel at the pianoforte and in the use of the watercolors?

She even excelled in a sport he admired, for she was a fine horsewoman. He had taken her out riding strictly to discover for himself the extent of her abilities.

To this day, she did not know why, on the last day of the London season, in June of 1813, he had simply left, without a word, without a missive to express even a particle of his sentiments, and— most horrifically—without an offer of marriage.

She had cried her heart out the remainder of the summer.

"No," she reiterated to her husband. "It would

be unthinkable to disoblige His Royal Highness in this manner."

They passed through the doorway into the corridor, the blue bamboo and pink walls bringing a rush of pain throbbing at her temples. Really, she despised the decor of the Pavilion and had always wondered what maggot had got into the Prince's head that he would ruin his home with such a ridiculous collection of Chinese statues, lanterns, and absurd bamboo furniture.

Her gaze sought one of the objects of her obsession instead—Miss Amberley. At a distance, she saw her brown curls through which a string of pearls had been wound quite expertly and wondered how it was that with her ridiculous fainting episode in the banqueting room some two weeks earlier she had actually been able to arouse Stoneleigh's interest.

Stoneleigh had once looked at her in that manner, as a buyer at Tattersall's does when purchasing a hack—examining each of her attributes and flaws in turn.

She stared at the back of Miss Amberley's head, a feeling so like despondency overtaking her that she did not hear her husband until he pinched her arm lightly. "My darling?"

"Yes, what is it?"

"I can see that you really are not well. We should go," he whispered.

Her head had never quite bothered her this badly before. She wondered if it were possible Miss Amberley could be *the one*.

Her heart seemed to draw up very tight of a sudden. She couldn't let that happen.

"Christopher," she said, drawing very close to her husband. "I promise you that I will be perfectly well throughout dinner, but I have just been thinking that it would be quite lovely to invite several guests to join us at Longreves for the forthcoming weekend."

Lord Purcell was quiet for a moment before answering, "Do you think, then, that your *headache* will be cured forever if we do?"

There were times when her husband was more perceptive than she wanted him to be. She therefore ignored his question entirely and thanked him sweetly for agreeing to a scheme which she knew would give them both a great deal of pleasure.

Twenty

Charlotte gently touched the sleeve of her father's bottle-green coat. "Papa," she said, addressing her quiet parent, "I have never seen you appear so forlorn before." She paused before adding with a smile, "Have you perchance been crossed in love?"

He was staring out the window of the town coach, oblivious to the easy sway of the carriage as it made its way through the Sussex countryside. His gaze was fixed on nothing in particular, the slump of his shoulders and downward turn of his mouth shouting at Charlotte that something dreadful was amiss. She was seated next to him, completely perplexed. From the moment they had met over breakfast, with Henry already gone sea-bathing in the company of Nurse, he had been clearly in a brown study.

"Crossed in love," he murmured, a note of sadness in his voice. "Hardly. I was once, last year, but nothing to signify. The truth is, I have given up hopes of ever finding a woman like your mother. No, it is nothing so simple as being crossed in love."

"I wish you might tell me what is troubling you. A few days ago, you were convinced your fortunes had turned. Has something happened to mar your confidence that the Prince will support you in Parliament?"

He snorted angrily. "Indeed, it has. And I have only one man to thank for it. You may very well guess who that might be!"

Charlotte felt a constriction of her chest. She knew the answer before uttering it, yet for the life of her she could not quite comprehend why she wished it were anyone else but the viscount.

"Stoneleigh?" she whispered.

"Who else! It would seem that man has interfered in my affairs yet again. Apparently he persuaded Prinny that I was not an appropriate risk for such a venture and I have received word that unless His Royal Highness can be assured of the nature of my company and other pertinent aspects of the operation, he feels he can't recommend to Parliament to grant the Charter."

Charlotte was not fully conversant with matters of trade, of shipping, of the methods by which charters were granted and fulfilled; but she had heard her father say nothing which seemed necessarily unreasonable to her. "Forgive my ignorance, Papa, but is there some reason why this information could not be assembled and given to the Prince?"

"Much you know about it!" her father snapped, turning angry blue eyes upon her and stamping his cane on the floorboards of the carriage. "This is a matter of honor, of my honor! When was an Amberley's word not sufficient? Forgive my temper, Charlie, but I am out of reason cross that Stoneleigh has achieved his end once more. He is sworn to break me, you know."

"What?"

"You heard what I said. He intends to ruin me, and where will that leave Henry? Though you have a fortune of your own to depend on separate from mine, little Henry hasn't a farthing except what is entailed to him through the estate. And much of that will be lost if Stoneleigh has his way."

Charlotte took a deep breath. These were harsh words, words she did not want to hear, nonetheless believe. Why had her father become an object of such spite, such malice? "Does he despise you so much, then, to have actually *vowed* to ruin you? But why?"

Sir John was silent apace, his gloved fist tight about the balled end of his cane. When he spoke, it was with some effort. "It is not a matter I can speak of easily. Let us just say that he, in his meddling manner, cut up my hopes forever that I would bring home a wife to Amberley again. I had meant to once—no, not last year—but four years ago. Stoneleigh ruined everything."

"I see," Charlotte returned uneasily. Her father was saying so much, yet so little. Who was this woman and how had Stoneleigh been able to manipulate her away from her father? What would have prompted him to do so in the first place? But then, did he need a reason? Some men were simply cruel by nature, seeking to harm others for their own pleasure.

Charlotte winced as she turned to look out her own window. In the past several years, particularly those since her mother's death, she had come to know a great many people from a variety of backgrounds. She knew she had acquired some measure of discernment where a person's character was concerned; and, though she might believe Stoneleigh capable of an unfeeling attitude toward the eligible ladies of his acquaintance, she found it difficult to believe he would set out to destroy another man for no reason. And that was the rub, for her father was that man.

She felt deep within her she had questions demanding answers, yet she could not bring herself to ask the questions. To do so would be to bring her father's character under scrutiny, and, after all, wasn't it a matter of honor?

The vibrant greens of the Sussex downs, as the coach rolled easily over macadamized roads toward Lord Purcell's home just a few miles northwest of Brighton, eventually began to soothe Charlotte's tormented mind. The gently sloping, grassy hills all around her were ridged and marked with rock walls. An occasional oak rose to draw the eye to its wide, spreading beauty. The steeple of a parish church would peek from behind a hill, announcing the presence of a village that might have once seen the troops of William the Conqueror some eight hundred years earlier.

For the smallest moment, Charlotte wished she were back in the safety of Amberley Park's familiar sights and smells; of hearing the housekeeper rattle her keys when she entered a room; of smelling Cook's apricot tartlets fresh-baked from the oven; of sitting quietly in the morning room, which overlooked her best flower beds, and reading or embroidering or merely reclining on her favorite velvet sofa and listening to the robins chatter nonsense to one another. Everything her father had said to her had effectually cut up her peace, particularly since there was so little she could do about any of it.

He ground his teeth, so distraught was he. When he at last spoke, it was venomously. "I should have called him out! Damme, I should have. Now, look what a pass everything has come to, and all because I—I played the gentleman and ignored the insult."

"I shall speak with him," Charlotte stated, unaware she had even made such a decision until the words were out of her mouth.

"No," Sir John countered hastily. "I mean, it

145

wouldn't do to have you mentioning such matters to Stoneleigh. It wouldn't be proper."

Charlotte wanted to argue with him, but to what purpose? He was a stubborn man and no amount of even the most erudite argumentation on her part would serve to convince him otherwise. But in her heart, she decided she would broach the subject with Stoneleigh. After all, he was the one intent upon getting up a flirtation with her—he had kissed her wrist on the Steyne; he had dressed up in lady's flannels at the sea-bathing machines; and he had drawn her apart in the Red Saloon only two nights previously. And last night, at a ball held at the Castle Inn, he had gone down two dances with her—their quarrel at the Pavilion set firmly behind them—and more than once sought her out to converse with her.

She had been a little surprised that he had even spoken with her, nonetheless danced with her, since she had aired her opinions so ruthlessly to him at the Pavilion. But he had explained his willingness to forgive her because he knew, to some extent, she had been right. Even Emily had told him so, and the whole of it had been an awakening of sorts to him.

She had eyed him with surprise. "Now you have confounded me," she said.

"In what way?"

"Well, I was prepared to be ignored for the remainder of the summer. Instead, I find you a little penitent and willing to admit a mistake."

"You do see me as a rather hopeless creature, don't you?" he responded.

"Not completely," she replied. "Any man who will risk his reputation by wearing a lady's sea-bathing costume is not completely beyond hope."

"You are straining my patience," he retorted, with mock severity.

"Excellent."

Charlotte could not help but smile a little at the memory of this exchange, but her heart could not be easy as she again glanced toward her father. She felt that her whole world had shifted a step or two to the right in the past sennight.

Though neither Maude nor Selena would credit it, she had ceased her campaign against Stoneleigh's heart—indeed, in her own mind, she had never launched it. The moment she had run from the music room, she had dispensed with all her intentions to undo his heart. That Stoneleigh seemed taken with her afterward was the workings of Fate alone and nothing of her own design.

How serious his intentions were toward her, she could not tell. But whatever they were, she intended to seek him out and discover, if she could, more particulars regarding his animosity toward her father. Perhaps if she learned the nature of their quarrel, she could serve as a mediator and help resolve their differences that Stoneleigh might in turn support Sir John in his desire to acquire a charter for his joint-stock company.

With this last thought, she found some peace and could at last look upon the forthcoming weekend at Lady Purcell's country home with some pleasure.

As the carriage reached the top of a rise before descending into a charming valley, Amberley stated, "Longreves."

Charlotte drew in a deep, appreciative breath, for there, sitting prettily on the side of the hill opposite the rise, was a beautiful manor house, built up and refigured over the years to vie with the majesty of even the loftiest of mansions.

"How sweetly the trees and landscaping are shaped about the house."

"Repton, of course. Some of his best work. Entirely in the picturesque."

"We shall pass a delightful weekend here, Papa, I'm sure of it."

"Not if Stoneleigh is present, as I believe he means to be."

"Then I suggest you ignore him completely, as I shall do if he is not civil to you."

Her father merely harrumphed as the postilion eased the horses down the gentle grade toward Longreves.

Twenty-one

"My dear Miss Amberley!" Lady Purcell cooed. "Oh, pray let us not be on such formal terms, especially here in my home. Will you permit me to call you Charlotte?"

Charlotte felt Lady Purcell's thin, delicate arm wrap about her own; she smelled the hint of lilac clinging to her shawl and summery gown of embroidered muslin; she heard the gush of words begging to be on intimate terms with her, but she could not credit it. She was only barely acquainted with the baroness and felt that the request was premature. Lady Purcell, however, was her hostess, and to refuse would be unkind and uncivil.

"Yes, of course," she returned, blinking up at the taller, more sophisticated woman.

"And you must call me Anthea."

"As you wish, *Anthea*," Charlotte responded politely.

Lady Purcell attempted to smile warmly upon her, at least Charlotte was certain that was her intention. But there was just such a demanding light in her eye that Charlotte knew an instinct, if not to flee precisely, then to take care.

"You will adore Longreves," Anthea gushed a little more. "It is the finest in the county—save

Stoneleigh's home, of course. I have been blessed beyond any worthiness on my part and am so *grateful* that Fate has permitted me this lot."

Charlotte remembered the quotation, *the lady doth protest too much* and believed it could possibly apply to this instance.

Lady Purcell led Charlotte from the expansive entrance hall of black and white tiles through a charming antechamber—in which a rectangular, rosewood pianoforte and a harp had been nicely arranged—to a large, open chamber flanked on two sides by row upon row of Elizabethan windows. The chamber was all light and radiance, the morning sun, though not directly on the windows, suffusing the room in a wondrous glow.

The windows were each draped with gold-fringed lengths of medium-blue silk-damask, under which sheer, white muslin curtains helped to extend the sunlight into the chamber. A large fireplace, completely worked in plaster scrollwork and carved wood, then painted white, was a vision, particularly topped by two Sèvres vases and a large, flat arrangement of gladioli and lilacs against a gilt-edged mirror.

"Madame—that is, Anthea," Charlotte began awkwardly, a blush of discomfiture warming her cheeks. "I have never seen refinement, elegance, and symmetry come together so beautifully in a chamber. Your sense of beauty is remarkable. When Mama was alive, we spent hours pouring over furniture catalogues and conferring with painters and linen-drapers, but I daresay the final effect of any of our efforts was not half so *perfect.*"

"Just so," Sir John agreed, his quizzing glass fixed to his eye as he also scrutinized the chamber.

"You are both too kind," her ladyship replied uneasily. Charlotte felt she had distressed Lady Purcell somehow, for her smile grew fragile, and if Charlotte had not known better, she would have supposed the baroness was ready to burst into tears. "Well, then, I do believe I hear another carriage on the drive, so let me direct you both to places of the most promising amusement while the remainder of our guests arrive." She led them through another antechamber toward the back of the house and into a long gallery, adorned with the portraits of dozens of Purcell ancestors. It opened onto a wide sloping lawn, carefully scythed and groomed.

"Charlotte, your friends are already enjoying an *al fresco* luncheon as you can see and, as for you, Sir John, a little sherry, cold chicken, and fruit along with a billiard table may be found by following the line of the gallery into the hall and listening for my husband's voice."

She then departed after expressing her hope that all their desires would be attended to during their brief stay at Longreves. She then disappeared through a doorway leading back to the entrance hall, her light, embroidered muslin skirts billowing slightly out behind her as she hurried away.

"*Anthea,*" Charlotte murmured. "Papa, why ever would she wish to have me address her so informally? I am not at all acquainted with her."

Sir John grunted. "You are forgetting that I know her quite well. I believe it was all meant as a compliment to me."

"I suppose so," she responded. "But it still seems quite odd."

"It is just as I suspected," he said. "You've become abominably stuffy. Now, do as your hostess bid you—join your friends on the lawn and pray do so before they see you and come running. Can't abide either of them. They gabble too much."

He then gave her a gentle push toward the long

French doors and headed toward the billiard room.

Once Charlotte passed through the doors and stepped from the stone terrace onto the lawn, both Maude and Selena let out squeals of delight and raced toward her—just as her father had said they would. In the distance, where servants hovered around an enormous rush basket and a dark blanket spread out on the grass in the shade of a fully-leafed lime tree, she could see that a gentleman, unknown to her but one of an age with her father, had been entertaining her friends.

Both young ladies caught her up on either side and, with their joint energy, hurried her toward the blanket.

"He is so droll," Maude whispered.

"You will adore him," Selena cried.

"He is a marquis. Thaxted," Maude whispered, lower still.

"And he is not married," Selena rushed into her ear.

"You are both being absurd," Charlotte responded, a little irritated that their first consideration in introducing the marquis to her had been his eligibility.

The Marquis of Thaxted rose to greet her, took her gloved hand in his, and—rather than merely bowing over it—placed a kiss upon the back of her hand. "How do you do, Miss Amberley?" he said slowly, looking at her from rather sleepy brown eyes. "I believe I am acquainted with your father. Sir John Amberley. Am I right?"

"Indeed, yes, you are," Charlotte returned.

"Do sit down," he said, gesturing with a sweep of his hand to the blanket on the grass. Both Maude and Selena arranged themselves, one on each side of him, in attitudes which bordered on worship.

"Thank you," she said, choosing to sit opposite

him in order to better observe him. She knew little of the Marquis of Thaxted by reputation, only that he was a childless widower and that Emily's son, William, was his heir. Emily had only mentioned him once, but her faraway look when she had spoken of her uncle gave pause to Charlotte's potential enthusiasm in having at last made his acquaintance.

He was teasing Maude and Selena in turn about anything and everything but most particularly about Maude's statuesque beauty and Selena's fiery curls.

"Are you one of Michelangelo's creations come to life?" he asked of Maude.

Then to Selena, "Is your heart as full of passion and vigor for life as your beautiful hair most surely suggests?"

His smile was warm, his tone gentle, his words kind and complimentary. He gave no indication of passing the bounds of propriety and, though he pressed a glass of champagne upon each of the ladies, he refused a second one for himself. "The disadvantages of age," he explained, directing his comment to Charlotte. "The gout. Even His Royal Highness suffers from it occasionally. An abstinence of Bacchus' pleasures is the only remedy, most unfortunately."

"I feel most acutely for you," Charlotte said sympathetically. "My father, as well, has been known to sit for days in anguish, his foot bound up in linens." The gout was a painful malady in which the body only enjoyed relief once it had rid itself of the poisons which caused the swelling of, often humorously, the big toe and frequently the ankle joint.

The marquis nodded, an acknowledgement of her concern, then asked the servant to bring him a glass of water that he might drink to the ladies' health.

Charlotte was not certain why, but in the same manner she questioned Lady Purcell's effusive desire to befriend her, she did not quite like Thaxted. He was dressed suitably in a dark blue coat, buff pantaloons, and a buckskin waistcoat. His neckcloth was tied to perfection, and his shirt-points rose to a moderate height upon each cheek.

Perhaps it was his cheeks which daunted Charlotte's enthusiasm to proclaim him the delight her friends obviously felt he was. His skin was finely patterned with little red lines and even the whites of his eyes were slightly red. Beyond this indication of the manner of life he lived, he was indeed a fine-looking man. His brown hair, which he kept cropped short and close to his head, was only barely silvered with gray. His brows were a dark brown, like his hair, but neither bushy—which occurred frequently in men of fifty and more—nor so thin and wispy that he might give the appearance of a milk-fed parson without use for anything but his books. His eyes were brown and would have been deemed handsome had the lids not been kept almost permanently at half-mast, giving him a bored look. His chin was firm and in his youth he must have presented an awesome presence, for even now, so many years later, as he sipped the water the servant had just given him, his frame was powerful. He reclined on one elbow, not a hint of excessive flesh apparent in his firm, muscular legs, nor in what could have been an unhappy bulge of his waistcoat but what was instead decidedly flat and smooth, nor in a doubling of the chin above his neckcloth.

Again he teased Maude, then Selena, both of whom were enjoying their champagne a little too much, each falling into bursts of laughter.

He addressed himself to Maude. "Surely I know you, Diana the Huntress!" he cried.

154

To Selena, "Are you a woman of Celtic ancestry and would you fight beside your man in battle like your forebears?"

How long this nonsense would have continued, Charlotte would never know, for just as he began turning back to Maude, something behind Charlotte caught his eye and a strange, dark expression overcame his face.

He murmured, "The man's a millstone about my neck!"

At the very same moment, an unearthly crashing sound was heard coming from the direction of the long gallery. Charlotte turned around, startled, her heart racing with sudden fright. She was horrified to see her father, stripped of his coat and black boots, sword in hand, lying on his back in the midst of the debris from one of the French doors—a door now hanging precariously on its hinges and shed completely of its glass.

He picked himself up with great agility, his temper hot, and was on his feet instantly. "By God, Stoneleigh, I'll have your head if it's the last thing I do!"

Twenty-two

By the time Charlotte reached the gallery, the quick, rasping and sliding of metal against metal could be heard, a sound that sent the blood racing from her head. She felt dizzy and ill and thought with malicious self-condemnation that it would be true to form for her now to swoon.

She willed herself, therefore, to watch what was going forward. Somewhere in the distant reaches of her hearing, she knew that Lord Purcell was shouting to both men to put their weapons away, that ladies were present, that it was no compliment to his wife that they conduct themselves so terribly.

Directly across from Charlotte, Lady Purcell appeared in the doorway. Behind her, Mr. and Mrs. Knight stood, their mouths agape, along with Mr. and Mrs. Wyndham. Charlotte's gaze was drawn back to Lady Purcell. She watched a veil cloak her ladyship's eyes, her sentiments entirely inscrutable, save for the marked rise and fall of her breast as she in turn watched the duel. After a long moment of scrutiny, Charlotte felt she comprehended something of the baroness.

She is enjoying this, she realized with some horror.

She returned her attention to her father and

Stoneleigh. The two men shifted around the gallery, banging into tables, overturning chairs, their socked feet alternately padding across the carpet and, where the carpet would end, sliding dangerously over polished wood.

Everything happened so quickly.

Already Stoneleigh had a bloodstain on his shirt over his left arm. Her father's face poured sweat as if he had been marching in a hot sun for miles on end.

Stoneleigh lunged, trying mightily not to strike but to catch her father's blade and tear it from his hands. But Sir John was a skilled swordsman and easily fended off his opponent's attempts to disarm him. She could see her father was enraged, that he was beyond himself, beyond reason. She also knew that Stoneleigh was trying hard to end the terrible duel before more blood was drawn and honored him for it.

"Coward," Sir John muttered viciously.

"End this," Stoneleigh cried, breathing heavily. "For God's sake, man. This is not the place!"

"You're a coward and a liar!"

There was nothing for Stoneleigh to do but continue. No man of honor could turn aside such an insult.

One or the other could die, Charlotte thought, her heart thrumming in her ears. The swords were wretchedly sharp. It was only a matter of time before someone was seriously wounded or killed.

"Do stop," she cried out breathlessly, her ears aching with the noise of her own heartbeats.

But her effort availed nothing. Both tempers were too high. The gentlemen were like wild dogs in a vicious fight. Only submission on the part of one or the other would end the confrontation.

And neither would submit.

Charlotte heard Maude and Selena arguing be-

157

hind her. "Do move a little to the right, I can't see anything!" Maude cried.

"Stop shoving me!" Selena returned.

Charlotte began backing up, since the men seemed to be moving closer and closer in her direction. Stoneleigh had locked her father's sword arm about his; and, while Amberley strained to disengage the hold the viscount had upon him, the pair moved steadily toward the French doors.

The next moment, Maude moved past Charlotte, brushing her shoulder. As she turned around to pull a face at Selena, Amberley lost his footing. Stoneleigh stumbled forward, his sword arm outstretched in losing Amberley's resistance; and before Maude could utter a sound of protest or move out of the way, his sword pierced the flesh of her right shoulder.

"Oh, my God," Stoneleigh cried, withdrawing his sword carefully and letting it clatter to the wood floor. "Fetch a surgeon!" he cried over his shoulder. "Dear God!"

To Charlotte's horror, her father was scrambling to his feet, ready to continue doing battle, his choler still commanding his senses.

"No!" she screamed as he leaped toward Stoneleigh. At the same moment, she saw a blur from the corner of her eye, a quick, unearthly movement, as Thaxted catapulted himself between Amberley and the now-defenseless viscount. "Enough, man! Miss Dunsfold has been hurt!"

He was pressing against the full force of Sir John's body, preventing him only with a tantamount effort from reaching his quarry. When her father's eyes, however, fell upon Maude, who was now sitting in a heap on the floor near Stoneleigh, blood seeping into the peach-colored silk of her gown and forming a pool on the wood floor beside her, only then did his reason seem to return.

He backed away from Thaxted. "Good God," he murmured out-of-breath, his chest heaving from his exertions.

Maude wept quietly. "I'm bleeding," she said over and over, between unearthly sobs.

Charlotte scanned the assembled company and saw that, as one, the guests stood in a sort of deathly stillness, frozen into inaction by the horror of Maude's injury, their combined attention fixed on her. No one moved; not one eye blinked. The only sound that disturbed the pervasive silence was the sudden ripping of fabric.

Charlotte was as immobile as the rest and turned to watch in mute fascination as Stoneleigh tore a ruffle from the bottom of Maude's gown and began wrapping it tightly over the top of her shoulder and beneath her arm. "It hurts," she said.

"Yes, I know," Stoneleigh responded quietly. "But you must be brave. It is only a flesh wound. You have nothing to fear."

"It hurts."

This last pathetic cry somehow brought the room alive again. A murmuring and a bustling quickly ensued as Lady Purcell recommended that the gentlemen retire to the billiard parlor and the ladies upstairs to the yellow drawing room.

Charlotte quickly went to Maude and comforted her as best she was able. Selena joined her but could do little more than sit on the floor and weep alongside her friend. The baroness came forward and said that she would see a surgeon was brought immediately from the village but that it would be best if Maude were taken upstairs to her bedchamber.

"Let me do it," a masculine voice called sternly from the doorway.

Charlotte's gaze was instantly drawn in the direction of the voice, and she was stunned to find that Harry had arrived. She had not even known he had been invited. His face was ashen as he looked at Maude, his lips compressed tightly together, his eyes blurred with unexpressed emotions. Without being asked or given permission, he picked Maude up from off the floor, lifted her easily into his arms, and headed toward the entrance hall. "Only tell me where to take her," he commanded over his shoulder.

"Turn right at the top of the stairs," Lady Purcell responded.

Just as he was about to cross the threshold, Mrs. Bosham appeared. "Merciful heavens! I have just received word little Maudie was struck down by Stoneleigh's sword. Has she been killed?"

"No, of course not," Harry snapped. "You can see that she has not."

"I am not dead," Maude whispered.

"Thank heavens for that. Your mother would have never forgiven me!" Mrs. Bosham was a birdlike woman with round eyes that even in the calmest of circumstances gave her a frightened appearance. Of the moment, confronted with the serious wound Maude had sustained, she gave every indication she would soon suffer a spasm as she clutched at her side.

"I can't bear the sight of blood," she whispered to Charlotte as Harry bore Maude toward the staircase. "Oh, dear. Oh, dear! Margaret Dunsfold will have my head! She will blame me for having gotten her daughter killed. Where is Selena? There you are my dearest! Did Stoneleigh attack you with his sword as well?"

"No, he did not!" Selena cried, bursting into a serious bout of tears. "Oh, Mama, it was all so horrible!"

Since Selena was obviously in need of comfort, Mrs. Bosham's attention was happily diverted to the less painful task of supporting her own, un-injured child.

Charlotte followed after Harry, with Lady Purcell beside her. The baroness slowed her pace a trifle, letting Maude and Harry gain a few feet in front of them both.

"I don't understand what possesses men to take up the sword in the first place," she murmured quietly to Charlotte. "But leave it to one of them to begin a quarrel in a gentlewoman's home. I am astonished that Stoneleigh—who is generally the most considerate of guests—would actually duel with Amberley, and in my gallery! I suppose it is the fault of all these rumors—ah, well, there will always be gossip, no doubt. For now, if I can but see Miss Dunsfold settled comfortably in her bed and her wound tended to, I can rest easy. I wonder how I will possibly compose a letter to her mother. She will undoubtedly worry herself ill when she hears that her daughter has been wounded. But then, one does worry so about one's children, though I don't suppose you can know what that is like." She looked at Charlotte and eyed her speculatively. "But in this I am mistaken, am I not? For Emily Hastings was telling me of your little brother, whom she says you have raised like your own son. Dear Charlotte. You've not had a normal life for a young woman. By now you should have enjoyed a half-dozen seasons and been married some six years at least, with children of your own. You ought to marry, and the sooner the better from what I've heard. I suppose nothing much can be done for little Henry, though he might perhaps consider a naval career when he is older. There is always a war to be fought for England somewhere in the world."

Charlotte did not know what to make of Lady Purcell's speech. "A naval career?" she asked, mystified.

"Well, yes. Now there is no need for you to pretend, Charlotte, when we are such excellent friends. The entire *haut ton* knows of your father's debts. It is said there will be nothing left for your little Henry in the end."

Charlotte did not know what to say to the baroness and so remained silent. She had no interest in either confirming or denying what was quite obviously both a rumor and a lie. The conversation did have the effect, however, of causing Charlotte to wonder if her father owed more to the moneylenders than he had originally told her. Whether or not he did, it was none of Lady Purcell's concerns.

As Harry entered Maude's bedchamber, Lady Purcell stopped Charlotte just outside her room and prevented her from going in. It would seem that *Anthea* had not yet said enough.

"I know this is not the best moment in the world, my dear, but I do feel I ought to give you a hint in another quarter—Lord Stoneleigh is not for you. Please trust an older woman's judgment in this. Now, pray do not fly into the boughs when I have meant nothing but kindness in offering you my advice. Surely Maude and Selena have told you what he is like."

Charlotte was too angry to speak, for the impertinence of her *advice* was beyond bearing. She lowered her eyes and nodded in acknowledgement of having heard her, hoping that the baroness would take her hint and let the subject drop.

Apparently, she was not wishful of doing so. "There, there! I can see I have quite piqued you. Well, never mind. We have enough troubles for the present; only if later on you find yourself in the basket because you have not heeded my advice, you will at least have been warned and can perhaps save yourself from complete disaster.

Now, I beg you will inform Maude that I am sending for the surgeon."

With that, she breezed down the hallway on a bright step, turned the corner, and disappeared from sight.

Charlotte relayed her ladyship's message to Maude, whose color had returned to her cheeks, and afterward queried, "You look as though you feel a little better. Do you, dearest?"

Maude glanced shyly at Harry, then back to Charlotte. "A little, yes."

"I'm sure Stoneleigh was correct when he said it was only a flesh wound."

"Is that what he told you, Maudie?" Harry asked. "Then you may be certain it's true."

Maude smiled into his eyes, and Charlotte was struck both by the sweetness of her expression as she looked at Harry and by the fact that Harry was already on such terms with her friend that he had called her Maudie. When had the unlikely pair found time in a mere three days to view one another with such affection?

She realized quite readily that she was neither needed nor wanted in the sickroom and retired in good order.

Besides, it was time to find her father and to discover, if she could, what had possibly prompted him to set his sword against Stoneleigh.

Twenty-three

Just as Charlotte reached the bottom of the stairs, Lord Purcell appeared, having come from the direction of the gallery, his face red from exertion and fright, a kerchief pressed to his round face.

"Such a terrible deed. The house is in an uproar. Is she—is she dead?"

"Oh, no, no! You mustn't think. . . . The bleeding has stopped, I assure you."

"With so much blood pouring from her, I didn't expect her to—well never mind that! But you mustn't blame Stoneleigh, my dear. No man could have stood the insults that—I don't like to speak ill of your father, Miss Amberley, but I hold him responsible. He pressed too hard and literally tore my swords from the wall and cut Stoneleigh's arm before Stoneleigh would pick up the gauntlet. Oh, dear! Oh, dear! Excuse me, but I must see Miss Dunsfold's condition for myself. The whole house is in an uproar!"

"Where is my father?"

Lord Purcell was already past her and taking the stairs two at a time before she got the words beyond her lips.

"I don't know. I don't know." He did not even look back at her as he spoke.

Charlotte returned to the gallery but saw no one there save three servants busy repairing the damage to the carpets and furniture and mopping up the stain on the floor. The house seemed strangely quiet suddenly as Charlotte looked around her. There was not even the smallest sound emanating from the corridor connecting to the billiard room.

She was prompted to approach the nearest servant, an older man in a white powdered wig and the Purcell livery of scarlet and gold.

"Where is everyone?" she asked quietly.

"I don't know precisely, Miss," he said, righting a hall chair covered with gold damask. "But I believe all the ladies went upstairs, retiring to the yellow saloon on the first floor with Lady Purcell. The gentlemen spoke of going round to the stables to see a servant properly dispatched to the village."

"Was Sir John Amberley among them?"

"I can't rightly say. There is still one gentleman in the billiard parlor. That might be he."

"Thank you."

Charlotte walked quickly through the doorway of the gallery into a long hall at the end of which she could see another wide doorway. Through this aperture she noted the green-velvet pocket of a billiard table on the far side of what appeared to be a large, expansive chamber and quickened her step.

A crimson carpet, patterned in gold and black geometrics, bespoke a gentleman's haunt. When Charlotte reached the threshold, she had an instant impression of dark-grained woods, of a massive cabinet containing hunting rifles and pistols, and of several trophies of deer, fox, and boar mounted on the walls.

But for all these points of interest, her eye was drawn immediately to the quiet form of Lord

Stoneleigh, clad in buckskin breeches and a white, bloodstained shirt, sitting very still in a black-lacquer Empire chair at the far end of the room. He was near a wide window overlaid with green velvet curtains drawn back at an angle by gold cords. Through the window, visible below the angle of the drape, was the home wood rising gently up the side of the hill behind the house and, above the hill, a deep blue sky unmarred by even a hint of clouds.

How gray the figure appeared against the bright setting, his countenance slumped. One knee was outstretched farther than the other for balance; his expression was blank, his gaze fixed to the carpet. One hand overlaid his neckcloth, which was wrapped loosely about his arm. Charlotte could see the task of tending to his wound was unfinished.

The impulse she felt at the sight of him was to help, nothing more.

She was beside him before the viscount knew anyone had joined him in the room, for he looked up at her from startled, yet red-rimmed, blurred eyes. "Is she all right?" he asked urgently, his voice choked.

Charlotte was stunned by his appearance, by the pain she saw in his face—in his eyes—and heard in the obvious constriction of his throat.

"Yes," she said firmly, dropping down beside him and taking the ends of the torn neckcloth from what she now perceived was his shaking hand. "It appears the bleeding has stopped."

"Thank God," he said, covering his face with his free hand for a moment before wiping at his eyes. "There was a great deal of blood."

"You told her it was a flesh wound. Were you speaking the truth?"

"Yes, but one can never be sure. Not completely."

Charlotte carefully tied the bandage over his wound.

"Thank you," he whispered, removing a kerchief from the pocket of his breeches and blowing his nose soundly. "You are at liberty to think me anything you wish at this moment, Miss Amberley. I wouldn't have the right to argue with any ill-opinion you might put forth." He struggled to control his feelings. "Oh, God I could have killed her," he cried, shuddering and burying his face in both hands.

"But you didn't; and even if you had," she responded, placing a firm hand on his shoulder, "there is not a single person present who would deny you were trying to restrain yourself and to urge my father to desist. What happened to Maude was an accident. Nothing more."

"Nothing more," he laughed, again blowing his nose. "The outcome could have been so different. I should never have forgiven myself."

He seemed inconsolable for a long moment. Only in his silence did Charlotte become aware that she was touching him and that the shirt beneath her hand was damp from his exertion. Her gaze followed the line of the shirt to the points of the collar hanging open at his throat due to the absence of his neckcloth. His black hair was wet with perspiration, clinging to his neck and in odd wisps to his ear and to his face where he had wiped his kerchief across his dampened forehead. She smelled the soap, familiar to him, mingled with the starch of his clothes and the leather of his breeches. The latter, she noted, were dotted with blood.

For the barest moment she felt faint again, certainly dizzy, but from what cause she was uncertain. She knew she was not ill, but she rather thought the slight pleasurable queasiness which assailed her had more to do with the clinging

167

damp of Stoneleigh's shirt and the feel of his shoulder—separated only by the thin, white cambric—beneath her hand than by the awful reasons for his distress. Or perhaps it was the whole of what had happened and a culmination of who this man was, of having been kissed warmly by him before, of having seen him move in unearthly agility around chairs and tables—sword in hand— fending off her accomplished father's attack, of seeing him now horrified at what might have been. These were perhaps the more likely reasons for the odd way her heart was behaving as she kept her hand where it was, connected to Stoneleigh's warmth.

"Do you blame me?" he asked quietly.

Charlotte knelt beside his leg and rested her arm on his knee. "No," she said.

At that he looked at her, giving his head a small shake. "You should."

"I have been given to understand by Lord Purcell that this fight was forced upon you and that my father wounded you when you were unarmed."

"That much is true, but only in essentials. Ours is a quarrel of long-standing. I have provoked him by my determination to do him ill."

Charlotte looked away from him slightly, trying to comprehend these two men—her father whom she now felt she had never known, and Stoneleigh, whom she knew only but a little and whom her father hated.

"Will you tell me," she began slowly, her finger lightly touching the delicate gilt lion's paw which shaped the arm of the chair, "why you despise him so very much? You see, since my arrival I have heard morsels of gossip and a little of my father's difficulties from his vantage point, but I can't make sense of the whole. What is the nature of your quarrel? I wish to help if I can."

He looked at her steadily for a long moment before answering, "If your father has chosen not to speak of it, I have no right to say anything; but know this, Charlotte Amberley, my heart is hard towards your father and can never be anything more."

Charlotte could not conceive of what her father could possibly have done to have incited Stoneleigh's malice so completely. She turned her gaze to the lacquered arm of the chair and again touched the gilt lion's paw. Her father had spoken of a love interest. Could this be the source of their quarrel?

"Was it because of a woman?" she queried.

He did not respond at once, but after a moment, he spoke in almost a whisper. "In a manner of speaking I suppose you could say so, but not in the way you might think."

Charlotte shifted her gaze quickly back to the viscount. There was a meaning hidden in his words—but what? She knew he did not wish to say more and so did not press him. She determined in her heart instead to ask her father later to reveal the truth to her. She could do little to rectify the situation after all until she knew precisely what had gone awry.

"Charlotte," Stoneleigh began, employing her Christian name for the first time, but sounding deeply distressed.

"What is it?" she asked.

He placed his hand over hers. "Why is it," he began. "Why is it *you* had to be *his* daughter? Why couldn't you have been anyone else's child? Are you come to make me curse the day I was born?"

"Why do you speak so?" she cried, feeling as if her heart were being torn from her. "Only tell me why he insists you intend to ruin him if you can? What has he done to you?"

169

"You must ask him the reason. I will not tell you, nor is there anyone else who can tell you—he and I alone know the truth. But tell me this—are you in league with him? Are there others involved? Did you come to Brighton to a purpose?"

"Yes," she whispered. "My task was to distract you that first night—when I was so very ill and swooned at your feet. My father wished to speak privately with the Prince and believed you would not permit him to do so. When you followed after me, he was able to request His Royal Highness to support him in his quest for a Charter for a joint-stock company. I succeeded in distracting you though, didn't I?"

"Then I was not mistaken," he responded, his hold on her forearm tightening. "And yes, you succeeded, for you have quite driven me to distraction—that night and every night since!" He leaned toward her, searching her face, her eyes—letting his gaze linger upon her lips.

"Whether you believe me or not," she said, "I don't care. But I promise you that I have done nothing since my arrival in Brighton except stumble blindly over the wishes of my father and my friends. If I have *driven you to distraction,* it is not by design. I find I am far too naive and too susceptible to swooning to be of much use to Papa—or to anyone else. I did not expect to find your eyes so blue and the sound of your voice as welcome to my soul as the rich strains of the cello. The scheme was present from the beginning, the execution a farce which for some reason, beyond the poor pathways of my mind, seems to have had an effect. Or am I mistaken?"

"No, you are not mistaken," he said, his face—his lips—close to her own. "Perhaps I shouldn't, Charlotte, but I do believe what you have told me." He rose suddenly, sliding upward easily from the chair and catching her up in his arms at the same time.

She found herself buried deep within the circle of his embrace, pressed against the cool dampness of his body, his lips hot against hers.

She was lost, completely, forever.

Every ability to reason, to place her thoughts logically one before the other, swirled around her brain in disjointed bliss. She ached for him, giving herself to the passion of his arms as if in doing so, she could relieve the ache she felt. He was so strong, holding her fast one moment, then stroking the length of her back possessively the next. His hand held first her neck, then her face, gently before he swept his mouth over hers and kissed her again.

At first she had been still, allowing him to touch her, to kiss her, but when he spoke her name, *Charlotte*, yet again and breathed it against her ear over and over, her stillness disappeared in stages as her fingers found their way into his hair, then slid across his cheek and touched his lips. He kissed her fingers, the softness of his tongue a whisper against her skin. She closed her eyes to feel the soft, sensuousness of his touch, burying her face into his neck, and revelling in his closeness, in his strength, in the tender expressions of his affection.

His hand joined her hand, fingers slipped between fingers as he held her tightly to him. He kissed her again. And again. The passion seeming to subside only in slow, necessary stages, thoughts overpowering the inexplicable burst of unspoken sentiment.

Charlotte knew a feeling of desperation so keen, a need to remain close to him so profound, that she drew in a breath which sounded very much even to her own ears like a sob. What was happening to her?

She pulled away from him, longing to remain in his arms, yet fearing him the longer she remained. He had the power to hurt her deeply, she realized with dreaded awareness.

With that, her feet obeyed her fear and retreated from the room. She put her hands over her ears that she might not hear the voice she was growing to love calling to her, "Charlotte. Wait."

In the antechamber which adjoined the billiard room to the library, Lady Purcell stood unseen beside the darkened doorway, her hands wrapped tightly about a porcelain bowl filled partially with water, a towel draped over her arm. She looked down at the water and saw that it was jiggling strangely, then realized it was because her hands were shaking as she held the bowl.

She had come purposely to the billiard room, intending to shower Stoneleigh with her careful, *motherly* ministrations. She knew the men were gone. She had watched them all depart to the stables and waited to perform her task only until she had told Purcell to join them there and to wait for the surgeon to return.

How carefully she had made her plans.

How easily another female had stolen the fruits of them.

She had arrived on the threshold, a flirtatious smile on her lips designed to enchant him, a dozen or so words readied on her tongue with which to chide him for disrupting her little *fete*, and a demure lowering of her eyes rehearsed to let him know she didn't truly mind in the least, since he had relieved her heart entirely of its deepest fears by surviving Amberley's horrific attack.

Only what should she find, instead of Stoneleigh,

alone and in need of her gentling and coddling, but the viscount kissing that horrid little vixen, Charlotte Amberley—and so thoroughly!

She had not known what to do and so had slipped out of sight, leaning her back against the cooled, wainscotted wall in the antechamber, her hands quivering with rage, her heart full of a jealousy so profound she thought each fibre of it would tear her heart apart if she drew one more breath.

"How dare she!" she whispered into the empty air of the small chamber.

She began taking deep breaths in order to regain her composure.

A minute passed, then another.

Finally, she moved away from the wall, away from the billiard room, sloshing water as she went, not caring that it spilled onto the front of her gown and the flowered carpet beneath her feet.

In a rage, just before she left the antechamber, she dumped the remaining water over an arrangement of roses and watched with satisfaction as the weight of the water bent several of the red, velvety heads. She would have liked to have thrown the porcelain basin against the wall, but she had enough of her wits about her to know that that would only stir up unwanted gossip.

She paused for another minute or so, supporting her trembling limbs with a hand held firmly against the doorjamb, and waited for her full composure to return. Only then did she make her way to the yellow saloon where she pretended to listen to Mrs. Knight complaining of the vicar's last sermon and all the while she weaved her next scheme.

Sir John Amberley stood on the stone terrace, leaning against the wall, just out of sight of the broken French door. He had only barely escaped Charlotte's notice as she came out of the billiard room.

In the aftermath of his contest with Stoneleigh, he had been filled to overflowing with guilt—a resounding, echoing, pulsing contrition that seemed to have had the effect of clearing, perhaps only momentarily, his ability to see things properly.

What the devil had he been about?

What had he been thinking when he attacked Stoneleigh in Purcell's billiard room? By God, he had been behaving like a callow youth still wet behind the ears. All Stoneleigh had done was quietly give him a hint to stay away from Walker's Library and *rouge et noir* for Charlotte's sake.

Something in him had snapped, all his hatred for Stoneleigh and the viscount's easy path among the *haut ton* rioting up within his chest until, before he knew what he was doing, he had a sword in his hand and had pricked the viscount on the arm, drawing his blood with a quick slice to his flesh and forcing him to do battle.

Now, an hour later, he saw the extreme stupidity of giving in to his animosity toward the wealthy peer. But when he had learned from Harry Elstow the night before of the extent of Stoneleigh's wealth—that the man had vast trading interests in America, in the West Indies, in India, and in China—a root of jealousy had taken hold within his heart. Stoneleigh was not merely the seventh viscount of an ancient family with ties back to William the Conqueror, but a man of considerable means beyond comprehension. That he was a man of influence and of Trade—an arena he had himself intended upon entering in order to restore his fortune—seemed to cause the root to grow, to flower, and to blossom in the most hideous manner.

Hence, he had forced him to duel.

A half-hour later, he had come upon him holding Charlotte in his arms.

Charlotte! It seemed so impossible.

An alliance?

Possibly, but unlikely. Stoneleigh had an ungenerous reputation among the women of their mutual acquaintance. He had even heard rumors that the viscount would put any prospective bride through her paces—a series of tests, as it were—before asking for her hand. He had done so with Lady Purcell. She had failed and had taken her fall hard.

He leaned his head against the stone wall, the scent of climbing roses nearby causing him to feel giddy. Then he smiled. He would like to see Stoneleigh attempt to put Charlotte through her paces. She would give his head a washing he had never experienced before.

He understood something then, something, if not wondrous, then perfect. He could not lose now. He had but to exert the mildest influence over his daughter—one direction or the other—and he would have either his Charter or a fortune. In either case, his mounting difficulties would be solved.

Knowing that Charlotte had disappeared through the doorway leading to the stairs, he now had a choice to make. He could stay at Longreves or he could leave. He chose the latter, knowing in so doing he would be giving Charlotte an opportunity of getting to know Stoneleigh better.

His decision made, he left at once, without returning to his chambers, without seeing his belongings restored to his portmanteau, without saying goodbye to Charlotte.

He merely strode through a break in the yew hedge and headed to the stables, where the rest of the gentlemen had congregated. He had his horses put to; made his apologies all round; begged his host to forgive him; asked Colonel Hastings, who had just arrived, to take charge of his daughter; then simply climbed aboard his carriage and left.

"What do you make of it?" Colonel Hastings queried of Lord Purcell, giving his head a shake.

"A rum touch, that one. He was playing deep at Walker's Library only a few days ago, you know. *Rouge et noir* and a thousand pounds in vowels. Saw him there m'self."

The Colonel whistled low. "Incredible. I hear he is in debt to the moneylenders. Some say as much as forty thousand pounds. Of course, it is all conjecture."

"Miss Amberley is ignorant of his affairs, I suppose."

The Colonel snorted. "Amberley is ignorant of his affairs," he stated derisively. "How could his daughter, therefore, know anything about it, however clever I believe her to be."

"Pity. He has a young son, I understand."

"Indeed, he does. But he won't have been the first child to inherent a ramshackle estate—if anything is left of it by the time he attains his majority. We live in terrible times when a man can deprive his family of even the roof over their heads by a patronage of the East-End hells."

Twenty-four

Charlotte did not go immediately in search of her father but instead returned to her chamber where she sat in a lovely flowered-chintz chair and looked out over the valley. Her room faced southeast and she knew beyond the downs, just five miles distant, was the sea. She closed her eyes and pretended for a moment that she could feel the warm sun on her face and hear the lapping of the waves as they slowly rolled over the shingle beach, pulling noisily, greedily, at the land as the tide drew the wave back to its bosom.

Once her spirits were calmer and her heart had settled down to a steady pulse instead of the hammering which still afflicted her, she meant to coax her father to return this afternoon first to Brighton, then to Amberley Park. If she could separate him from his interests here in the seaside watering-place, she believed she could get him to divulge his secrets to her.

For now, however, she would dream of the sea, of its calming effect on her soul, and wait. Then she would discover the truth for herself.

She was now convinced something terrible was wrong, but what she couldn't imagine. He had told her of his debts and had a simple plan—a business venture with notable, experienced partners. His loss of fortune was a problem to overcome, and she was certain he would do so. But what mystery had Stoneleigh referred to, what terrible rift had occurred between the two men that Stoneleigh must vow to destroy her father—what could Sir John have possibly done to have incurred the viscount's wrath so completely? Though she did not pretend to fully comprehend Stoneleigh's mind, she believed she knew enough of him—particularly because of his genuine remorse regarding Maude's injury—to comprehend that he was not a man lost to a sense of honor. Indeed, she believed, he was capable of all the finer sentiments. What then had happened?

If only her father would speak to her.

She opened her eyes and placed a hand on her bosom. Her heart was quieting in her breast. On the bed was laid out for her an evening gown of violet sarsenet, the wrinkles already pressed from the delicate fabric, even the narrow tucks across the length of the décolleté bodice free from the smallest crease. Her mind wandered away, her thoughts given to conjecturing whether or not Stoneleigh would like her gown. He would, she thought with a gentle smile, for it was simple and elegant and quite feminine. A fine point lace trimmed the very hem of the gown, points which would touch just the tips of her white silk slippers once she was fully dressed. The same point lace edged the bottom of the gown's puffed sleeves and trimmed a violet silk ribbon which she would wear in her hair à la Grecque, very much like a crown.

A sadness enveloped her.

But she wouldn't be here this evening. She must take her father away to help quiet the scandal he had caused already, to see if she could determine in what manner she could best help Sir John in his difficulties with Stoneleigh.

How was it, she wondered, letting her gaze drift about the pretty bedchamber decorated in fine mahogany furniture and in royal blue and dark rose fabrics, that her holiday in Brighton had come to such a pass as this—her heart nearly torn in two, her nerves in shreds, and poor Maude wounded?

Could anything worse ensue?

Impossible.

After a few minutes more, Charlotte left her bedchamber and descended the stairs where she found, to her delight, Emily Hastings chatting quietly with her husband and with Lord Purcell. After the gentlemen greeted her and Lord Purcell begged the Colonel to have a glass of sherry with him, Emily drew Charlotte across the black-and-white tiles toward the blue drawing room.

"For you must know I needed a word in private with you. The Colonel has spoken with your father. He is gone, Charlotte, and has left you in our care."

"What?" she cried, stopping their progress just before the doors of the drawing room, near the harp and pianoforte.

"Yes, it would seem he felt it was best and did not wish to spoil your amusements. Only tell me everything. Did Stoneleigh actually pick up the sword?"

Charlotte allowed Emily to take her arm and lead her into the drawing room. "Only after my father provoked him in the most reprehensible manner. Emily, do you know why so great an animosity exists between the men."

"I don't, or at least I know in part that it had something to do with Stoneleigh's sister."

It seemed very strange to Charlotte that no one had hitherto mentioned the viscount's sister. "I had supposed he was without siblings. Why has no one spoken of her before?"

179

Emily sat down on a settee near one of the large windows and gestured for Charlotte to join her. "Elizabeth was never quite well. She is kept secluded in the country and has been for these ten years and more. She is older than Stoneleigh by perhaps as much as eight years. Prior to her seclusion, she went the usual rounds of the *haut ton,* but her antics grew more and more erratic as time went on. She was known to go about town dressed as a boy—much like Caro Lamb and with very much the same results, poor thing. She set fire to her bedchamber once and went about the streets in her nightgown. But I believe the last was the worst, when she was found trying to cast herself in the Thames. Her madness, Charlotte, was caused by a disease from birth. Do not concern yourself that Stoneleigh might be similarly afflicted. I only mention the matter to you because you have asked about your father and, though I know none of the details, he was connected with Elizabeth in some way."

"Was he in love with her?"

"No, I don't think so."

"I am surrounded by mysteries and hints and gossip. I can't discern the whole from so many pieces. I had wanted to speak with Papa, to persuade him to leave with me, and now I find him gone—"

Emily narrowed her eyes and appeared as if she wished to say something, then bit her words back.

"What?" Charlotte asked, taking hold of Emily's arm. "Tell me what you are thinking?"

Emily's hazel eyes shifted toward the remarkable plaster-work ceiling. She sighed deeply and said, "Though I have been about town for so many years, I still do not always know when to speak and when to be silent. But I am choosing silence now because I fear forcing decisions upon you which you are not yet ready to make. If you have a hint of grievous trouble ahead of you, you are right—and that from more than one quarter. You chanced, my dear Charlotte, to come to Brighton at the worst possible moment. The irony is that you are undoubtedly going to affect the outcome of everyone's objectives in the most unexpected ways. I don't want to change that, because I believe you will have a good effect on those objectives. I have seen a possible future for you that, if you were to act now, might end any chance of securing that future—which is why I shall remain silent. This I will say, enjoy your weekend here at Lady Purcell's home; and, when you return to your father on Sunday, ask him about Elizabeth. Until then, with all my heart, I implore you to follow the leadings of *your* heart."

Charlotte knew she was referring to Stoneleigh, and she strongly suspected that Emily Hastings wanted her to fall in love with him. This knowledge warmed her heart, coming so close on the heels of her recent encounter with him. If the truth be known, she was very close indeed to tumbling head over heels in love with him.

But what was this course she would embark on if she knew all that Emily knew?

"Tell me," she whispered urgently.

"No, I will not. It is not my place, nor do I believe this is the proper time. Sunday will arrive whether I tell you or not, and I am convinced Sunday is soon enough for you to know all."

A gentleman's lethargic voice intruded, "Ah, Emily, my dear niece. How do you go on? I see you are acquainted with the beautiful Miss Amberley."

Charlotte watched Emily's complexion pale. "Hallo, Uncle. I am very well, thank you; and, yes, Charlotte has become my newest friend in Brighton."

Lord Thaxted narrowed his eyes curiously, first

at Emily and then at Charlotte. "But how intriguing! Have you taken up that truly wretched art of matchmaking then? Poor Stoneleigh. It was you he always loved."

Emily's jaw stiffened alarmingly. Charlotte had never seen her choler evoked before, but a few words from Thaxted and even Charlotte could feel the air prickling between uncle and niece.

"You are being absurd," Emily retorted, keeping her temper. "As you always are."

"Of course," he responded. "But did Miss Amberley tell you of all the excitement we have suffered?"

"Yes, as did Lord Purcell."

"Quite a display," he said. "Though I believe Stoneleigh had a slight advantage, they were for the most part well-matched. Had Miss Dunsfold not intruded, I believe we could have witnessed some adequate swordsplay—not truly exceptional, but adequate."

"You are, of course, a judge of such matters."

"I am," he said.

Charlotte felt a chill wrap itself neatly about her spine and travel down its length. She was so newly acquainted with Lord Thaxted that she scarcely knew what to make of him, but the manner in which these two words had been spoken left no doubt in her mind that he considered himself an adversary of some skill.

Emily was apparently unwilling to listen to more, for she rose and addressed Charlotte. "I have not yet unpacked. Do join me in my chambers—I wish you to help me select a gown for this evening."

Charlotte needed no prodding, not even the slightest roll of Emily's eyes, to oblige her hints. Rising to her feet, she said, "And you may do the same for me. I have a violet gown I thought

182

I might wear, but a blue one which Papa says enhances what he calls my *fine eyes.*"

"Do excuse us, Uncle," Emily said, slipping her arm about Charlotte's and drawing her back toward the entrance hall. Charlotte was surprised to find that her friend was trembling.

The ladies had not gotten far when Thaxted called to Charlotte. "Miss Amberley," he said, but did not finish his thought until both ladies had turned to face him. "I feel compelled to inform you that you have blood on your gown."

Instinctively, Charlotte searched for it and could not find it. Emily did the same and whispered, "It is on your back."

Charlotte realized much to her mortification what had happened and felt a blush burn her cheeks. "Oh, my," she said, knowing the stain could have only come from Stoneleigh's arm when he had embraced her.

"Just so," Thaxted murmured with an accusing laugh. "But how deliciously intriguing."

Emily literally ground her teeth. "Pay no heed to him, Charlotte. Come. We shall have you fixed up in a trice. Blast that man."

Once in the entrance hall and mounting the stairs, Emily began to giggle. "Oh, you turned the color of a beet—a dark, rich, ripe beet, poor thing! So he kissed you, did he! I hoped he would, but leave it to Stoneleigh to do so and mark you because of it. Was his wound on his left arm?"

Charlotte could only nod.

"Silly goose," Emily cried. "I hope he tumbles violently in love with you, I do! Oh, I do!"

Charlotte lifted her skirts as she climbed the stairs. "It was not the first time, either," she whispered. "I feel very wicked, indeed. I am wicked. How could I permit a man to kiss me, a man to whom I am not even remotely promised!"

Emily sighed dreamily. "I have never told anyone this, but the real reason I married the Colonel was because he was the only one of my suitors—Stoneleigh included—who would catch me in hallways and antechambers and the box at the opera and steal kisses from me. I still shiver with pleasure at the thought of it. Am I shocking you? It is a hopeless failing of mine that I have always longed for romance."

Charlotte glanced at the proper lady next to her and could not imagine the stoic Colonel Hastings doing anything so daring.

Emily smiled broadly and laughed. "Don't you see. He couldn't help himself, and I loved him for it. I still do. If a man can't lose some of his self-mastery when he is around you, then what is the point?"

Charlotte could give her no answer at all, particularly when the nature of the conversation forced her to remember in exquisite detail the kisses she had recently shared with the viscount—his hands, the strength of his embrace, the lightness of his breath in her hair, the moist warmth of his lips. She must have sighed, because Emily pinched her arm and again called her a silly goose.

Once in the hallway connecting several of the bedchambers, Charlotte said, "You do not seem to get on well with your uncle."

Emily took in a deep breath. "No, I do not. I cannot. He—he is not a man I admire. Had I known he was to be in attendance this weekend, I should have sent my regrets to Lady Purcell."

"I am a little surprised she did not tell you she had invited him."

Emily lifted her brows. "One thing I know of her ladyship, she thrives on contention and controversy."

"Then why did you come?"

"Because I adore Purcell. He is a darling and has gotten a bad bargain in his wife. But there it is Charlotte—he, too, loves to the point of distraction. That she is unable to return his affection is very sad, not just for him, but for her as well."

Twenty-five

"So, tell me, Charlotte," Lord Stoneleigh queried in a low voice. "Did my kisses overset you?" He was standing next to the low railing of the terrace overlooking the dark hills. Lady Purcell had set out a dozen Chinese lanterns in the gardens and already moths were gently buffeting the sides of the lamps.

Charlotte was surprised by his question spoken into the night air, his words directed away from the other guests milling about the gallery and the terrace in anticipation of dinner.

She stood next to the viscount, begowned in her violet sarsanet, a white beaded reticule dangling from her gloved wrist, her heart suddenly beating strongly in her breast. She had not expected him to speak of their earlier encounter, yet found herself approving of his candor and what she believed was his genuine concern.

"Completely," she responded quietly, also turning into the night and the Chinese lanterns, her back away from Emily and Lord Thaxted and Mrs. Knight. "I only wish I knew what devilment was astir in my heart that I should long for you to take me in your arms again."

She heard him utter an astonished gasp, as he turned to look down into her face. She enjoyed teasing him. "Why do you now gape at me? Did you expect me to dissemble and to utter maidenly protests? I am past the age of such schoolgirl nonsense. Besides, you must know you are mightily skilled in the art of, er, hugging."

"You little wretch," he responded, not in the least vexed. His eyes were sparkling too nicely for him to be actually experiencing displeasure in this moment. "I don't know whether to believe you and be dumbfounded or to take you over my knee and give you the punishment you deserve for provoking me."

She moved past him, circling just behind him. Holding her fan to her lips, she whispered, "Not over your knee, that would be most uncomfortable, I'm sure. Besides, you would crease my new gown."

He followed along, first behind her, then quickening his step to fall in stride beside her. "It's a very pretty gown and most becoming."

When she stepped from the terrace onto a pathway leading through the lanterns, she thanked him for his compliment. "Now, *you* must tell *me*," she commanded lightly. "Did my kisses overset you?" She stopped abruptly upon posing the brazen question and turned to face him.

If she hoped to again give him a severe shock, she was mistaken. "Overset is not the word," he returned easily, as if he had been giving the matter a great deal of thought. "I don't even feel as if I were caught off my guard, though I certainly had had no intention of accosting you. But somehow, when you are near, I experience an inexplicable—well, perhaps not wholly inexplicable since I find you a deuced lovely female—but I seem to get this sort of dizzy sensation when you are near, and the next thing I know, I am importuning you. Perhaps Cupid is at work, performing his magic against all my sense of decorum and propriety.

Does that answer your question? And, yes, I know it was wrong of me to take such grievous advantage of you, which only causes me to wonder why my inclination to do so has become a familiar aspect of my relationship with you. I am always taking you in my arms."

She wished he would keep speaking of it forever. She liked the way it made her feel. First, that he would speak of it at all; then, secondly, that he admitted she had an effect upon him, just as he had an effect upon her. She thought of Emily's words and how Colonel Hastings was always reaching for her when he hoped no one was looking. She smiled at the thought.

"What are you thinking?" he asked. "For your brown eyes have a decided glint to them and you are smiling. I can see as much, because the lantern over my right shoulder is lighting up your face in the most delightful manner. Damme, but you are a beautiful woman. I only wish we were alone; at the same time, I'm grateful we're not. Now, tell me, vixen, what are your thoughts?"

She was spared the necessity of having to enlighten him, however, by the appearance of a servant announcing that dinner was served.

Twenty-six

On the following morning, Charlotte approached the doorway to the yellow saloon. Hearing her name, she stopped abruptly and listened.

"Yes, I am speaking of Miss Amberley," Mrs. Knight whispered from between pinched lips. "And again, I ask you, have you seen how he looks at her?" She nodded once quite solemnly before continuing. "I tell you he is about to put her to bridle. Then we shall see."

Mrs. Wyndham tugged nervously on her red curls and blinked at her friend of many years. "You are not serious. Whyever would he have formed an attachment to Miss Amberley when her nearest relation is a man he detests?"

"I tell you it is true. Did you not see him with her on the terrace last night, dancing about her skirts as he was used to do with you, Eugenia, if memory serves."

Charlotte should have made her presence known long since, but both her heart and her stubborn feet remained immobile as if the latter were stuck fast to the floor and her heart had simply stopped beating.

Put to bridle?

Goodness, what a truly reprehensible expression, but whatever did Mrs. Knight mean by it?

"Someone ought to warn the girl," Mrs. Wyndham said with an inexplicable smile on her lips.

Mrs. Knight, humor being reluctant to appear anywhere on her cold features, also surprised Charlotte by smiling, however thinly. "Indeed, someone ought to." Then both women burst out laughing as if they shared a great joke.

Charlotte knew now it was impossible to enter the yellow saloon and so backed slowly away from the entrance. She did not flee, precisely, for that would have set the servants' tongues to wagging, but to have discovered that for one reason or another she had become the brunt of Mrs. Knight's and Mrs. Wyndham's amusement caused her to wish she could run away from Longreves.

She sought refuge in the rose garden, where the fragrant flowers—in rich reds, pinks, and delicate whites—joined with the sunshine and created a welcome ambience. She seated herself on a stone bench near a sundial and let the warmth of the sun bathe her entire body. She felt calmed, peace restored to her distraught mind. She knew the ladies had referred to Stoneleigh. He was the only man who had spoken to her on the terrace, nonetheless *danced about her skirts.*

Is that what it had seemed to everyone else?

She knew now she had been indiscreet. She seemed to lose herself when he was around, forgetting that eyes were always peering and minds, prying and conjecturing.

She smiled to herself, remembering what she and Stoneleigh had discussed beside the lanterns. Would Mrs. Knight have fainted had she known they were speaking of shared kisses? Undoubtedly. *Put to bridle.*

She shivered, even in the balm of the sunshine. She did not know what Mrs. Knight had meant by it, but somehow she was convinced the meaning could not be a happy one; nor did the analogy conjure up the best of visions.

"So tell me what you suspect, Lady Purcell?"

Charlotte heard Selena's girlish voice coming from the direction of the morning room, which was situated just behind the rose garden.

"Only that if your friend does not take care, she will soon lose her heart to one who cannot give his in return."

"Charlotte would never be so bird-witted," Selena reassured her hostess. "Maude and I have both spoken at length of his unfortunate conduct with the women of his acquaintance. She will not lose her head."

"I am so happy to hear you say so. Really, my confidence is restored. I had intended upon giving her a hint myself, but I see now it is completely unnecessary."

"Oh, entirely. Indeed, she came to Brighton only to break his heart—a sort of mission on behalf of the ladies of our fair watering-place. Did you see her work her clever spell with him last night? He was fairly bounding about her like a puppy. It is Stoneleigh who ought to be warned."

A tense moment ensued, when Charlotte, unable to see either lady, waited for her ladyship's response. When it came, she felt certain she could see Lady Purcell's wide eyes blink rapidly several times. "Indeed, someone ought to."

Another shiver snaked down Charlotte's spine as she rose to her feet and left the now oppressive garden and began marching toward the hills and the home wood. Once there, she was surprised to find Harry not twenty feet down a woodland path, collecting an armful of ferns. "Whatever are you doing?"

"Charlie!" he cried, his face lighting up at the sight of her. A light blush immediately followed, coloring his cheeks to a marked contrast with his fine, white shirtpoints and elegantly tied neck-cloth.

"But how dashing you look," Charlotte returned, smiling teasingly at him. "Is that a new style of cravat? I have not seen it before. Is it perchance called *trône d'amour?*"

Harry scowled, then thrust an armful of ferns at her. "You've guessed it then, hm?"

"It is only because I have known you these several years and more that I would dare to twit you. Besides, I could see how it was with you from the beginning. Have you seen her this morning yet? I was with her shortly after breakfast. Her color is completely restored, and she was pinching at her bedclothes as if she wished to be rid of them."

He shook his head as he tugged at more ferns. "No, not yet. But I mean to. Lady Purcell sent me to gather some ferns for her. She said she would make a particularly pretty bouquet for Maude, if I so desired. I daresay I turned the precise shade of a radish, for she pinched my cheek and sent me up here as if I were a silly schoolboy."

"You do blush easily, you know."

"Dash-it-all! Why couldn't my fault be more manly, like a fiery temper or a tendency to jostle other men in doorways and demand satisfaction in duels?"

"Pray do not speak of duels," she cried, accepting more ferns from him. She then gave a cry and, holding the ferns away from her, exclaimed, "Do get this spider off me! For heaven's sake, Harry, couldn't you have at least checked for insects?"

He brushed the harmless spider from her arm, then told her not to be so missish. "So, tell me, are you in love with him?"

Charlotte bit her lip. There was, after all, one

disadvantage to teasing one's friend about being in love. "Am I what?" she asked, pretending not to understand his question.

He was bent over and looked up at her, peeping around his shoulder with a devilish smile on his face. "There, now you are blushing as well. The shade of an early apple, I think, but deepening. Do you love him, goose?"

"No," she answered flatly.

"Don't pitch that gammon to me. Remember, I know you better than anyone. Besides, I wasn't the only one who noticed how he was dancing attendance upon you last night. Take care, Charlotte. He has a considerable reputation for taking a lady's heart and leaving it lying carelessly behind him when he moves on."

"I thought you were his friend."

"I am. I admire him more than any other gentleman of my acquaintance, save my father, of course. Stoneleigh is a great man, but I suppose you already know as much. But where women are concerned, he—well, let me say only that his expectations are beyond belief."

"And you don't think I quite meet them?" Her heart strained to know Harry's response. She trusted him as she trusted few others and knew that his opinions were nearly always correct.

With his arms also quite full of pungently fragrant ferns, he faced her squarely. "I can have no notion what his thoughts are. I only know that I doubt there is a lady present who has not admitted at one time or another to having had hopes of becoming the next Lady Stoneleigh. Though I think you are extremely well-suited for him, Charlotte, no one here really knows who or what he is. If he expects a great deal from the future mistress of his estates, he has some right to. From what my father has told me, his concerns are not only those of a gentleman in possession of one of the oldest titles in England and a place in the Lords but are extended throughout the world." Harry lowered his voice as if he were maligning Stoneleigh's character, "His connections in Trade are nearly as broad as my father's. His influence—his ability to gain information from any part of the world within days—is unheard of. Add to all this that he has the ear of the future King, and you can readily see there is no height to which he could not aspire if he wished for it. He has a right, therefore, to be selective; and for that reason, I cannot say what he thinks of you; I only want you to take great care not to give your heart when—when you might be found wanting through no fault of your own."

He then looked down at the ferns and laughed. "How absurd," he cried, his laughter growing more intense.

"Are you mocking me?" Charlotte queried.

"No. Oh, no! Never! In my opinion, dearest Charlie, he is unworthy of you if all that I have heard of him where the ladies are concerned is true. I am mocking myself. Here I am telling you not to give your heart when you might be found wanting, and all the time, mine is already given and residing in the hands of a young woman whom I know can only despise me because of the nature of my father's fortune."

"Oh, Harry," Charlotte sighed. She slipped her free arm about his waist and hugged him. She laid her head on his shoulder and murmured. "Aren't we a hapless pair? But you are right. I believe my heart is given—though I am reluctant to admit as much—given to a man whom I know for some reason has cast aside nearly every woman I know."

A summer's breeze caught the hair at the nape of Stoneleigh's neck and buffeted the brim of his beaver hat. He was some thirty yards away from Charlotte and Harry; and only as the couple began descending the hill toward the house did he realize his fists were clenched so tightly he had been hurting himself.

He knew they had a fondness for one another—he had seen as much the day on the Steyne when Harry had surprised Charlotte by his sudden appearance in Brighton. He also knew by all that Harry had told him of Charlotte, his eyes glowing with affection, that theirs was a deep, abiding friendship.

Had it now blossomed into a mature love, a *marriageable* love?

He felt the blood rush to his head and pinch the back of his eyes. Was Charlotte so unsteady that she would give her kisses one moment, then hug another man in the next? At the same time, he knew the worst desire to tear Harry Elstow limb from limb and to ask him if this were how he repaid his kindnesses in bringing him forward into the highest circles of the *ton*.

He hurried back up the hill, from whence he had come, setting his boots marching along at a clipping pace. He had not known such a rise in temper for a long time; even when Amberley had provoked him in the billiard room, he had not been so much angry as annoyed with the man's lack of self-control.

He walked quickly, leaving the home wood and reaching the ancient tracks on top of the downs, taking deep gulps of the fresh air, redolent yet of the sea. In the far distance, he could see a blue-gray line and wished he could dive into the cool ocean and dampen the fire still burning angrily in his veins, in his limbs, in his mind.

How dare Harry touch Charlotte Amberley! his mind cried.

Only after some twenty minutes of setting one

dogged foot in front of the other did his sense return to him.

Undoubtedly, the embrace was perfectly innocent. In fact, the more he considered the matter, the more he knew it was true. Harry had said he simply knew *Charlie*, as he liked to call her, much too well to tumble in love with her. She was stubborn and managing and once her will was crossed was a formidable adversary. She had once locked him into a shed for a day and a whole night because he had ridden her horse without asking permission. Of course, Harry had admitted to doing it because he wanted to see her angry, but he had never expected to be locked up all night. Evidently, her remorse, however, had been great, for she had come to him at dawn, in tears, and said she had merely fallen asleep in the library and had meant to release him at midnight.

Stoneleigh stopped and turned around in a full circle, looking up at the deep blue sky, now dotted with fast-approaching clouds, to the rolling hills of the downs to the valley below to Lord Purcell's fine country house.

Where would all this end? he wondered. Was he in love with Charlotte? What was this persistent need he felt whenever she was near to catch her up in his arms and to never let go? He had never before experienced such a powerful sensation toward a woman. Not even toward Emily, whom he believed he had always loved. No, not even Emily had turned his head so completely and shaken his world to the roots of every solid belief. But Charlotte had, causing him to wonder if he were wrong about her father and if, perhaps, all this time he had rejected matrimony not because the women were lacking but because he had not known love with any of them.

The devil take it! He could make sense of none of his thoughts or feelings.

All he knew was that watching Charlotte nestle her head in Harry's shoulder and take comfort from him had caused his blood to boil. He had felt primordial in that moment, prepared to club Harry to death for daring to touch a woman he had claimed as his own.

Yet he had not claimed her as his own.

He had only kissed her.

Somehow in his mind, however, as never before, a claim and a kiss had become inseparable.

Twenty-seven

"Oh, it is too wonderful!" Charlotte breathed, viewing Lady Purcell's ballroom swathed in white tulle, gold artificial leaves, and the dazzling light from scores of candles. She was standing near the windows at the far end of the exquisite chamber which overlooked the hill behind Longreves. Selena stood next to her but apparently did not share in her enthusiasm for, though she glanced around the ballroom, she neither exclaimed over the decor nor once smiled.

Already the ballroom was filling fast with not just the weekend guests but with neighbors and friends living nearby. Lady Purcell had kept the event a secret until the very conclusion of dinner, when carriages began to approach the house, visible in the dark as a line of swaying carriage lamps and announced by the clopping of horses hooves and shouting of coachmen. Only then did her scheme emerge that she had planned a surprise ball.

Lady Purcell had clapped like a child, her husband smiling fondly at her antics and afterward rising to join her in the greeting of her new guests.

A moment later, orchestral music from the ballroom resounded through the house, causing the men to give up forever their hopes of being able to sit 'round the dining table with their port and snuff and enjoy their mutual, masculine company while the ladies retired to the drawing room.

No, it was clear to them all that now they would be required to do the pretty and to dance until the ladies could dance no more.

Charlotte was delighted, wishing only that Maude had been well enough to join them. She was an indefatigable dancer, and Harry would undoubtedly have enjoyed securing a waltz with her that he might thereby hold in his arms the woman of his heart. But it was not to be. She remained abed.

Selena's interest in the festivities was decidedly lacking. "A ball," she whispered dully. "How utterly charming."

Charlotte looked at her and saw that she was watching Stoneleigh. She understood suddenly something of her friend and, taking her arm, guided her away from the crowds, closer to the windows. "Do you remember that young man you wrote me about summer last?"

Selena shook her head, an innocent expression on her freckled face.

"His name was Alfred Knight, I think," Charlotte informed her, though not believing for a second that Selena was truly unable to recall him to mind. "I believe he was our Mr. Knight's nephew, if I am not mistaken."

"Oh, yes, now I remember."

"You seemed very fond of him at the time. And quite appreciative of his sense of humor. I believe you mentioned him in no fewer than two dozen of your letters."

"He could be very amusing," she said, tapping her fan on the palm of her hand, lifting her chin and attempting to appear indifferent.

"Whyever did you not encourage him to see you again?"

Selena did not look at her directly but let her gaze fall to the shoe-roses on Charlotte's silk slippers.

"I don't know," she responded quietly. "He did not please me after a time, I suppose."

"Did not please you!" Charlotte exclaimed. "To my thinking, a lady who fills each of her correspondence for weeks on end with lines and crossed-lines regarding a young man she has just met does not suddenly find he doesn't please her. There is another truth, Selena, and you know very well what it is!"

"Whatever do you mean?" she cried, her gaze flying to Charlotte's face, her blue eyes flashing.

"In your next letter you wrote two lines about your beau. They went something like this. *Alfred has decided to take Holy Orders after all. I daresay I shan't see him again.*"

Selena compressed her lips. "I don't know why you should remind me now—a year later—of something that hardly signifies. I was only acquainted with him for a month or more. We enjoyed a brief flirtation and—after a time, he did not please me. I found him coarse, frequently boring, and—and, oh what difference does it make?"

"A great deal of difference, because during that month your heart was full to overflowing with thoughts of him. At the time I received your letters, I was convinced you had fallen head over heels in love with Alfred. Was I so much mistaken?"

"Of course you were. There is only one man I have ever truly loved—you know his name. *He* is why you came to Brighton. Which puts me in mind of something I felt I ought to give you a hint about. You seem perilously close to commit-

200

ting the very same error that Maude and I did—or have you done so already?"

"Do you mean, have I developed a schoolgirl's *tendre* for Lord Stoneleigh?"

"Yes! I mean, no, of course not!" she whispered crossly. "Not a *tendre*. I certainly feel more than a mere *tendre* for his lordship."

"There I believe you are sadly mistaken and have been for the longest time, even to the point of pushing from your life forever a real and lasting love."

Selena gasped. "I—I thought you were my friend," she exclaimed, on her mettle. "How dare you cast my affections for *someone* in such a horrid light."

"You have worn the willow too long, Selena, for something that never existed. And you cast Alfred away because you wished—as did Maude— to make a brilliant match. Instead, each of you is perilously close to becoming an *ape-leader* if you do not take care."

Selena gasped again and unfurled her fan with a snap. "I didn't know you could be so cruel. And if we are to speak of *ape-leaders* and the like, I wish to know how old you are, Miss Amberley, and precisely how many proposals of marriage you have cast to the wind."

"Then I am the chiefest among us, being the oldest, but at least it will not have been for having deceived myself about being in love with a man when I was not."

Selena struggled with her composure for some time, then finally straightened her shoulders. After casting Charlotte a scathing glance, she quit the ballroom.

Charlotte watched her go, thinking she had probably ruined herself in Selena's eyes forever. But she had not been in her company more than five minutes upon arriving in Brighton, nonetheless the past fortnight, without having comprehended the sad state of her heart and of her unhappy mind. Selena was convinced she loved Stoneleigh. And though she never said as much, her eyes followed him everywhere and always with a look so painfully sad as caused Charlotte to want to slap her. She was convinced Selena had fallen into the habit of believing herself crossed in love—not that Maude had not done everything she could to support Selena in this conviction. But the truth was, moving among the insularity of the *beau monde*, Selena had become cut off from more enduring values—of honest love, of occupation beyond the ballrooms and drawing rooms of Mayfair, of work among the poor, of common sense. Her whole existence had become devoid of purpose.

Her thoughts were abruptly interrupted. "Well said, my dear."

Charlotte turned quickly around and, from the shadows of the open window, Lord Thaxted moved into the glittering light of the ballroom. "Oh," she cried. "I did not know you were there. Well, I suppose you heard everything. And if I may say so, my lord, you ought to have made your presence known."

"What? And miss so exemplary a dressing down? You were positively right, you know. Miss Bosham has believed herself in love with his lordship for these many years when, in truth, she has only been in love with *love*. Poor child."

Charlotte did not like him. His tone was insolent, cold, and unfeeling. "And you are overflowing with sympathy, aren't you?"

"So tell me, Miss Amberley," he countered, ignoring her question. "Are you in love with society's darling as well? Did his kisses sway your heart—and do not protest you did not kiss him for, if you remember, your gown was proof enough of his embraces. At least, only tell me, did his kisses turn your heart as they have so many—or do you fancy yourself the first, or if not the first, the best? I don't like to mention it, but you seem to have a great deal of pride. Not unlike your beloved parent."

"I find your manner of speaking intolerable. I bid you good evening and beg you will not approach me again."

"As you wish," he said, strolling by her. Moving away from her, however, he whispered, "But I believe our paths will cross again; and if you can set aside *your* foolish *tendre*, you may just acquire everything you have ever wanted."

Charlotte could not restrain herself. "One moment, if you please, my lord," she said. Thaxted paused, a look of satisfaction written deeply on his face. Drawing near to him, she queried, "And what is it I have always wanted that—dare I say it—you could give me?"

Charlotte was surprised by the intensity of his expression as he touched her gently just above the elbow. "To be a marchioness. You would have one of the highest positions in our society. You would have wealth and an estate to match few others. You would have power, Miss Amberley."

"And this, you believe, is what I want?"

"Tell me it is not so? Is not your dogged, quite unmaidenly pursuit of Stoneleigh proof of your designs? You cannot tell me you are in ignorance of the extent of his wealth."

His gentle touch had become firm and demanding, his hold on her arm almost painful.

Charlotte narrowed her eyes at him, refusing to look away from his penetrating gaze. "You are grievously mistaken, Lord Thaxted. And I daresay if I told you what I truly wanted, you wouldn't comprehend it in the least."

He was evidently surprised by her response. Releasing her arms, he said, "And do you now mean to expound upon the virtues of poverty and the romanticism of bearing your children in a hovel as long as you can be with the man you love?"

"I would be utterly foolish to say anything of the sort. At the same time, as a woman of means, I am fortunate not to have to rely upon a marriage alliance in order to secure my future and, therefore, perhaps more than others, can place *love* at a higher priority than most. But you still have not come close to my true heart's desire."

"What then, pray tell? An orphanage for the less fortunate brats born in even lesser circumstances. No? Let me guess again. You do not wish to see children go down the holes in the ground and plow coal from the bowels of the earth. Or shall we discuss slavery?"

"Is your heart so dark, then?"

"Have I hit upon it?" he queried facetiously. "You are a philanthropist."

"Not in essentials," she responded. "My concerns have kept me too close to Amberley Park to do more than manage my father's household and to share in the raising of his son. But what I want, from my heart, is something I know you could never give."

He seemed perturbed, unable to fathom her meaning. With an exasperated sigh, he said, "Then tell me at once what it is, for I vow I am in a state of painful anticipation."

She laughed, some of her dislike of him easing away. "If you must know, what I wish for most is honesty, uprightness, and kindness. Give me these, and I shall be content. Can you give me as much, my lord? These are my heart's desire."

"Easily spoken when you have a fortune," he sneered. "Would you had none that you might know how hard such virtues are to come by when the stomach is empty."

"I would not deign to guess what my heart would wish for were I wallowing in a poverty not of my own making. But since that is not the case, the point is moot. I'll ask again, can you grant my heart's desires, you, who have so much?"

His eyelids resumed their place at half-mast, and he responded in a bored voice, "You are far too virtuous for me, I am sure."

"You have said it, sir, not I."

Twenty-eight

"Emily overheard you arguing with her uncle," Lord Stoneleigh whispered, holding Charlotte close in the easy, rhythmic movements of the waltz. The hour was past midnight, and Lady Purcell's ball showed few signs of being on the wane. "And I want to know what you said to him. Yes, yes—I admit I am being impertinent, and Emily equally so to have repeated the whole of what she heard to me—but I am fully intrigued. She said you pressed him rather hard about *honesty*, was it?"

"Yes, it was about honesty, in part, but Emily is mistaken if she believes I was arguing with Lord Thaxted," Charlotte countered defensively. "It was just that he made a very wrong assumption about my principles and I did not wish for him to continue in his misapprehension."

Stoneleigh narrowed his eyes at her as if trying to make her out. "You are so very different from any lady I've ever known. Honesty over position?"

Charlotte nodded, looking up into his face. She saw that his interest was entirely sincere. "But I did add that because mine has been a blessed existence—I have wanted for nothing all my life—it seems not a difficult prospect at all to keep one's values close to one's heart. I have never known poverty—I don't think I ever shall. Were I poor and struggling to see my children fed, I daresay I might hold a different view of the matter entirely—valuing bread over honesty, perhaps."

"You do not do yourself justice, Miss Amberley—the discussion of poverty excluded. I know a dozen ladies who shared the same advantages as yours but who have grasped eagerly for a handle to their names without the smallest consideration of the character of the man to whom that handle was attached."

"I can speak only for myself and do not wish to judge others—at least I try not to. But, it seems to me, I was also fortunate in my mother. She spared no pains in showing me an abundance of affection nor in seeing that my heart and my conscience were planted on a path she thought proper and right."

"You have been fortunate, indeed."

She smiled at him. "Very!"

The well-lit chandelier overhead, as she looked up at him, caught the periphery of her vision time and again as the gently flowing strains of the music ordered her feet to turn, then to turn again. The candlelight cast a glow about Stoneleigh's finely brushed black locks, lending him an unearthly appearance as he whirled her around and around.

She loved the waltz, the latest addition to the art of dancing, and had been in the habit of performing the steps for every occasion required at the local Bedfordshire assemblies. She rarely sat out a waltz.

"You excel in your mastery of the steps, Stoneleigh," Charlotte remarked. "I do love a waltz."

"And you are an easy partner to guide—the best I've ever known."

She nodded in acknowledgement of his compliment. He was silent apace, leading her with care and grace around the perimeter of the chamber. After a time, he reverted to the original subject. "Are you much acquainted with my Lord Thaxted?" he queried.

She wondered if, like the patterns of the dance, he meant to lead her back again and again to Thaxted.

"No," she responded. "Not really. I met him for the first time only yesterday afternoon."

"I see. Yet you had assessed him enough to counter his effrontery with what Emily described as a masterful rebuke."

"I beg you will forget Thaxted and what I said or did not say to him," she cried. "And if you don't mind my mentioning it to you, Stoneleigh, you seem rather obsessed with him."

"I wish you would call me Edward," he said, nearly causing her to miss her steps. "Stoneleigh somehow seems much too formal to my ears."

Charlotte felt her heart quicken alarmingly in her breast. "Edward?" she asked, stunned. "You wish me to call you, Edward?"

He smiled faintly, yet Charlotte could see that his color was heightened as if he had just realized the import of his request. "That is my Christian name, after all," he said.

Charlotte could not continue to look into his eyes, at least not for the moment. She let her gaze slide to the diamond pin stuck into the folds of his neckcloth. Her thoughts seemed to jump about in her mind like wildly bolting horses. Whatever did he mean by making such an intimate request of her? Should she refuse? Should she now beg him to call her Charlotte?

"Have I distressed you?"

"Yes, of course you have," she responded with a laugh. "I have not heard even Emily address you with such familiarity."

"She does, privately. If she were to do so

openly, it would set the tabbies to caterwauling even more loudly than they already do regarding my friendship with *Mrs. Hastings.*"

"I understand."

"I knew you would. But I would like it above all things if you called me Edward," he said, his voice low and warm near her ear. "At least while we're dancing the waltz and when we are alone together in billiard rooms or outside of clock shops or when you are awakening from a swoon and I am holding you in my arms."

Each memory he culled forth reminded her of how frequently she had been held captive in his arms, how often he had kissed her. She looked into his eyes and saw there a familiar light, a longing, an intensity which further disrupted her peace. Taking a deep breath, she tried to quiet the trembling which she could feel had begun as a slight quivering sensation round the whole of her heart and was beginning to radiate even to the tips of her fingers "Edward," she breathed.

"You are trembling."

"It is nothing," she said, odd tears smarting her eyes. She felt overwhelmed by his nearness, by how tenderly he held her and continued to guide her about the floor.

"No, you are mistaken," he said, drawing her near and whispering in her ear. "I believe it is everything."

"How can you know as much," she queried, frightened.

He ignored her question. "Only tell me what you told Thaxted—what you wanted more than position or wealth—besides honesty."

"Kindness," she responded, grateful this time he had returned to his original question. "And uprightness."

She could see that her words were having a

profound effect upon him. "Just as I thought," he said cryptically.

Charlotte would have asked what he meant by it; but at that moment, the music drew to a close and, before she could speak, Lady Purcell descended upon them both, her fan fluttering quickly over her features. She drew Stoneleigh away with her, immediately begging him to partner a young lady who had just come out. "You will excuse us, Charlotte," she said brightly. "But I have promised him. His mother is one of my dearest friends."

"Of course," Charlotte responded, feeling terribly unsettled. She moved to the perimeter of the ballroom and watched Stoneleigh bow over the hand of a blushing young lady barely emerged from the schoolroom. She found her heart so full of admiration and affection for him that her eyes again began to fill with tears she could not quite explain.

"Only promise me you don't mean to put her through her paces as you did the others," Emily begged later that evening. She was standing next to Stoneleigh and whispering to him urgently behind her fan.

He watched Charlotte go down a country dance with her host. She was politely oblivious to everything that went on around her save her partner. He approved heartily of her manners and even enjoyed the way she made her opinions firmly known when she believed herself right. "I daresay it wouldn't matter in the least," he responded to Emily's plea. "She would probably tell me to go to the devil if I attempted to do so."

"Then you will not?" she asked hopefully.

"I didn't say that. After all, I do want to be

certain and I'm 'fraid the stable is not at all what it should be."

Emily sighed. "You can be the most provoking creature—stable, indeed! I feel I ought to warn you, however, that you will make a grave mistake by putting Charlotte Amberley to the test. What little I know of her, she will not take kindly to the notion at all."

"She will know nothing of it," he countered. "I do not precisely take out an advertisement in *The Times* announcing my intentions. She would be none the wiser before it was all over, unless you tell her, of course."

"You know I wouldn't, but there might be others who would comprehend what you were doing and inform Charlotte."

He was surprised. "To whom are you referring?"

"I can't readily say, Lady Purcell, perhaps—she has known you the longest. But you must know you've only to lift an eyebrow and speculation runs rife. Your interest in her is already being bandied about on every tongue, especially belowstairs—and you know what that means."

When the servants were gossiping, it was generally understood that either a scandal of delightful proportions was in the making or a match was in the offing.

"I see," he responded. "Though I suppose it would be silly of me to express too much surprise at this juncture. I have hardly ignored the chit these several days and more."

Emily laughed. "No, you have hardly done that."

"What does the Colonel think? Does he approve?"

"He thinks she is too good for you, and I agree."

"Wretch."

"Well, I shan't offer you another morsel of advice, only take care that you do not put your bird to flight with all your clever schemes."

"Perhaps this time I won't do it," he mused, frowning slightly.

"That's what I want to hear. Besides, you must know her by now. She is an exceptional young lady. She became a mother to little Henry when her own mother died. This alone ought to tell you all you need to know of her character. But, beyond this, her interests in general are so far removed from profit and gain that to *put her through her paces* seems an absurdity."

It was an irony to Stoneleigh that, for all of Emily's fine reasonings, she had succeeded not in affirming his instinct to offer for Charlotte without benefit of a test of her character but had persuaded him instead to proceed. She had mentioned Henry, which served to bring a wave of doubts flooding his mind. Charlotte must be aware that Henry's inheritance was coming apart at the seams moment by moment under Amberley's misconduct. Wouldn't *gain*, therefore, be her primary consideration?

No. He would proceed, as he had countless times since Emily married her colonel, if for no other reason than to ascertain once and for all whether or not Charlotte had escaped her father's hapless influence.

Twenty-nine

On the following evening, Charlotte found the opportunity for which she had been waiting—Sir John was staying at home. When she had seen him settled, stretched out full on the Grecian couch of gold and white silk near the fireplace, when she had delivered into his hands his favorite Madeira, and after she had played several Bach preludes for him on the pianoforte, she drew up a footstool and seated herself next to him.

"You're a very good girl, Charlie," he said, looking at her fondly and smiling. "However, I have not known you all these many years without being aware that such kindnesses as you have poured out upon me just now were to a purpose. Are you wishful that I send round a note of apology to Stoneleigh for having badgered him at Longreves? I have already done so and sent a second apology to Lord Purcell. I don't know what came over me that I came to conduct myself like a witless halfling—brandishing my sword about like a Turk. I am glad, though, to hear that Maude is recovering well."

Charlotte found herself surprised by her father in this moment. She had expected belligerence from him, certainly an argument, but not a humble affability. She would have questioned his sincerity, since he was speaking in a manner so unlike him, but she could see by the warm light in his eye that he meant what he said.

She did not try to dissemble. "There is something I wish very much from you, Papa," she said, laying a hand on his sleeve of black superfine and squeezing his arm gently. "Do you recall our journey to Longreves and how sorely distressed you were over Stoneleigh's interference in your affairs?"

"So, that's it, eh?" he queried, nodding in response to her question. "You want to speak of Stoneleigh, then."

Charlotte drew in a deep breath, shifting her gaze for the moment away from his. "In a manner of speaking," she responded. "More to the point, I wish you to tell me of—of Elizabeth."

Only then did she return her gaze to him. His reaction to the name was instantaneous. He dropped his glass of wine and spilled the dark red contents onto the gold and white couch. He rose quickly from his reclining position and withdrew his white cambric kerchief from the pocket of his coat. In brisk strokes, he began to wipe at the red, bleeding stain. "I have ruined it!" he cried, his attention focused entirely on the unforgiving silk fabric.

The moment the glass had fallen, some of the wine splashing onto Charlotte's dark-blue silk gown, she had leapt to her feet and moved out of the way of Sir John's tall form. When she saw how distressed he was, she said, "Papa, let Mrs. Glover tend to that in the morning. If she cannot remove the stain, then I'm certain a new fabric can be found to recover the cushion."

"Of course," he said, returning his kerchief to his pocket.

"Now, do sit down," she coaxed him. But the moment was lost, for he paced the chamber twice before excusing himself, saying he had just re-membered a most important matter he had to tend to immediately.

Charlotte could do nothing more than let him go. If her effort on the morrow proved equally fruitless, she was not surprised. She attempted several times to broach the subject, but the more she pressed him, the more elusive he became—both in how cleverly he switched subjects and in how he finally began to disappear each time she arrived home from her habitual outings.

She did not know what to think of his extraor-dinary conduct. He never once told her he did not wish to discuss Elizabeth, nor did he ever ap-pear angry. When three days had elapsed and she saw no possibility of running Sir John to earth on the subject of Stoneleigh's sister, she discon-tinued her efforts. For one thing, she had noticed a profound change in her father when she did speak with him for a few minutes here and there—he was more congenial, more at ease, more affectionate than she had ever known him to be. What's more, he told her outright that if she were to contract an alliance with Stoneleigh, he would do all he could to mend the breach between him-self and the viscount.

Charlotte needed no more assurance than this—whatever the history of Elizabeth entailed. In her experience, once goodwill was put into play, the rest followed in time.

Besides, for the past three days since arriving home from Longreves, Lord Stoneleigh had shown her every attention she could have wished for; and every hour spent with him increased both her admiration of him as well as her general enjoyment of his company. She found they shared many interests which, in the normal course of be-coming acquainted with an individual, she had previously found entirely lacking.

One of his most heartfelt endeavors was an orphanage which he hoped to make so effective in its operation that no child was turned away from the door. In her own village, Charlotte had always made every effort to see any child that had been unfortunately bereft of its parents placed in a good home.

Stoneleigh worked diligently in the House of Lords to seek legislation enacted that veterans were better provisioned following service to their country. He had approved heartily and with great praise of her and Harry's brickworks scheme.

Charlotte had said, "You've no idea how dreadful it is for me to see a vagrant, crippled man wearing a tattered uniform, only to learn he served in the Peninsula but came home to his country to be simply ignored—no work, no relief, no future."

"A great irony, isn't it?" he responded. "They served our country, ended Boney's domination of Europe—and, therefore, his persistent threat to England—then they arrive home to be forgotten."

On only one occasion had Charlotte felt uncomfortable in her discussions with Stoneleigh. She had been quite enthusiastically listing Henry's accomplishments in the schoolroom, when she came to realize the viscount was not responding as she might have wished him to. He had grown very quiet and did not look at her but appeared to be thinking about something altogether different. She did not know what to make of it, save that since Henry was not connected to him in any manner, it was very likely he found an enumeration of the child's talents and abilities to be something of a bore. She immediately brought forward a new subject, but it was a few minutes before his former animation returned.

* * *

On the following day, Charlotte found herself in Walker's Circulating Library, fatigued from having been awakened by Henry in the early hours of the morning with the earache and listening in astonishment as Stoneleigh attempted to brangle with her.

"I do beg your pardon, Miss Amberley; but, though I am always reluctant to correct a lady, I am persuaded this book is a dark shade of blue, not brown," he said, regarding Charlotte with a cool, blank stare. He had come upon her in Walker's Library and, from the moment he first approached her, had seemed desirous of challenging her every opinion—from her belief that Jane Austen was the finest novelist of the day to her prediction that the afternoon would be sunny and cloudless to the color of the cover of the book he meant to purchase for Emily.

Charlotte returned his gaze, surprise causing her to remain mute for a long moment. "Blue?" she queried. He was holding a brown, calfskin novel in his hand, one of the five volumes of Fanny Burney's *Cecilia*. It was not blue, not even by the wildest stretch of anyone's imagination. It was a rich, dark brown.

She looked around her and saw that Lady Purcell was nearby and had apparently overheard Stoneleigh's remark. Her expression was equally blank, save for the hint of a smile at just the corners of her mouth. Glancing back at Stoneleigh, she now recognized his expression for what it was, since she had seen it a hundred times on Henry's little face whenever he wished to provoke her into a quarrel. Henry was at just that age that if she said *yes*, he would say *no*.

But what did Stoneleigh hope to achieve by behaving like a boy still confined to the nursery? What could he possibly mean by insisting the cover of the book was blue?

She could not resist responding with precisely what she would have said to Henry under similar circumstances.

"Are you feeling bilious, m'lord? If you are, I have a purgative at home which often relieves Henry of the same symptoms. There are very few fits of temper, I have found, which a strong dose of purgative will not cure."

His mouth fell open and he gave a decided start—a response Henry usually exhibited when she recommended the very same remedy for his unexplained bouts of peevishness.

She glanced out the window. "I can see by the angle of the sun the hour is advancing. I must, therefore, bid you good day. I'm sorry I can't remain to converse with you upon the color of this book, but I have more pressing concerns. I was up very late last night. Henry had the earache, and I must pay a visit to the chemist before I return to West Street."

She strolled away, a package tucked beneath her arm containing a small wooden horse, uncertain what to think of Stoneleigh's odd conduct. She was content, at least, that she had dumbfounded him, if nothing more. He had approached her not five minutes earlier, his jaw set in a rather mulish manner, and apparently desired to engage her in an argument—but to what purpose?

It hardly mattered. If he meant to behave in an absurd manner—whatever his reason—he had every right to do so. She simply did not have to remain in his company and bear his obnoxiousness. *The book is blue!* How absurd.

Besides, what she had told him was very much the truth. Henry had cried himself to sleep in her arms only a few hours earlier, his ear having caused him great pain in the middle of the night. She had patronized Walker's Circulating Library this morning strictly because it contained a selection of toys, and she had purchased the horse for Henry, hoping to cheer him up.

She might, therefore, have been more distressed by Stoneleigh's curious conduct had she not herself been quite weary.

Two hours later, when she arrived home, she was greeted by her father, who clapped her gently upon the back and cried, "Well done, Charlie! I hear you have recommended to my Lord Stoneleigh that he make use of a purgative to cure his defects of temper."

Charlotte was stunned. "How on earth did you hear of that?"

"It would seem you have become an object of great interest in Brighton society, my dear, and as such—particularly when you cause such a personage as Stoneleigh to appear foolish—your exploits are bound to be repeated like fish escaping the net. *Are you bilious, m'lord?* Well done! Well done, indeed!" He then cleared his throat and whispered, "However, I am not so certain such a mode of speaking to one so proud will do much to engage his heart!" He then chortled, enjoying the whole of it prodigiously.

Charlotte couldn't credit her ears. It had not occurred to her that her silly remarks would be repeated—though, now that she gave the matter some thought, she realized Lady Purcell had undoubtedly had overheard the whole of her conversation with Stoneleigh.

"Oh, dear," she murmured.

"Now don't go pulling that Friday face. It will do Stoneleigh a great deal of good to have received just such a setdown as you delivered him. *A purgative!* Quite brilliant, m'dear."

"I fear I was so distracted by Henry's earache that I spoke the first thought which came into my head. He was arguing with me over the most ridiculous things—you can have no idea! Like

219

whether or not it was likely to rain in the afternoon. I said the skies would be cloudless, and he insisted—even in the face of the sun shining brightly against an unmarred expanse of the deepest blue sky—that there would certainly be a downpour. I suppose I simply lost my temper."

Sir John grunted in his disinterested manner, apparently having had his fill of the conversation and closed the subject between them by saying, "Oh, by the by, I cannot attend Mrs. Hastings' dinner this evening. Pray send my regrets." He then bethought himself and inquired, "You do mean to attend anyway, don't you? I dare say it wouldn't be polite if both of us failed to make up her numbers." Charlotte wanted to point out that it was hardly polite that *he* inconvenience Mrs. Hastings at so late an hour, but it would have been useless. Sir John would probably have just grunted at her reproof and walked away.

Charlotte sighed. "Yes, Papa, of course I mean to go."

"Excellent!" he responded, rubbing his hands together as if happy to be rid of the matter entirely.

Charlotte could not imagine how her father spent his time in Brighton, for he was rarely seen on the Steyne, never beneath the sheltered piazzas, never at the circulating libraries, not once at any of the Castle Inn balls. He had already vowed that he would never set foot in the theatre again, and only occasionally was he seen astride his horse taking the air. What, then, occupied his time?

She had been wondering as much for several days now and had been able to learn from Miss Fittleworth that all Puckley would tell her was that he arrived home every night past three o'clock in the morning.

Undoubtedly, he had a set of friends about

which she knew nothing. But then, so had it been all her life. Sir John had his own, private interests to which she was simply not privy.

As she ascended the stairs of the town house, heading toward Henry's bedchamber, her thoughts turned toward her encounter with Stoneleigh. Again, she murmured, "Oh, dear," wondering if he would be able to forgive her for making him appear the complete gudgeon. But then, what had possessed him to pinch at her as he had?

That evening she travelled alone in her father's town chariot and was set down in front of the Colonel's house. She could not help but feel she was a sort of *Daniel* entering the lion's den. Lady Purcell was among the guests attending Emily's dinner, and Charlotte was convinced she was the very one who had set the interchange between herself and Stoneleigh firmly about the *beau monde.*

As the butler opened the door, she knew by the sounds of general laughter and conversation that most of the guests had arrived. The next moment, when she ascended the stairs, she found herself being embraced heartily by a laughing Emily and an equally jubilant Colonel Hastings. After she delivered her message from her father, Colonel Hastings could no longer keep silent regarding her adventure at Walker's.

"By Jove, what a fine afternoon you have given us both," he cried. "I never laughed so hard in my life as when my wife told me what you said to Stoneleigh. Damme if you didn't fix him right and tight! Poor devil! I imagine he has suffered all manner of abuse since this morning."

These words, which she believed the Colonel had spoken with the sole intention of praising her, instead struck fear into her heart. She wished now she had not been quite so fatigued from her night's exertions with Henry and had tempered her speech with Stoneleigh.

"Don't applaud my insolence," she returned in a low voice. "I fear I spoke heedlessly because I was very tired. Henry had had the earache the night before."

"I shall praise you if I wish," he retorted gleefully. "You are in my house, and if I choose to— my, but isn't that gown becoming. And I do like that feather in your hair—very charming, indeed!"

Charlotte wondered why he left off *praising* her, but was grateful for it whatever the reason. She glanced upwards and could see from the corner of her eye the silky, fluffy white ostrich feather just topping her brown curls. "Thank you," she said. "I have never worn one before, and I rather feel like a bird."

From behind her, a low, resonant masculine voice intruded, explaining the Colonel's sudden shift in subject. "Not a bilious bird, I hope?" Lord Stoneleigh queried.

Charlotte whirled around and found the viscount standing behind her only just arrived. Amusement, pure and simple, danced in his blue eyes.

"You are not angry?" she cried, unfurling her fan and holding it in front of her face as if in doing so she could protect herself from him.

He leaned toward her and, with his hand, gently closed her fan into her palm. "No," he whispered. "Not in the least. Your words cured my, er, fit of temper. So you need no longer have a concern about my health."

"But the incident has been bandied about all over Brighton—as I am persuaded you are already aware. Are you certain you are not out of patience with me?"

"Yes," he responded. "I am certain."

Since his good humor was obviously restored

to him, she could not keep from asking, "Why were you behaving so badly?"

"I shan't tell you," he responded, then moved past her to embrace Emily and place a kiss on her cheek.

Emily laughed at him, not once but twice. "Served with your own sauce!" she cried. "I, for one, am grateful Charlotte has come to move amongst us. Perhaps she may show us the way yet to undo your wretched pride."

When Stoneleigh appeared nonplussed by her words, she drew Charlotte forward and led her into the blue drawing room where, to her mortification, she was greeted with applause and laughter, which only increased all the more when Stoneleigh appeared in the doorway. For a half-hour it seemed little more was discussed than the detrimental effects of biliousness on one's temper and character until even Colonel Hastings had quite had enough.

"If you will all now be on your very best behavior, my wife has promised to swell her voice with song."

A general round of enthusiastic cries filled the drawing room and, as the ladies disposed themselves upon chairs and sofas and the gentlemen ranged themselves nearby or against the farthest walls, Emily took her place beside the pianoforte.

Charlotte felt comfortable in a manner she had not known in a long time. The general ease and mutual consideration—and not a little good-hearted teasing—with which the Hasting's circle of intimates related to one another pleased her immensely. Even Lord Stoneleigh seemed more relaxed than she had yet witnessed him. She sensed that here was very little jealousy and ill-feeling, only the conviviality resulting from like minds, kind hearts, and goodwill.

Emily's voice was a great pleasure to hear—lyrical, sweet, and strong enough to carry each note to the deepest corner of the chamber and back again. Lady Purcell accompanied her, keeping excellent pace with Emily's style of phrasing.

Chancing to glance across the chamber, Charlotte saw Stoneleigh watching Emily with a warm smile of appreciation on his face. She felt a familiar tug of attraction for him and something more, of longing, which seemed always to afflict her when he was near. Did he know her thoughts or sense her feelings?

Was it some remarkable intuition which caused him to turn at precisely that moment, when she was asking these questions of herself, and to return her gaze until Emily's song drew to a close?

What was he thinking? Did he feel as she did, that the more she knew of him, the more she wanted to be with him, to see him smile, to hear his rich voice, to feel his arms wrapped tightly about her? His indifference to having become the brunt of a great joke at her hands impressed her probably more than anything yet had. Only a man comfortable with himself could have so easily dismissed the veritable hounding he had received from the moment he had arrived at the Hastings' town house.

Thirty

Two days later, as dusk was falling upon the town of Brighton and a cool evening sea-mist crept along the Steyne, Charlotte took Lord Stone-leigh's arm, but warily. Something in his demeanor warned her all was not well.

Over the course of the past two days, Stone-leigh had made a point of spending a good deal of his time with her and with Henry. On the first afternoon, he had paid her a *morning visit*, then later that night danced with her at a ball at the Ship Inn. The next morning he took Henry—along with William and George Hastings—to the sea-bathing machines, followed by a repast shared with Charlotte and Henry at the Castle Inn. At which time he instructed Henry on some of the finer points of each horse that trotted by, much to Henry's delight. Later in the afternoon, he had taken her out for a ride along the downs in his shiny, black curricle.

On each occasion, they had fallen into their for-mer easy discourse, conversing about everything and nothing, discussing the merits of Mr. Brown's idealistic concepts of Pantisocracy, then wagering whether the fly on the window would touch the top sill or the bottom sill first. They argued over estate management and how fully to combine the skills of the butler and the housekeeper without offending one or the other. And, at odd moments during these two days, several times in mid-sentence, Stoneleigh had fallen silent, only to look at her in his wondering way, the intense expression on his face a strong indication that had they been alone, he would have kissed her yet again.

His attentions to her, kindly and generously given and greatly enjoyed, suggested to her in the strongest way that he had fully recovered from his ill-humor at Walker's Circulating Library. The more he paid her court, the more she came to depend upon his growing interest in her.

But now, as they progressed down the Steyne, with Colonel Hastings and Emily not far away, Charlotte sensed trouble was again brewing not unlike the episode which had occurred at Walker's. He wore the same somewhat mulish expression he had worn then and did not look her directly in the eye when he spoke to her.

She wondered suddenly if the same affliction which had caused his sister to behave so erratically, so dangerously, at times also beset the viscount.

He held her arm tightly about his own and did not look at her as he began to slow perceptibly in his steps until, just like the last time they had walked together on the Steyne, Emily and the Colonel had far outstripped them.

When he fell silent in addition to slowing to a snail's pace, Charlotte decided to address the situation. "Do not tell me you are feeling bilious again, Edward," she suggested, hoping to tease him of what she thought was perhaps a fit of the megrims.

He turned to look at her and lifted his brows as if mildly annoyed. "No, I am not. However, I would appreciate it if you would quicken your step a little to match my own. I don't enjoy walking about like a tortoise."

"A tortoise?" she responded, taken aback. "Quicken my step? But I was following *your* lead, or so I thought."

"Well, you were wrong, weren't you?"

Many, many hot words sprang first to her mind and then to her lips, but she kept them all in check. She had no intention of brangling with him if she could help it. Controlling her temper with considerable effort, she responded, "If you prefer to walk faster, I shall be happy to accommodate you."

"Excellent," he said, smiling as he began increasing the length of his stride.

And increasing it again!

To Charlotte's mortification, it wasn't long before she was struggling to keep up with him. She was nearly running! What in heaven's name was he thinking? Perhaps he was mad, after all, like Elizabeth!

Finally, she cried, "Enough, Stoneleigh. This is quite absurd! I am not a horse! I am a woman with shorter legs than you." She came to a complete halt on the brick pathway and did not pay the least heed to several *tonnish* personages who eyed her curiously as they passed by.

He seemed surprised and displeased, his blue eyes flashing as he turned toward her. "I know very well you are not a horse, but I do think you underestimate your abilities. Are you saying then you are unwilling to keep stride with me?"

She took a moment to catch her breath and at the same time stared at him in bewilderment. He must have gone mad.

"Well?" he queried.

His expression was imperious, and she began to feel a little more than annoyed, her choler rising. When he crossed his arms and sighed impatiently, waiting for her response, she was instantly in the boughs.

Still, she took two very deep breaths before saying evenly, "You are being a brute, and you know it. I am not certain why you are conducting yourself in this entirely thoughtless manner, unless of course you simply wish to be rid of me. If that is the case, then there will be no love lost between us, I can promise you that. If you wish to apologize—"

"Apologize?" he queried, astounded. "Of all the absurdities, when I did nothing more than pose you the question *are you unwilling to keep stride with me.* You have only to answer it. I don't comprehend your belligerence in the least."

"My bellig—" she stopped herself before she said the next two or three unkind and unladylike thoughts which had just popped into her head. "I see," she responded at last. "It would seem I have made a grave error, after all."

He seemed to relax, mistaking her meaning entirely. "That's better," he said, staring at her from insolent eyes, his arms still crossed over his chest.

"Do you think so?" she asked facetiously. "Perhaps you are right." She waited only a second more before she turned on her heel and began walking away from him.

To her surprise, he caught up with her immediately, tugging upon her arm and forcing her to stop. "You are leaving?" he asked, dumbfounded. "I shan't permit you to go."

"Shan't permit me?" she returned, astonished. "You have no claim on me, Lord Stoneleigh. And even if you did, I would still walk away. Your conduct is completely unacceptable to me."

"You are not to leave me standing on the pathway like a commoner."

"How dare you," Charlotte breathed, incensed. "How dare you tell me what I am or am not to do, especially when you are being damnably ill-mannered. Edward—no, I refuse to do you the honor any longer of addressing you by your Christian name." She began again, more formally, "My Lord Stoneleigh, I don't hesitate to tell you that a commoner would treat me with greater respect and consideration than you have just shown. So, let me hear none of your assertions that your rank demands that I defer to your miserable conduct, because it does not—and never will!"

He started to speak, but she lifted her hand imperiously. "I will hear none of it, Stoneleigh! I have wondered for some time now how it is that a man of excellent breeding, fortune, and rank has been unable to coax even one lady of his acquaintance to accept of his hand in marriage. I now comprehend the whole of it completely. Good night, sir."

She retraced her steps and, as soon as she was able, found a hackney who could convey her back to West Street in good order and was gone.

Stoneleigh let her go, his thoughts running quickly together and keeping his feet immobile. His mouth was agape as he stared at her retreating back. He remained for the longest time in the very spot where she had left him. He wanted to laugh uproariously. Did she know how ironic her last fiery remark had been? He didn't think so, but he believed he would treasure it forever as one of the highest points of his courting of her.

He knew he had seriously wounded himself in her eyes. He whistled low. His apologies would have to be effusive on the morrow if he hoped to regain her good graces. He sincerely doubted she would forgive him readily and decided he ought at once to set himself to the task of determining how best to go about offering his apologies to her.

This last thought prompted his feet to begin moving again. As he ventured down the Steyne, toward the Colonel and Emily, whom he could see barely outlined in the fading sunlight, he smiled, his heart lighter than it had been in years. He took in a large gulp of air and wanted to shout to the heavens that here was a woman worth every guinea of his fortune.

How many times had he practiced the same truly wretched misconduct on the hopeful ladies of his acquaintance only to have them bow meekly to his wishes. Maude Dunsfold had actually run along beside him rather than object to his mistreatment, and Lady Purcell had burst into tears, hoping by doing so he would be moved to pity.

Not once, in the past seven years since Emily had married her Colonel, had a lady dared to confront him and to call his conduct what it was—an outrage. If he felt a twinge of conscience in having deliberately provoked her, he quickly set it aside. After all, he was certain he could explain all to Charlotte once she passed his third and final test.

Until then, he had to discover if he could find some way of compelling her to forgive him for his truly wretched manners.

The following morning, Charlotte sat in the *morning room* of her father's town house, contentedly sipping a cup of chocolate and drying her hair with a towel. The window was open, and the fresh sea air filled the small chamber. She sat at a square mahogany table, an arrangement of fragrant roses settled in front of her. The chamber was decorated in a simple manner, a light-blue damask adorning the walls and forming a valance over sheer muslin under-drapes billowing out from the window. A watercolor showing a perspective of Brighton adorned the wall opposite the fireplace.

She had already been sea-bathing with Henry, who could not seem to keep from splashing her thoroughly every morning and subsequently soaking her hair. However much she might not enjoy the prospect of drying her hair and having it restyled after their trek to the seaside, Charlotte had come to rely upon the daily ritual as much as Henry. The sea was having a happy effect upon her, just as so many faithful sea-bathers had insisted it would.

As she sat perusing the various columns of the *Morning Post,* willing herself to set aside the painful memories of her terrible confrontation with Stoneleigh the evening before, she found herself feeling wondrously calm and refreshed. Nurse was taking Henry on an excursion into the countryside, Fittle was preparing the curling tongs, and Cook was creating her famous macaroons, which were a favorite of hers. She was left, then, to the enjoyment of her solitude and the promise of warm cookies in a half-hour or so. What more could any lady wish for?

So absorbed was she in her reading, in drying her hair and sipping her chocolate, she did not hear the commotion in the hallway until it burst in upon her.

"There you are!" Lord Stoneleigh called to her, nearly stumbling over the butler as he entered the morning room.

"I am sorry, Miss," Puckley cried, staring angrily at the viscount. "But I told him you were not *at home.*"

"How dare you, Lord Stoneleigh?" Charlotte began, wrapping her towel securely about her head and rising from her chair. She would gladly help her father's butler cast the verminous creature from her house if need be. "How dare you come into my home with neither Sir John's permission nor mine. Does your conceit know no bounds?"

"Just as I thought," Puckley said, rubbing his hands together as if preparing for a mill.

Stoneleigh leaped away from him and raised his fists. "I've boxed with Jackson," he said, an exuberant light in his blue eyes.

"And I once went a round with Molyneux," Puckley countered mulishly.

"Ah," Stoneleigh breathed. "A man of excellent science, he was. Well, then, let's see what you've got!"

The men began to move slowly in careful circles.

Charlotte was stunned and quickly intervened. "Oh, enough, the pair of you! For heaven's sakes! Stoneleigh, leave him be—have you gone completely mad? Puckley, pray be so good as to close the door behind you on your way out—I'll see to him. And speak of this to no one. If his lordship is not gone in five minutes, you may return and throw him through the window with my blessing!"

"Yes, Miss Amberley," Puckley said, controlling himself with some effort. He bowed politely enough to Charlotte, but his expression was murderous as he cast a final scathing glance upon Stoneleigh before quitting the morning room.

Charlotte spoke first, the moment the door snapped shut behind the butler. "My hair isn't even dry, and you come charging into my home as if you've a right to be here—which you most certainly do not! In fact, I cannot even imagine why you've come, for you must know I haven't the smallest desire to even speak with you! Let me warn you, then, if you've come for any other purpose than to apologize for your horrendous conduct of last night, you might as well leave on the instant!"

Before she knew what he was about, he had rounded the table and dropped to his knees before her, a quick, startling movement which caused Charlotte to back away from him. "Whatever are you doing?" she cried.

"Forgive me," he pleaded. "You assessed my intentions to a nicety. I did come for no other reason than to offer you my humblest apologies."

When she backed away from him farther yet—disturbed once more by his bizarre conduct—he followed after her, quite absurdly on his knees, until she felt the wall behind her.

"It was very wrong of me to press you so hard last night, Charlotte. I don't know what came over me, some sort of madness just as you have said. Only I promise you I have come to realize how wrong I was, how cruel and unthinking, and need only to hear you tell me you will forgive me to be restored to complete sanity."

Since he was now holding the skirts of her yellow, silk morning gown in each hand, Charlotte did not know what to think of his conduct.

"Are you making sport of me, then?" she queried.

"No, never," he said, his expression softening. "I am entreating you not to think worse of me than you already do and to find it in your heart to forgive me that we might begin again. As I have said before, I don't know why I behaved so *unkindly* to you last night. All I know is that I was wrong. Horribly, wretchedly wrong!"

Why did she believe him, Charlotte wondered as she looked down into his eyes. She had sat up half the night fussing and fuming over his errant misbehavior and had decided he was too flawed for her to hope he might actually be a man she could share her life with.

233

Now, she did not know what to think, except that already her heart was fluttering in her breast as it always did when he was near and she was feeling dizzy again.

"You are such a simpleton," she responded, giving in to a smile and daring to trace his cheek with her finger. "I know I shouldn't, but I forgive you."

He needed no further encouragement but released her skirts and rose to take her in his arms. "I deserved every word you said to me last night. I am sorry, my darling Charlotte."

"What did you say?" she murmured, wanting to hear him speak her name again with so wondrous an endearment attached to it.

His lips were nearly upon hers as he repeated, "My darling Charlotte."

"Oh," she breathed as he kissed her full upon the lips, pressing her firmly into the wall. She slipped her arms about his neck, her former grievances forgotten completely in the gentle search of his mouth and the arm which sought out her waist and drew her so close that she thought for a moment she might simply disappear into him forever.

After a moment, he released her and looked seriously down into her eyes. "I am giving a ball at my home on Saturday next. Will you come?"

"Of course I will."

"Your—your father, too, if he wishes for it."

"I shall ask him, though I cannot speak for him since I do not know if he has a previous engagement."

He was silent for a moment, his fingers gently touching her cheeks and the line of her chin. "However absurd I have been this morning," he said sincerely, "I want you to know I am sorry for my conduct of last night—deeply sorry."

She again touched his cheek lightly. "I can see

that you are, and I promise you I have forgiven you as long as you promise never to behave so badly again."

"I shall cut out my heart first."

"Excellent," she responded with a smile, "though I feel compelled to warn you that if you don't, I will."

Somehow these words, which were hardly lady-like, brought his lips slanting down hard upon hers and she was forced yet again to submit to his embrace.

Puckley, who had been standing in the hallway and fairly studying his pocket watch, waited only for the second hand to reach its objective when he snapped the silver lid shut and pushed open the door.

He was about to speak, to order the viscount to raise his fists again, when he realized he would not get to discover if Lord Stoneleigh had pitched a bit of gammon when he boasted of having boxed with Jackson. He was quite downcast as he retreated from the morning room at the sight of Miss Amberley, a towel about her head, locked in the embrace of Brighton's greatest swell.

Damn and blast!

He hadn't enjoyed a good bout of fisticuffs in too many months to be remembered.

Thirty-one

The next sennight floated by for Charlotte like mist through a vale. Each day scarcely made an impression on her as she awaited the arrival of Saturday and Stoneleigh's ball. She knew her name was being bandied about in every drawing room in Brighton—much she cared! Her only consideration was that her heart was as light as a feather; and if her feet touched the earth as she walked about, she simply wasn't aware of it.

She was in love, deeply, wondrously, madly, completely.

Henry asked her if she had the stomachache because he said she was always staring at nothing in particular and looked as if she were in some sort of pain.

She had caught him up in her arms by way of response and tickled him until he laughed raucously.

Miss Fittle expressed her concern that she was pinning her hopes on a man who had never before been brought up to scratch, even by the most fashionable ladies.

Charlotte merely smiled and said she didn't give a fig for what had gone before. Lord Stoneleigh had expressed his love for her and that was all that she required.

"He told you he loved you?" Miss Fittle queried, surprised.

"Well, no, not in so many *words.*"

Miss Fittle gasped. "Have you permitted Stoneleigh to *kiss* you? Oh, please, Miss, say you have not! Oh, dear, oh dear. You shouldn't have, and you most certainly should not mistake a bit of kissing for love. We haven't spoken much of the gentlemen, Miss Charlotte, but you do know they are quite fond of kissing for its own sake, don't you?"

Charlotte laughed, told her to stop fretting, patted her cheek, and floated away. Stoneleigh may have kissed many women before, but surely not the way he had kissed her. Not with such meaning and intent. Surely not!

The day of the ball arrived, and Charlotte set out alone in her father's carriage to Lord Stoneleigh's home—Ashurst Hall. Though Sir John had declined accompanying her because of a previous engagement, he had wished her well and hoped that her evening would be a prosperous one.

Charlotte assured him dreamily it would and climbed into the carriage. Miss Fittleworth had packed her best rose-silk-and-tulle balldress in a trunk, and she felt very much like a princess going by command of the Prince to the castle. Once arrived at Ashurst, a maid would be appointed to her to help her dress.

Two hours later, when the coach rounded a tree-shrouded hill and Ashurst came into view, Charlotte suffered a shock. She had heard the viscount's home was elegant and knew that Stoneleigh was a man of substance, but still she was not prepared for the sprawling mansion which greeted her eyes.

"Oh, my," she breathed into the dusky air. "I hadn't thought—"

Another carriage preceded hers; and as her

own conveyance turned up the drive, she saw Lord and Lady Purcell descending the baron's elegant travelling coach. Longreves did not begin to rival Ashurst, and Charlotte had thought Longreves a house of unequalled beauty. She had been wrong.

She counted the windows of the mansion as her carriage rolled inexorably toward the front door and realized Ashurst must contain thirty, perhaps forty, bedchambers. Goodness gracious!

Once her senses had become somewhat accustomed to the awe-inspiring structure, she let her gaze travel from the fully-leafed lime trees staggered in a picturesque manner down the length of the drive to the large lake flanking the house on the left and graced with an abundance of beautiful, white swans. On the far side of the lake was a temple in the Greek mode and, because of the almost careless yet perfect placement of shrubs, conifers, and banks of flowers around the lake, she knew that the hand of Repton had been at work—just as at Longreves.

Serenity and beauty filled every soft angle of the estate, no matter how close the horses drew the carriage to the front door.

It was not long before she stepped past the portals of Ashurst and was nearly overset by the vision of the double staircase rising upward, leading her gaze to a large skylighted dome overhead.

"Edward," she breathed, her arm held tightly in his as she advanced into the spacious entrance hall. "You've a lovely home. Truly magnificent. Amberley Park seems like a country cottage by comparison."

"Thank you," he murmured.

She looked up at him and felt a rush of affection so strong for him as she gazed into his blue eyes that for a moment she couldn't speak. He seemed equally affected, gazing back at her intently, his eyes unwavering, his lips parted slightly as if he wished to say something to her but could not find the words.

"I'm glad you've come," he said at last. "And now, permit me to introduce you to my housekeeper, Mrs. Burnell."

He drew her toward the staircase, where a lady gowned in stiff, proper black bombazine awaited her. She was motherly in appearance, her figure—as a woman of advancing years—round and soft, her gray hair thick and swept tidily into a loose chignon atop her head. She wore a small watch on a silver chain draped about her neck, and her general air of poise invited confidence.

Charlotte found herself immediately impressed with the directness of her gaze as Mrs. Burnell regarded Charlotte from light blue, perceptive eyes.

Once in her company, however, Charlotte became aware of a certain reticence on Mrs. Burnell's part. That good lady was perfectly willing to answer any question Charlotte put to her, but offered no information beyond that which was strictly required by the nature of the question. Charlotte began to feel uneasy, sensing that, for reasons of her own, Mrs. Burnell had deliberately chosen to refrain from sharing liberally with her on a subject which she was convinced must have been close to that lady's heart—namely, Ashurst. Charlotte had known many excellent housekeepers, and they all shared the same quality—a love for the home whose care had been given into their hands.

Mrs. Burnell took her to the bedchamber assigned to her, and Charlotte saw at once that it was special. She turned to her and could not keep from exclaiming, "You must tell me something of this room, for I can see by the elegant gilt-work and the fine tapestries on the walls that it is of some significance. Surely.''

As she watched Mrs. Burnell's bosom swell with pride, she knew her initial impression of her had been a true one. She did love Ashurst Hall. '' 'Tis called the Queen's bedchamber. No less a personage than Elizabeth slept in these quarters.''

"Elizabeth!" Charlotte breathed. "Oh, my!"

"Precisely so, Miss Amberley,'' the housekeeper stated. She smiled, then, for the first time since making Charlotte's acquaintance, and it seemed that an understanding passed between the two women.

"Elizabeth,'' Charlotte intoned again, advancing slightly into the august chamber which was decorated in red-velvet curtains about the elaborately carved, gilt four-poster bed and cascading on either side of the two tall windows across from the door. She felt a river of gooseflesh travel completely through her as she imagined the virgin queen and her attending maids preparing for dinner, a ball, and later for bed.

"I'll leave you now, Miss Amberley. Katherine will attend to you.''

When Katherine drew her balldress from the trunk, she cried, "Oh, you'll look just like a fairy-princess, miss—sheer tulle over rose silk—how lovely. A fairy-princess, indeed. And I have a way with hair. See if I don't!''

The maid's enthusiasm was infectious and, before long, Charlotte was regarding her reflection in a long mirror. Katherine had drawn her brown locks into a gentle knot atop her head, permitting a dozen curls to dangle down the back in a loose wave. She kept a soft fringe across her forehead and through the whole she wound narrow gold and pink silk ribbons. When she had donned her gown, she believed Katherine's prediction had come true—she did look like a fairy-princess.

"You've arranged my hair to perfection," Charlotte said.

"Thank you, miss," she responded, clasping a necklet of diamonds about Charlotte's throat.

Afterward, she handed Charlotte her long white gloves and said, "I wish you the best of luck, Miss Amberley."

Charlotte could not mistake her meaning and felt a blush warm her cheeks. "You're very kind," she responded, looking away from the eager young maid and hoping her high-color would quickly fade.

Within a few minutes, Charlotte left her bedchamber, where she chanced to find Lady Purcell passing by.

"Oh, Charlotte, don't you look pretty," her ladyship cooed. "Are you prepared to descend the stairs and see the grand salon? You will not credit your eyes. Stoneleigh, it would seem, has benefitted from the Prince's prestige and has been able to purchase a great deal of French furniture through his influence. The revolution was a terrible thing for France's aristocracy, but a benefit to our poor island—their furnishings have quite enhanced many of our great drawing rooms. I have a chest of drawers in my own bedchamber which was said to have belonged to a prince."

Charlotte responded that it was indeed a most unfortunate circumstance that France's noblemen and women found it necessary to sell their belongings in order to remain alive. She would have warmed to the theme, but, having reached the top of the stairs, Lady Purcell caught her wrist suddenly and stopped her progress. "I know I oughtn't to interfere, Charlotte, but someone must warn you. If you believe you have been brought here in order for Stoneleigh to introduce a future bride to his staff and to his home, you are mistaken. The truth is—"

241

But she got no further, for at that moment, their host appeared at the bottom of the stairs. Lady Purcell was instantly all smiles and, taking Charlotte's arm, said in a commanding voice, "You will find that Ashurst goes on for miles and one finds oneself weary in simply walking from one end to the other." She then laughed and whispered, "I will tell you more later."

Charlotte did not know what to think, though she was honest enough with herself to believe that Stoneleigh had brought her to Ashurst in order for her to see his home and to meet his servants. Was she as badly mistaken as Lady Purcell would have her believe? Had he another purpose in mind? If so, what?

When an hour had passed and the guests were all assembled in the grand salon, the ladies wearing gowns of the finest silks and the gentlemen coats fashioned by the hands of Weston and Stultz, Charlotte sensed that something was amiss. Lady Purcell had not been able to complete her warning, but the concerns she had expressed were not what was disturbing Charlotte now. For one thing, though she was chatting easily with Emily and the Colonel, she had noticed that Emily's gaze frequently drifted toward Stoneleigh, her hazel eyes full of meaning, as if she wished to convey some critical message to him. Stoneleigh for his part, appeared to be ignoring her. She wanted to ask Emily what was troubling her, but the occasion simply did not present itself. The chamber was too full of guests to permit private discourse.

Then she chanced to notice that one after another of the guests had begun glancing at the charming Apollo clock on the plasterwork mantel over the fireplace. She wondered what the significance could be and saw the reason for general concern—dinner was late. The appointed hour had arrived and gone by a full forty-five minutes!

Glancing at Stoneleigh, she noted that he seemed distressed now as well.

"What is wrong?" Charlotte whispered to Emily. When Emily did not immediately respond, Charlotte looked at her and happened upon an exchanged, very private glance between husband and wife. Emily seemed angry, but why Charlotte couldn't imagine. The Colonel merely gave his head a resigned shake.

"Oh, now you must tell me!" Charlotte whispered. "Whatever is amiss? The pair of you look as if you're about to face a brigade of cannon."

Emily laughed, a shade too brightly, Charlotte thought. "Nonsense," she responded. "Only it would seem sometimes the housekeeper does not always have full command of the kitchens."

Charlotte was very surprised. "Indeed," she remarked. "I would have thought Mrs. Burnell a very competent woman. I wonder what could have gone wrong."

Emily pinched her lips together and directed her statement to her husband. "I could only wish Stoneleigh had found a way to manage his affairs better."

"No sense throwing stones now, my dear."

"It's that bad, is it?" Charlotte asked, truly stunned, for though Mrs. Burnell was not as forthcoming with her as she could have wished, there was not a chamber Charlotte had viewed which indicated a home less than immaculately well-maintained.

"I think it completely reprehensible!" Emily whis-pered, her voice sounding anguished. "Can't you do something, dearest? He is your friend, after all."

"Enough Emily," the Colonel corrected her. "Stoneleigh must do what he feels is best, even if you and I don't agree with him."

From that moment Charlotte knew that they

were not speaking of the housekeeper or of the cook or of dinner being late. But what? More than life itself, she wanted an answer to the riddle of their provocative exchange.

But at the same moment, before she could press either for an explanation, the door opened and the butler appeared begging a word with his lordship. Another moment later, and Stoneleigh approached Charlotte. "I need your assistance," he said quietly. "Will you come with me?"

He held his arm out to her, and Charlotte hesitated only a moment before taking it. But during that moment, she chanced to catch Emily's eye and saw a look of hostility—directed wholly toward Stoneleigh—which caused her heart to quaver in her breast. What on earth was going forward? Had Lady Purcell not tried to warn her of some impending doom and had Emily not spoken in such an anguished voice, Charlotte would have been *aux anges* at having been singled out to help the man she loved.

As it was, her knees trembled as she walked beside him.

Whatever did it all mean?

Thirty-two

Once in the entrance hall, Stoneleigh, whose manner seemed strangely reserved of a sudden, said, "You've had considerable experience, Charlotte, in managing an estate. It would seem mine is in an uproar, of the moment, and I am in desperate need of your help."

Charlotte looked up at him as they walked through the broad doorway between the double staircase. "I would have thought either Emily or Lady Purcell would have been a better choice in such a situation, Edward. It is true I have seen to Amberley for many years now, but Lady Purcell in particular has maintained a home closer to the size of Ashurst. As I told you before, Amberley Park, compared to Ashurst, appears more like a cottage than the large manor house it is."

He glanced down at her, a speculative look in his eye. She wondered what he was thinking and for a moment it almost appeared, as he slowed in his steps, that he was considering taking up her suggestion. Finally, he said, "No, it is your help I want. I'm certain you are as capable of offering the sort of advice I require as either Emily or Lady Purcell. Please, won't you help me?"

"Of course," Charlotte responded. She should

have been flattered; instead something nagged at her. It was as if a small gnat had crept into her brain and kept itself hidden most of the time, but every now and then, the little flying monster would creep out and flutter across her eyes. She kept hearing the anguish in Emily's voice and Lady Purcell's words, *someone must warn you*. Warn her of what?

She found herself in what she believed was Stoneleigh's office, a small but neatly fitted chamber at the back of the house. "What is wrong precisely?" she queried, advancing into the room.

"It would seem my chef was found in his cups not an hour ago and the courses only but half-prepared. I have thirty guests awaiting a dinner which is not ready. I don't know what to do." He gestured for her to sit down in a gold winged chair near the fireplace.

"Oh, my!" Charlotte responded, startled. When she had seated herself, she said, "I'm very sorry to hear it. Well, it is a difficult case, but not an impossible one. What do you intend to do?"

He seemed surprised by her initial response and leaned against the edge of his desk of fine, light-grained satinwood. "I suppose I was hoping you might be able to instruct Mrs. Burnell or even to take complete charge, if necessary."

She wondered what she would do if such a situation ever arose at Amberley Park. She thought of her housekeeper, who was in charge of Cook, who in turn ruled over the kitchens, and knew instantly what she ought to recommend to Stoneleigh. "I'm not certain what I could accomplish if I *took charge,* but really, Stoneleigh, I would not presume to interfere in the management of either your kitchen or your staff. You have spoken with Mrs. Burnell, haven't you?"

He shook his head. "No, as it happens I have not. The butler informed me of the crisis, and I brought you here hoping you might be able to help me."

"Well, it seemed to me, when I met Mrs. Burnell earlier this evening, that you were in the hands of a most excellent housekeeper. I would strongly advise you to leave the matter to her. I know that our housekeeper at Amberley has every eventuality planned for. You might discover she already has a scheme of her own in mind."

"This is the only way you feel you can help me in this situation?" he queried, astonished.

"If you feel more is necessary, I suppose I could speak with her myself."

"Please," he said, appearing genuinely desirous of her doing so.

"Pray be so good, then, to summon her."

He did so with alacrity and, in five minutes, Mrs. Burnell was standing before them both. Lord Stoneleigh returned to the satinwood desk, a curious expression on his face as if he longed to know what next would happen.

As Charlotte regarded him for a moment, she really could not understand why he wasn't more distressed, given the nature of the crisis. He had thirty guests awaiting a dinner that gave every appearance of not making it to the table, yet he truly did not seem particularly concerned. In her opinion, he should have shown a little more anxiety.

The gnat flitted before her eyes again, then disappeared.

She turned to Mrs. Burnell, who she could readily see was suffering acutely—but not so much from anxiety as from anger. Her appearance was quite wooden, almost hostile. Her lips were pinched tightly together and she did not look Charlotte in the eye as she addressed her. "You wished to see me, Miss Amberley?" she queried politely.

She felt the gnat again flit across her vision

and absently tugged at one of the curls on her forehead as if she could make the imaginary creature disappear by doing so.

Charlotte spoke softly and kindly to her. "Lord Stoneleigh tells me that your chef is not feeling well."

"Yes, Miss," she said, nodding firmly. "That is true."

"And dinner is in a state of *half-dress,* shall we say?"

The housekeeper glanced at her and frowned slightly, as if she were slightly perplexed, before nodding.

"Well, the odd thing is," Charlotte said, "though I have been in the way of managing my father's home for many years since the unfortunate death of my mother, your master seems to think I know a bit of magic to perform on uncooked meat or the like."

She saw the housekeeper's lip twitch just slightly as her eyes slid toward Stoneleigh and back. "I—I wouldn't know precisely what my master thought you might accomplish, Miss Amberley."

"They never do know, do they," Charlotte said smiling. "Sometimes I think men believe that Cook waves her hand—or his hand, whichever is the case—invokes a few magical spells, and twenty courses appear. And why in large houses they expect everything hot to table, I cannot imagine, but it is always the way, isn't it?"

"Yes, Miss," the housekeeper said, now smiling without reservation and this time looking her directly in the eye.

"Am I correct in believing you already have a scheme of your own in mind by which this unfortunate situation might be remedied?"

She saw the housekeeper's bosom swell. Charlotte suspected that the daggers which appeared in her light-blue eyes were meant not for her but for her master, but she dared not throw them in his direction. Instead, she clasped her hands together quite firmly in front of her and said, "As it happens, I've a fair notion precisely how to correct the situation."

Charlotte turned toward Lord Stoneleigh and, with a shake of her head, said, "Stoneleigh, I don't like to mention it, but you've a singular failing in this instance. From the moment I entered your house, I could see there was not a whisper of dust to be found anywhere. And though I have not had the pleasure of sleeping in one of your beds, I would suspect that all the linens are in excellent order. Your gardens are groomed to perfection; your staff is prompt and exceedingly polite. Your serving maids, in particular the one who attended me, are a delight. And I've yet to see even a bit of wainscoting that is not glistening with French polish." She heard the housekeeper give a grunt of satisfaction, and she dared not look at her for fear she might burst out laughing. "This is what I suggest to you in this situation, that you value your retainers a little more. There is nothing for me to do here except to tell you that I am persuaded if you will but give Mrs. Burnell permission to do so, she will manage this troublesome difficulty to a nicety."

Stoneleigh still had his arms folded across his chest as he listened to her. He did not seem in the least angry by her rebuke.

What is he thinking? she wondered.

"I can see I have made a grave error," he said at last. Turning to his housekeeper, he continued, "Mrs. Burnell, pray do whatever you feel you must do to see that dinner is completed for my guests. Only tell me how long I must beg them to wait, and I shall inform them myself."

Mrs. Burnell eyed him triumphantly. "I daresay a half-hour will suffice."

"Very good," he said and dismissed her with a smile.

But Mrs. Burnell did not leave immediately. Instead, she turned to Charlotte and, curtsying very deeply, said, "Thank you, Miss Amberley, for your confidence in me. I can see that your mother taught you very well, very well, indeed."

"She would be happy to hear your say so," Charlotte responded.

When Mrs. Burnell had quit the room, Charlotte eyed Stoneleigh askance and said, "I suppose I owe you an apology."

"What for?" he asked. Did he sound angry? Charlotte wondered. He continued, "I was very much at fault, and you've neatly put everything to rights with just a few well-chosen—and very generous—words. I am indebted to you."

He left his post by the desk and went to the door. He seemed distracted as he said, "I have something I want to say to you, but first I have a matter of some urgency to attend to. Will you wait here for me?"

"Yes, of course." She felt uneasy, as much by the strained tone in his voice as by the abrupt manner in which he quit the room and closed the door with a snap.

Again the gnat teased her, then disappeared.

A few seconds later, the door opened, and Charlotte rose from her chair, supposing Stoneleigh had returned, perhaps having forgotten to tell her something. But there, standing before her was not Stoneleigh at all, but Lady Purcell. She seemed almost panicky in appearance, a wild look to her eye.

"Thank heaven I have found you," she said breathlessly. "It is not too late, is it? He has not given you his famous setdown, has he?"

Thirty-three

"Whatever is wrong?" Charlotte cried.

Lady Purcell, a fluttering, beautiful butterfly in a gossamer blue gauze over a white-satin undergown, cried out, "Has he given you the final test yet—about his staff?"

"What?" Charlotte asked, the gnat appearing again, only this time to remain as a constant irritation before her eyes.

"Has he presented you with some insurmountable dilemma requiring your assistance?"

"Well, yes, but how did you know? Does everyone know his chef was in his altitudes?"

"Ah, yes, his chef. My dear, there is no time for you to lose. I ordered my carriage brought round, and it would be utterly perfect if you were to escape in it now—before he returns and gives you his *famous setdown*. When I saw him call you away, my dearest Charlotte, my heart grieved for you, for the humiliation you would soon be suffering. This was what I was trying to tell you about earlier—on the landing at the top of the stairs. Don't you see that he has *put you through your paces*? Has no one told you he does this to every lady with whom he becomes even mildly enamored?"

Charlotte felt as if a river of ice were streaming

over her in painful waves. Lord Stoneleigh has been putting me through a sort of test?" The gnat landed on her nose and laughed at her.

Lady Purcell nodded.

"He has done this before?"

"To me, to others."

"Mrs. Wyndham?"

Again the nod.

"Mrs. Knight?"

Another nod. "I believe poor Maude failed in her second test and he took her no further. She was never invited to a ball at Ashurst that I know of."

Charlotte thought back to the Steyne and to Stoneleigh's wretched conduct. She then thought back a little further still. "The bookshop!" she cried. "You were there. The *blue* cover. He was testing me then, wasn't he? Why didn't you tell me?"

"I enjoyed your answer so much I couldn't interrupt his schemes. You see, I have been harboring this hope that one day a young lady would come along with enough pluck to vindicate us all. He has tormented so many, you've no idea. And now you can serve him the turn he so richly deserves. That is why I had my carriage brought to the front door. Do heed my advice, Charlotte. Accept my coach before he returns to give you the setdown he undoubtedly means to confer upon you."

She turned toward the door and held her hand wide, beckoning Charlotte to go.

Charlotte remembered yet again Maude and Selena's tear-stained letters and why she had come to Brighton in the first place. She still could not believe it was true yet knew in her heart Stoneleigh had indeed *put her through her paces*. She felt queasy, sickened with disgust at the thought of how ill he had used her. It was no wonder Mrs. Burnell said she could have dinner ready in half an hour. Undoubtedly his chef was busy completing the meal just as he would have done anyway.

"I will go," she said quietly.

"You must hurry then, for I saw him enter the library with Mr. Elstow shortly after he left you. He will return any moment, I'm sure of it."

Charlotte needed no further prompting and walked quickly beside Lady Purcell, lifting the skirts of her gown and hurrying through the doorway beneath the double stairs toward an astonished butler and out onto the drive where, just as the baroness promised, her coach was waiting.

Lord Stoneleigh had not intended upon going into his library. He had originally planned upon retrieving the Stoneleigh heirloom diamonds from his bedchamber, always a wedding gift to the next viscountess, but Harry Elstow had arrived with an urgent dispatch from Rothschild's and had driven him off his path, if momentarily. Once he discovered what had caused Harry to set aside his hunting plans with Mr. Brown—though he strongly suspected his *plans* might somehow have involved Maude Dunsfold as well—he intended to present the diamonds to Charlotte and to beg for her hand in marriage. She had handled the false kitchen crisis in a masterful way, and it had been all he could do to keep from taking her in his arms then and there, kissing her hard and professing his love for her. But he wanted to ask her properly and to give the diamonds to her as a symbol of his devotion—he wanted the moment to be perfect.

Harry's arrival meant only a slight delay in the fulfillment of his intention to offer for Charlotte.

He broke the seal on the dispatch and read it through quickly. He felt his fingertips grow numb with shock as he clenched the accusing document in his hand.

"What is it?" Harry cried. "I knew it was of some import, but I vow, man, you appear as if the heavens have just fallen."

"Near to it," he whispered.

"What then? The letter from my father said it was an urgent matter. Does he know the contents?"

Stoneleigh shook his head, again scanning the damning communication. "There is a rumor circulating that someone is inciting the Turks to their nefarious activities again."

Harry whistled. "Tunis, Algiers, Tripoli—the Barbary Coast to rise again?"

"If this man has his way, yes."

"But I thought Lord Exmouth levelled the town of Algiers."

"So he did, but you must remember the Turks have been in North Africa operating their hostage and slavery operations for more than three centuries. Given a proper amount of capital, an enterprising Dey could gather his remaining supporters and begin again. All he would need is a few light *corsairs,* and the deed would be done."

"But who would finance such a venture?"

"A man who is desperate would," Stoneleigh began uneasily. "A man intent upon setting up a false joint-stock company. Although I think a man who seeks power would have even more interest in doing so."

Harry frowned. "You are not suggesting Amberley is the one. He may have come to a desperate pass, but he wouldn't be so wicked. He is only an unfortunate gamester, after all."

"I am suggesting another man who has chosen to use Amberley, one whose ambitions are beyond the reasonings of a sensible man, one who prefers the exhilaration of the hunt to nearly every other amusement."

"Do you know who it might be?" Harry asked.

"I'm not sure, though were I pressed to it, I would hazard a guess."

"Who, then?"

Stoneleigh shook his head. "Until I know more, I am unwilling to say. I do know this much, Sir John has one advantage he does not."

"His influence with Prinny," Harry stated. "Charlotte says her father has been friends with the Prince for nigh on thirty years."

"Precisely so."

"Hence Amberley's request for a Charter. A joint-stock company could raise all the money required to finance any business venture. But would Amberley actually pursue such a horrendous means of gaining a fortune? We are speaking of white slavery. He would be condemning his own countrymen and women to a fate worse than any imagining."

Stoneleigh weighed Harry's incisive observation. "I believe Sir John knows nothing about the venture he was so willing to go to the Prince for. I suspect he is a trifling pawn in a larger game. I only wonder what will happen when he has outgrown his use to his partner."

He then said, "You've been a good friend, Harry. Now tell me this, how is it I tumbled in love with Amberley's daughter and how am I now to reveal this awful truth to her?"

"Now there's a coil," he said, smiling crookedly. "What do you mean to do? Once the contents of this letter are made known, Amberley will be ruined forever. The last I heard through my father's agents, Sir John was in debt to the tune of sixty thousand pounds. He will never come about now."

"First, I believe I shall tell her all I know; and if she needs proof; you, your father, and an agent from Rothschild's can certainly confirm my tale. Then, I'll ask for her hand in marriage."

Harry's smile broadened. "I knew it!" he cried, taking Stoneleigh's hand and giving it a hard shake. "You will not regret having fallen in love with her, though I don't hesitate to warn you that she can be very stubborn. Whatever you do, don't cross her or she'll never forgive you. And as for *putting her through her paces—*"

"What?" he cried. "You know of that?"

"All of Brighton does."

"Good God!"

"Let me warn you, if she learns of it from anyone else but you, there'll be the devil to pay, make no mistake."

He grunted. "Then I shall tell her at once." His worried expression softened. "But she was magnificent just now. You should have seen her, Harry, giving me a rare trimming for not valuing my servants as I ought; and there was Mrs. Burnell, ready to pluck my eyes out, then satisfied beyond words that I had finally been set straight." He folded the letter up and locked it into the top drawer of his desk. "Say nothing of this to anybody. And now, you may return to Miss Dunsfold with my blessing."

Harry blushed and, after reiterating that he had left *Mr. Brown* awaiting his return as soon as possible, he expressed his desire that, should Stoneleigh require him again, he was at his service.

"Pray tell Maude that I hope she is feeling a great deal better. And Harry, I know for a fact Mr. Brown left on a pilgrimage to Bath over two days ago."

Harry smiled sheepishly. "Oh, the devil take it!"

Stoneleigh returned to his office and, before reentering the chamber, paused for a moment just outside the door. He whispered to himself by way of rehearsing a most dreaded speech. "You see, Charlotte, the reason I *put you through your paces* is because for so long now, I have been seeking precisely the sort of woman who could— oh, damn-it-all. Emily, I believe you were right. She'll never forgive me."

There was nothing for it, however, but to begin. Taking a deep breath, he pushed the door open. What he found startled him, for there, sitting atop the desk with her ankles fully exposed beneath a thin layer of rose gauze, was not Charlotte at all, but Lady Purcell.

"Your little bird has flown, my love," the green-eyed beauty cooed sweetly. "But I am here."

Thirty-four

"What are you doing here?" he cried. "Where is Charlotte?"

Lady Purcell kicked off her silk slippers and placed her stockinged feet flat on the desk, hugging her arms about her knees. "I told you. She left. I came in search of her, seeing that you were having a *very familiar* crisis in your household and hoping I could help. When I suggested to her that such a desperate situation had occurred before, she seemed to take exception to that possibility and desired to leave. Indeed, I would say her cheeks were quite pink and I have yet to see a lady flee a house so quickly. Only tell me something, Stoneleigh, tell me how she failed her final test that I might be comforted."

Lord Stoneleigh looked at her face, at the extreme brightness of her green eyes, and felt ill. "You are still angry with me, after all these years, even though you have a husband who is besotted with you, a fortune, a title, a house, a full nursery, and the envy of the entire *beau monde*."

"We ladies have very long memories. You may ask Mrs. Wyndham, if you don't believe me, or Mrs. Knight or even poor little Selena and her friend Maude; and we should all say the same thing—that we were ill-used. My only satisfaction has been in seeing that no lady since my time has been found worthy. That alone has been my comfort. So, relieve my heart again and tell me in what way Charlotte failed. As I recall, I made a spectacle of myself in the kitchens and berated your poor housekeeper, who to this day stares me down whenever I place my foot upon your hallowed entrance hall. I was even so foolish as to order your poor chef to leave your house. I trust Charlotte did the same?"

Stoneleigh felt the weight of his actions, the cruelty of them, bearing down on him not just from this one evening but through the years. He saw in Lady Purcell a manner of suffering he had never recognized before—that a woman's pride was no less fragile than a man's; but in a lady's case, she could find no reasonable outlet for such profound feelings. A man could challenge another gentleman to a duel for insulting him, but what could a woman do except scream quietly behind her fan, bite her lip, and wait for revenge?

"Charlotte gave me a dressing down for not valuing my servants properly."

Lady Purcell frowned ever so slightly. "I don't understand. She gave your head a washing? Do you tell me she did not run to the kitchens and try, as both Mrs. Wyndham and I did, to set everything to rights?"

He shook his head. "I don't know what I had ever hoped to gain by placing each of you in so hard a predicament; but the moment Charlotte ranged herself beside my housekeeper and extolled that good lady's virtues, I knew she was speaking precisely what I had wanted to hear."

Lady Purcell's cheeks flamed instantly and she swung her legs over the edge of the desk, clamping her hands about the scrolled wooden border. "Clever girl. I suppose if I had spoken harshly to you as she did, perhaps then you might have valued me a little more as well. You might even have loved me."

"I was wrong to have used you so poorly. I can see that now, but what shaped my blindness still remains. I don't believe you ever truly did love me."

She dropped lightly to the floor and ran to him, clutching his arms with her gloved hands. "Not love you! How can you speak so when I've always loved you and I always will? Terribly. You've no idea! How can you say I never loved you?"

"Is it love to tell all your friends you mean to bring me up to scratch by the end of the London Season? To flaunt my attentions to you in the face of even Emily Hastings? To tell the shopkeepers on New Bond Street that I was not quite up to snuff but once in your hands you would shape me to your will?"

Lady Purcell gasped. "Who told you such things?"

"One thing you underestimated, as I believe I have, is how our small society gossips. Do you deny you said these things?"

A tear trickled down her cheek. "But you would have been so much more a gentleman with my guidance."

"You've loved an ideal, Anthea. Not me. Perhaps that is the reason I intend to wed Charlotte Amberley, if she'll have me, because I believe she sees me neither as a man she wants to change nor as a god who has no right to be challenged."

"Marry her?" Lady Purcell queried, aghast. "You mean, she did not fail your test?"

"She showed me how foolish my conduct has been. I owe her a great debt and only hope I have not put myself beyond the pale through this evening's mischief."

"Marry Charlotte Amberley?" Lady Purcell burst

into a trill of laughter. "But how perfect, when you have set everything in train to ruin her father."

"He has ruined himself."

"Pray explain that to your bride. Oh, and one more thing, did you know why she came to Brighton?"

"Do tell me, Anthea," he said in a resigned voice.

"Selena Bosham informed me that Charlotte had come to Brighton for the sole purpose of breaking your heart. What do you think of your little *darling* now?"

"You have told me nothing she did not tell me herself. Anthea, you have been busy about my affairs for far too long. Now, let me give you a hint. Purcell is a good man; but, like most men who are treated with indifference, his affections will eventually stray. May I recommend you put your house in order instead of trying to bring mine down?"

"I don't know what you mean," she responded haughtily. "I am a very good wife to Purcell."

"Does a *good wife* always go about professing her love to another man?"

When Charlotte arrived home beforetimes, she stood in the entrance hall for several minutes as if she could not quite make sense of her surroundings. Her anger had long since been spent in the two-hour drive from Ashurst. But in its stead was a worse phantom, a silent dogged enemy that rode her heart hard—she felt grieved beyond words, beyond speaking, her pain as near the sensation of losing a loved one in death as it could possibly be.

She knew now how completely Stoneleigh had possessed her heart, for though he had used her so cruelly, still the thought of being bereft of his companionship forever somehow seemed a punishment beyond bearing. Even if he had not meant to give her a setdown, as Lady Purcell believed he would, the knowledge that he had, unbeknownst to her, held her up to the ridicule of the *ton* by testing her as he might a new horse he had bought was unforgivable.

She felt her throat constrict with tears and she swallowed hard, holding them back. Time enough to cry, she thought disjointedly, but not now. All she wanted now was to sleep; and tomorrow she could begin redirecting her thoughts and her life. She would set Stoneleigh behind her, of course. But where to go from here, when she left her heart behind her as well?

It was some time, so lost in her own thoughts was she, before Charlotte realized she was not alone in the house, but that apparently her father was entertaining a friend. Laughter erupted suddenly from upstairs as Sir John's footsteps sounded in the hallway above. His voice boomed down the stairwell, though Charlotte could still not see him. "We shall visit the linen-draper's tomorrow and purchase some brightly colored silk—orange and red is quite the mode, I believe. What do you say? A turban with a jaunty tassel, an embroidered vest, Moroccan slippers?"

Charlotte wondered who her father could be speaking to and knew by the fading of his voice that he was heading in the direction of his chambers. She was about to ascend the stairs when a sharp rapping sounded on the door. At the same moment, Puckley appeared, seeming quite confused by the sight of her.

"Are you still waiting here, then, Miss?" he asked, bewildered that she had not left the entrance hall upon her arrival.

"It must seem odd, I know. But, pray, pay me no heed. There is someone at the door."

"Yes, Miss. I'll see to it now."

He then straightened his powdered wig and opened the door just enough to peek his head through. She wondered who would be calling at so late an hour. It was obvious by the butler's discreet conduct he was not expecting anyone either.

A moment later, the servant closed the door holding a sealed letter in his hands. He looked at it for a moment and then glanced at Charlotte. "For your father, Miss."

Charlotte extended her hand toward him and took the letter. "I'll see that he gets it. Thank you, Puckley."

"Very good. The messenger indicated it was of some urgency."

When Charlotte began ascending the stairs, Puckley called to her. "Miss, I feel you ought to know that Sir John is not alone—he is entertaining my Lord Thaxted."

"Thaxted?" she queried, surprised. "Are you sure?"

"Yes, Miss. I've served your father a very long time and have lived in Brighton all my life. I would know his lordship anywhere."

"Yes, of course. Thank you." Charlotte watched the servant disappear down the hall and continued her ascent.

Thaxted. How very curious.

Thirty-five

Charlotte reached the threshold of the drawing room holding her tulle and rose-silk gown in one hand and the letter for her father in the other. She was struck at once by the musty smell in the air.

A large, ornately decorated and bejeweled box, full of snuff, sat on the pedestal table inlaid with brass and explained the presence of such a strong odor. Fine powdery grains could be seen on the lip of the gold box and in a light dusting on the polished wood. Glancing about the chamber, she noted that three bottles of Madeira graced the table of zebra wood near the windows—two empty and the third but partially consumed.

The drawing room, which appeared so light and classical during the day, seemed now to have taken on an entirely different ambience, particularly because of the snuff, the wine, and the fact that only two candelabra, bearing five candles each, had been lit. The chamber was dark, the shadows tall on the walls, and the portrait of Sir John over the mantel commanding.

She wondered where Thaxted was; and when her footfall made a squeak on the wood floor as she stepped into the chamber, he startled her by shooting bolt upright to a sitting position from the gold-and-white-striped couch nearest her.

"My goodness!" she cried, taking a step backward.

"I knew someone was there," he said, the red lines on his cheeks and nose more pronounced than ever. "To my knowledge, Miss Amberley, you were not expected back until quite late. I apologize, therefore, for my state of undress." He stood up; and Charlotte saw that he was lacking his coat, his neckcloth, and his shoes, but otherwise was fully clothed. He began donning his apparel as he spoke, starting first with his neckcloth, winding it around his neck carefully.

"Tell me how you found Ashurst," he began easily, as if he were used to conversing with ladies while putting on his clothes. "Though it is a full ten bedchambers short of my own house in Hampshire, I don't believe another mansion in the south of England can compare with the wonders Mr. Repton worked on the gardens. It is a country house transformed to a palace."

"Indeed, I found the whole of it to be quite magnificent," Charlotte responded, turning her gaze away from him. "It is groomed to perfection, and I certainly could find no fault with either the grounds or the house itself."

He paused as he began the intricate task of tying his neckcloth. "But perhaps a flaw or two with its master?" he offered hopefully.

Ordinarily, she would have ignored such a provocative query, but her disposition toward Stoneleigh of the moment was such—and Lord Thaxted's demeanor so engaging as he resumed tying his neckcloth—that she chose to respond, instead, "The master is indeed flawed."

She tapped the letter against the palm of her hand and glanced at it curiously. She wondered whom it was from and why its contents were said to be urgent.

Lord Thaxted had completed a fairly tolerable arrangement of his neckcloth—which he checked in a mirror beside the fireplace—and tugged on his shirtpoints. "So, are you disappointed in love, then? Or merely disgusted with Stoneleigh's methods of determining the worthiness of his women?"

"You know of his absurdity?" she queried, advancing into the room, again tapping the letter against the open palm of her hand.

He gave a mild snort of disgust. "Everyone of consequence in Brighton is aware of this folly. If I were on more amicable terms with Stoneleigh, I should have recommended he not proceed with his habitual scheme, for I knew you would not like it. Did you not, yourself, give me a proper setdown?" He turned toward her and slipped his black coat off the edge of a dark-blue silk-damask chair next to him.

Shrugging into it, he smiled kindly upon her.

She wondered if she had been as mistaken in her initial impression of Thaxted as she most surely had been in Stoneleigh. She thought anything possible at this point and so responded, "I very frequently offer my opinions before they are properly founded. I hope you will forgive me if I spoke unkindly to you."

"I assure you, I have forgotten all about it," he replied. "Do you care for a glass of Madeira?"

"Yes, thank you," she said. Charlotte took up a seat on the very sofa he had quit just a few minutes earlier. She turned her gaze to the grate, finding it cold and empty, a fire serving no purpose in the warmer summer months. She looked into it, seeing her heart and feeling as though every limb had become as leaden and as useless as the cold stone of the fireplace.

"Where is my father?" she ventured, again turning the letter over in her hand.

"What have you there?" Thaxted queried, pouring out a glass of wine for her.

"I haven't the faintest notion. It is for Papa and arrived but a moment ago. The messenger told Puckley that it was of some importance."

"How very curious," he commented, handing her the wine. He buttoned his coat and turned to begin looking under furniture for his slippers. "Ah, there they are," he murmured, dropping to his knees to retrieve his shoes from beneath the pianoforte. "Of some importance, eh? How very intriguing. But then, your father has been telling me that he has a business exploit he hopes to embark upon in the coming months—that is, of course, if he can secure a joint-stock charter from Parliament. I have been telling him I should be happy to use my influence however I might in seeing his company approved."

Charlotte watched the marquis ease into his leather slippers. "You will?" she queried. "How very kind of you."

"Your father is an admirable man, the very best of gentlemen, and has helped me out of more than one scrape, let me tell you. But mum for that! Ah, I hear him now."

Lord Thaxted moved smoothly toward the zebra-wood table and began refilling his own glass with Madeira, when Sir John's voice could be heard booming down the hall. "I hear every Dey has a harem of the fattest, prettiest women he can steal and increases the size of their flesh by feeding them bread dripping with honey. What the devil do you mean by waving your hands about? What are you trying to—oh, I say, Charlotte! My dear! Whatever are you doing here?"

Charlotte could make no sense of what she had just heard him say and supposed he was referring to something he had read. *Arabian Nights*, perhaps. But whatever the case, somehow the sight of him—carrying his favorite jar of Nut Brown snuff—was such a familiar figure that all her hurt seemed to rush in on her at once.

"Oh, Papa, he—he is a monster!" She was on her feet and, after setting her wine on a small table near the coach, hurried toward her father.

Sir John did not hesitate to catch her up in his arms. "What did he do!" he cried. "By God, I shall have his head if he harmed you in the smallest way! I shouldn't have permitted you to become associated with the Hastings or with that devil. Only tell me what he has done to you?"

Charlotte took a deep breath, pressing back a sob which constricted her chest. "He treated me like a horse he meant to purchase at auction, and then Lady Purcell came and told me he had done the same to her and that I would very soon receive his famous setdown which both Maude and Selena received at his hand. I detest him, Papa. He is cruel and deceptive and utterly wicked. I should have known when you were duelling with him at Longreves that he was not as innocent as he appeared, that you were not wholly to blame for the incident as Lord Purcell seemed to think."

"There, there," he soothed her, leading her back to the couch, where he insisted she reseat herself. He put her glass back in her hand. "A sip or two will restore your spirits. There, there, that's a good girl. Well, never you mind about Stoneleigh. If the truth be known, I am glad it is ended, for you are well out of it. What's that, Thaxted?"

"I don't mean to interrupt, but your daughter has a letter for you."

"From Stoneleigh?" Sir John asked, surprised.

"No, Papa," Charlotte said and pointed to the letter which, in her haste to be comforted by him, she had let slip to the floor. "There it is, under the other couch."

Sir John stared at it for a moment, then cried, "Good God! I have been expecting word from a shipping firm in Italy. This must be it!"

He fairly leaped for it, picking it up and breaking the seal. His countenance underwent a startling change; his face, which had been a burnished red from the evening's amusements thus far, turned the color of the chalk cliffs to the north and south of Brighton.

"What is it, Amberley?" Thaxted asked in a low voice.

"I—I don't know. This is very odd. You and I have been joking about purchasing a fleet of corsairs and setting up trade on the Barbary Coast, but look what my spies have sent me. Someone is trying to undermine our—that is, *my* real intent. It would seem the Rothschild house is convinced I've been consorting with the Dey of Tunis, that I intend to outfit him with a dozen ships. Of all the nonsensical starts—" He broke off for a moment, his blue eyes opening wide as if he suddenly comprehended the whole of it. "Damme, but if I don't know what it is. Stoncleigh! He vowed to destroy me, and this is clearly how he means to do it. He's told a pack o' lies to the Rothschilds and now they are setting it about as the truth. If the Prince hears of this, my Charter is finished and Stoneleigh damn well knows it!"

Thirty-six

"I believe I know what might be done," Lord Thaxted said. "But I prefer a word alone with you, Sir John—that is, if you wouldn't mind, Miss Amberley."

"Of course not," Charlotte responded, only half-listening to the men anyway. They had been discussing the horrific nature of Sir John's current crisis for several minutes; and, partly due to the wine and partly because she was greatly fatigued, she had very soon stopped hearing any of it. Their suspicions that Stoneleigh was behind the lies being told of her father she didn't know whether to believe or not.

When the two men quit the drawing room, her thoughts turned quite naturally to the viscount. She tucked her knees up onto the cushions and, leaning her head onto the back of the couch, began to review in quick succession every moment of their relationship from the accident outside the clock shop to the precise second she had fled his home just a few hours ago. She let her mind run about at random, scurrying to whichever memory called to her first—whether it was the time she had thought she was being kissed by a butterfly or the stupid manner in which he had spoken to her on the Steyne and had behaved so uncivilly to her or the way he had looked at her when she had ranged herself beside Mrs. Burnell and rebuked him for overlooking that good lady's qualities. She certainly could not respect his conduct on more than one occasion, but did any of his incivilities or disregard for her sentiments indicate that he would be so unscrupled as to actually start a rumor, such as her father believed he had, in order to ruin him?

She didn't know what to think.

She closed her eyes. How her heart ached, dully, persistently, painfully.

"Charlotte," her father said, placing his hand upon her shoulder and startling her. "I must speak with you."

She looked up at him, unaware he had returned to the drawing room, and wiped away a tear she had not even known had trickled down her cheek. He had not been gone much above five minutes, and she was surprised he had come back so quickly. He stood in front of her, an expression of grave concern on his face.

"What is it?" she asked. "Where is Lord Thaxted?"

"He awaits me in my library belowstairs but has sent me on a mission to you of some import. You see, we—that is, I—have great need of your help. You succeeded for me before, and I believe you can do so again. Thaxted has agreed to help me through this most pressing crisis and has suggested a very simple remedy to my difficulty. You do understand that Stoneleigh has mounted a slanderous campaign against me, setting it about that I mean to engage in the white slave trade along the Mediterranean?"

"I know that is what you believe, but are you sure? Is there not some other explanation for the letter you received? Another individual who might wish to do you harm? You know that I am grievously disappointed in Stoneleigh, but I am not fully persuaded he would do something so vile."

Sir John was quiet for a moment, taking up a place beside her on the gold-and-white couch. "Whether or not he is the author of this rumor, I cannot say. But one thing I do know for certain—he will be receiving word from the Rothschilds regarding these allegations, just as I received word from my associates. Charlotte, I don't know if I should tell you as much, but my debts are considerably more than I at first admitted."

At that, Charlotte sat up very straight, her heart beginning to thrum in her ears. "More than twenty thousand pounds?" She remembered what Lady Purcell had told her, that Henry could pursue a naval career since it appeared he would need to support himself somehow. She swallowed hard. "Pray tell me the whole of it, Papa. Holding nothing back, I beg of you."

"It is nearly seventy, now."

"No," she cried in disbelief, shaking her head, not wanting to credit the figure he had just stated. "No, Papa. You must be mistaken."

"Why do you think I have been reduced to engaging in trade—or at least attempting to?"

Charlotte felt ill, her thoughts spinning and spinning, first thinking of Amberley Park being lost to Henry forever; then how—through the difficult years since her mother's death—all her labors would be for nought, since the entire time her father had been gambling away his fortune; then her extreme gratitude that her own inheritance, coming to her through her mother's portion, had been kept separate from her father's.

"Rouge et noir," she murmured.

"Yes," he said, barely audibly.

Charlotte looked at the man sitting beside her. His eyes were red-rimmed from having imbibed so much wine during the course of the evening. His gaze was fixed on his hands, clasped loosely together on his lap; his shoulders were slumped, his brow creased with worry.

He looked very old to her all of a sudden.

"I don't know how the figure grew to be so large," he said, obviously bemused. "Some years it was hardly anything—and others, topping ten thousand. But this year, I seemed to have lost complete perspective until it was too late. Thaxted helped me more than once and finally suggested I do as all our ancestors must have done at one time, I suppose—engage in trade of some sort. I never meant to let things come to such a pass as this and now, when I think of Henry—dear God!" He buried his face in his hands and shuddered several times.

When at last he lifted his head, his face was wet with tears. "I've been wholly improvident. But Charlotte, you must help me. It is the only way!"

Charlotte had listened carefully to everything her father had said. He was not the first, nor would he be the last, to lose a fortune at the whims of chance. She took a deep breath, knowing that this was a time neither for lectures nor for recriminations. "If you wish me to *distract* Stoneleigh again, Papa, I tell you now I could not do it. I don't believe I could bear being in the same room with him—at least not for a time. I have had only one thought these past two hours—to return to Amberley."

"There will be no Amberley Park for you to return to, Charlie, unless I can come about. But I don't expect you to approach Stoneleigh in public. Could you perhaps be in the same coach with him, with no eyes upon you and the darkness of night to cloak your animosity toward him? Could you, as I desperately need you to do, lead Stoneleigh to a farmhouse near Lewes? I mean only to detain him for a night and a day that I might gain an audience with His Royal Highness and lay my case before him—before Stoneleigh can ruin any hope I have of succeeding."

"You want me to kidnap him?" she asked, stunned.

He smiled faintly. "I hadn't thought of it like that; but, yes, I suppose I do. But nothing to signify, I assure you, only a night and a day. Perhaps two, if Prinny is fully engaged. But I'm certain I shan't require more than that."

"Won't he seek some sort of revenge once he is set free?"

"Although he might wish to do so, my guess is that no one would take seriously his charges that a young lady had kidnapped him against his will."

"I see what you mean," Charlotte answered, thinking there was an amusing aspect to the idea of her actually kidnapping the viscount. "Will I be expected to stay with him?"

"Of course not," Amberley responded aghast. "I shall be waiting for you to arrive, and you and I shall return together to Brighton."

"Who then will guard him?"

"Thaxted has servants he trusts to perform that duty. But never you mind. We will attend to everything. All you must do is get him to the farmhouse."

"I don't know what to think, Papa. Kidnapping! Merciful heavens, we could all perish at Tyburn Tree attempting such an outrageous scheme."

"Where Stoneleigh is concerned, I have no compunction at all in serving him this hand. He deserves far worse, if for no other reason than for treating you so badly at his home. But do understand. If we do not act and Stoneleigh persuades the Prince that my venture is not only un-

274

sound but against the moral conscience of every blue-blooded Englishman, I have no hope of ever restoring the Amberley fortune. What then will little Henry do? What will he think of his poor papa?"

If Charlotte were wavering heretofore, the knowledge that unless she acted, Henry's future would be forever blighted decided her resolve. "I will do it," she stated firmly. "If not for my own sake or yours, then for Henry's. He has done nothing to deserve being cheated out of his birthright because of Stoneleigh's mischief. Now tell me what you require of me?"

At dawn's light, Stoneleigh was awakened by his valet, who shoved a tear-stained missive beneath his nose and said that there was a terrible uproar in the entrance hall. Sir John Amberley's man was refusing to leave Ashurst until he had received an answer to the letter he delivered.

"It is from Miss Amberley," his valet stated at last, holding the sealed letter directly beneath Stoneleigh's nose. The faint scent of lilacs took the last vestige of sleep from about Stoneleigh's brain.

He sat up quickly and broke the seal. "Tell Sir John's man I will have an answer for him directly," he said.

Stoneleigh did not know what to expect, but somewhere in his heart he had hoped for an apology from Charlotte for having quit his home so abruptly, leaving his guests to speculate far into the night precisely what had caused the lady he was pursuing to run from his house.

The dinner afterward and the ball had been the singularly most painful experience of his life thus far. He had been obliged as host to do the pretty with every lady present, and it seemed to him that at least a dozen of them had been waiting for this evening for a long time.

Served with your own sauce rang in his ears until he was ready to behead the next person who dared speak such impertinences to him.

Fortunately, Emily had rescued his failing sensibilities and restored his confidence in the goodness of his own character by pointing out that he could make up for his errant ways by spending the next few years as Charlotte's husband—providing he could persuade her to wed him—and doing everything he could to make her happier than even the angels could. Emily told him that she believed Charlotte was deeply in love with him and that with a little coaxing and a great deal of humility and consistency of proper conduct on his part, her heart and her trust could be won again.

He was not as certain, especially as he read through the letter and found few words of real encouragement. She spoke of needing desperately to speak with him, *privately*—underscored three times—and wishing to do so by having him escort her at night, in her father's town coach, to her aunt's house near Lewes. He could not recall her having spoken of possessing an aunt, nonetheless one residing near Lewes.

The letter continued, *would he please oblige her?* There was some sinister reference to her belief that her father had fallen under the influence of a very *bad man* and that she required his advice in knowing precisely how to manage what was proving to be an impossible situation. At the very end of her missive, she begged he refrain from speaking to anyone about her father's affairs until she had had an opportunity of laying the matter before him.

He left his bed and, after slipping on a purple brocade dressing gown, seated himself at a small desk in his bedchamber and began to write. After a few minutes, he had composed two letters—one to Charlotte and the other to Harry.

Charlotte read the letter, her heart pounding in her ears.

My dearest Charlotte, it began. *You will never know how grateful I am that you turned to me in your hour of need. I am not unaware of your reasons for leaving my home so abruptly last night, nor do I blame you. I was deeply at fault, but I can't entirely regret my actions only because I would not have missed for the world the sight of you supporting excellent Mrs. Burnell against my apparent ignorance of her abilities. Do I trespass on your sense of the absurd when I say that Mrs. Burnell has not let me forget a word of your speeches? She wrote them down in her diary and gave me a copy for my perpetual edification.*

I have waited a long time for a woman of your nobility of spirit to enter my poor existence, and I cherish the hope you will find it in your heart to somehow forgive my utter and complete stupidity in carrying out a scheme as silly as it was cruel.

As for the nature of your request, I will always be ready to lend you my assistance whenever you require it of me and shall be at the crossroads as mentioned in your letter at the appointed hour. Until then, God bless you. My heart is in your hands, Stone-leigh.

"Gammon!" her father cried, after having torn the letter from her hands and read the contents through quickly. "If I thought it were possible, I would think he was hoping to turn you up sweet. Is there no shame in this man?"

He threw the letter in the cold grate, from which Charlotte, once he had quit the room, quickly rescued it.

She read the letter again and felt sick at heart.

In all her anguish over having been ill-used by the man, it had not occurred to her once that he might be penitent. Her father may have spoken of the entire contents being gammon, but she was not so sure.

My heart is in your hands.

Oh, lord, why had everything become so complicated!

Thirty-seven

Charlotte shivered and trembled, then shivered again as she waited within the dark recesses of the coach. The carriage lamp played on the backs of the horses, who were stamping and snorting in the cool night air, anxious to be moving again.

But not more than she.

The hour of the appointed rendezvous wanted only ten minutes, but every second which passed by seemed an eternity. Finally, as she looked through the side window at the road behind her, she saw a flickering light through the hedgerow lining the curved lane. It gradually became more pronounced; but because the night was dark—a dense layer of clouds had obscured the moon and the stars—the road was nearly invisible in the blackness, which made the approaching, bobbing light appear both near yet far away.

She wished now she had not agreed to the desperate scheme.

Kidnapping Stoneleigh.

Had her wits gone-a-begging?

But then, what choices had been left to her? What would become of Henry if her father failed to secure his Charter? All that Sir John needed was time—a day or two at the most—with Stoneleigh hidden away.

Would Stoneleigh know he was being betrayed?

Charlotte turned away from the approaching light. She could hear Stoneleigh's equipage on the road behind her now, the pounding of horses hooves as they pressed against the earth time and again growing louder with each turning of the coach's wheels.

Squeezing her eyes shut, she heard the viscount's postillion call to his horses. She listened to the slowing pace of their hooves, heard the blowing of the team as they now passed slowly by her window. Stoneleigh had arrived.

She pulled the hood of her cherry-velvet cloak close about her face. She could manage well enough, she was sure of that, but only if she didn't have to look at him.

Then she heard his voice as he descended his town coach and issued orders for his postboy to return to Ashurst. She had forgotten how much she was always affected by the deep timbre of his voice. A few seconds more, she thought, her heart beating like the flustered wings of a moth getting too close to a lamp, and he would be with her.

The door flew open, and he spoke, his warm, rich tones filling the small enclosure. "Charlotte, my darling," he said. "Tell me everything. I am so grateful you asked for my assistance. You must know that I would do anything in the world for you."

Charlotte simply stopped breathing. In all her careful plans as she prepared for this rendezvous, she had not given a moment's consideration to the possibility that she could be moved by his voice, by his presence, or by the words he spoke to her. Her anger had been so great, the ache of her heart so profound at his mistreatment of her, that she had somehow, quite ridiculously, thought herself impervious to him. He had put himself beyond the pale with her—and there was nothing more to be said.

But she had not counted on his speaking so urgently to her nor so lovingly.

"Oh, dear," she whispered, lowering her gaze that she might not have to look at him.

My darling.

"Pray—" she began, her voice trembling as she initiated the kidnapping. "Pray command the postillion to put the horses to."

Stoneleigh did so. After closing the door with a snap, he asked, "How far is it to your aunt's home?"

"To my aunt's home?" she queried, wondering what he meant. With a start, she remembered that that was part of the ruse. How could she have forgotten? Goodness, she really must be more careful. "Oh, yes, to my aunt's home. I believe it is nearly five miles."

Charlotte glanced nervously toward him, caught a brief glimpse of blue eyes in the reflected light of the carriage lamps, and looked quickly away. The coach was very dark, and she could not precisely discern what he might be thinking or feeling.

He sought her hand among the folds of her dark-red cloak, but she pulled away from him.

"Please do not," she whispered, as the carriage wheels began to turn and the horses gained their stride, straining in harness. "I hope I have not given you a false notion in asking for your help. I do not seek your affections, only your assistance in an unhappy matter. The truth is, I had no one else I could turn to, otherwise I would never have written to you. That you must believe."

"I see," he responded.

How far had the carriage spun yet along the road—a tenth of a mile? Perhaps. Four and nine-tenths to go. However was she going to bear being in the same carriage with him?

Silence ensued. The brief images of momentarily illuminated hedges, stone walls, and fences came into view like grotesque figures, then disappeared as the horses continued down the highway.

"You are very angry."

Charlotte swallowed hard. "Yes," she responded, wishing she had been able to restrain giving him the truthful answer from her heart.

"You have every right to be, Charlotte," he said. "I realize that now. But would it help you to know that last night was probably the most trying evening of my entire existence and not just because I was bereft of your company?"

Charlotte fingered her velvet cloak, her eyes downcast. "Were you blamed for my having fled your house?" she queried, wondering for the first time what actually happened after she left.

He leaned his head against the squabs. "I received a rather just compensation, I think, for all the years I so wretchedly mistreated the ladies I pursued. At least a dozen women let me know the sum of their opinions of my character and conduct. Did you know that until last night, I truly believed no one was aware of the clever manner in which I *tested* the prospective mistresses of my house? Except Emily, of course. She had known about it for years."

In considering just how she thought the journey to the farmhouse might proceed, Charlotte had planned upon avoiding this subject completely. But learning that he had suffered at the hands of so many unhappy females—and all in one night—changed her intention.

"I cannot pretend that I am sorry you finally received your comeuppance. What I don't understand is whatever possessed you to begin in the first place?"

"I'm not certain precisely. Despair, perhaps," he began quietly, as the carriage swayed along the road. "In all your years since having come out, did a gentleman ever pursue you for your fortune?"

She thought back to the many times young gentlemen of limited means had shown an interest in her. She had been stunned when, during one of her earliest courtships, she had discovered her inheritance had been her singularly most compelling feature. He had been an officer in Wellington's army and had come home from the war lame in his left leg and with no prospects to speak of. She had enjoyed his company immensely and had believed herself falling in love—completely regardless of the disparity of fortune—only to come upon him one day quite by accident embracing a young lady of minuscule dowry. She had turned a corner in Mrs. Bosham's maze of yew hedges and nearly bumped into them.

She had been hurt and terribly disappointed, nonetheless disillusioned, when he explained the true nature of his sentiments—or lack of them—for her. In particular, that her fortune had been the chiefest of her attractions to him.

She had refused to be overset, however, and had viewed the incident in a practical manner, neither blaming the officer for considering her wealth of prime importance nor despising herself for being a woman of independent means and, therefore, the potential object of fortune hunters.

Since that time, however, she had taken greater care in whom she permitted to single her out. "Yes," she responded. "I have had many experiences as you have described."

"I don't mean to sound as if I am justifying my conduct to you, but I wish you will try to understand that my own situation, while similar to your own, is far more complex. My inherited title alone has made me a considerable object among matchmaking mamas. Add to that the fortune with which I was so profoundly blessed, and there came a time when I could no longer discern a lady's genuine interest from a false one. When the precise moment was that I decided to create a sort of test for those ladies who intrigued me the most I can't remember, but it was sometime after Emily married her Colonel. I did not compose such an unhappy stratagem out of a desire to hurt anyone, only from a wish that I could be sure I was marrying a lady whom I could trust, whom I could respect, and whom was not merely pursuing my possessions. Can you understand that?"

Charlotte at last turned toward him and pushed the hood of her cloak slowly away from her face. She took a deep breath before responding, "I suppose no one can truly comprehend what it has been like for you. We each walk about in our own slippers, scarcely ever able to see beyond our own desires. I had never before considered how harsh the Marriage Mart has been to you, season after season, until now. Yet, to have so cruelly raised the hopes of so many ladies only to dash those hopes—have you the smallest notion of the pain you have caused?" She pressed a hand to her heart and held his gaze steadily.

He also turned toward her, and this time she permitted him to take one of her hands within his gentle clasp. "Not until last night, and then I was informed of it to a vengeance." He smiled crookedly. "You would have been pleased if you had heard all the various dressing downs I received."

Charlotte allowed herself to smile in return, however faintly.

When his features began to take on that peculiarly intense look he always wore when he wished to take her in his arms, she shyly withdrew her hand from his and turned away. She might be grateful he had learned some humility, but she still could not trust him. Besides, she had a matter of much greater importance to attend to than the wishes of his heart.

"Am I not forgiven then?" he asked soberly.

"Of course you are forgiven," she said. "It is my Christian duty to *forgive* you."

"But not to forget?"

She looked out the window, watching the shadows of the trotting horses appear and disappear against the shrubs and trees lining the road. How far had they travelled? Two miles yet? Perhaps. Three to go.

She did not want to respond to his last remark and returned to the purpose of their journey. "Thank you for offering your help, Edward. My father, as I mentioned in my letter to you, has fallen under the influence of a very bad man. I was hoping you might be able to—"

He cut her off and stated, "You refer to Thaxted, don't you?"

Charlotte jerked back toward him, startled. Her eyes opened wide as she cried, "But—but how did you know?"

She had meant to lead him by stages, through a variety of carefully concocted whiskers, to the conclusion that the Marquis of Thaxted was the very man. The whole of it would have been an enormous lie which had been designed initially to lure him into the coach with her and later to keep her time with him occupied until they would arrive at the farmhouse.

Since none of it, not even the lie that her father had *fallen under the influence of a very bad man,* contained even a grain of truth she could not credit how it was possible Stoneleigh had known

285

her answer before she had even begun speaking her lies.

It seemed too much a coincidence!

Suddenly, she was afraid, a prescience that she had unwittingly stumbled upon a facet of her father's affairs which had hitherto been hidden from her. What did Stoneleigh know, then, that she did not?

Thirty-eight

"I have many sources, Charlotte, from which I glean information on a great many subjects. And I rarely rely upon just one in forming a judgment. But it would seem your father is in debt to Thaxted for a great deal of blunt. It would therefore follow that the marquis's hold on Sir John is great."

Charlotte felt her complexion pale as the blood rushed from her head. "Whatever do you mean? My father told me he was in debt to the moneylenders. He never said a word about Thaxted. Are you sure?"

In the faint light, Charlotte could see that Stoneleigh was weighing what he ought next to say. "According to one source, the firm holding your father's debts—some sixty thousand pounds— sold the whole of it to Thaxted two months ago."

Charlotte felt all of her resolution where the kidnapping was concerned fly upward once then land flat at the pit of her stomach where it lay motionless.

"This would be a hold, indeed," she replied, stunned. Could Stoneleigh be lying to her? But to what purpose? She could think of none.

"The most powerful hold possible. It is also believed that your father's pursuit of a joint-stock company was Thaxted's idea—that they have formed a partnership, only Thaxted wishes his identity to remain hidden."

The thought that she had intended upon telling a prepared set of lies about her father and the marquis now seemed both absurd and ironic. It had never occurred to her that the two men might have joined together to venture into Trade. However, if it were true Sir John now owed his horrendous debt not to the moneylenders but to Thaxted, she could not help but think that some terrible mischief was afoot. She did not believe her father was guilty of any nefarious intentions himself, but oh, how easily his friendly relationship with the Prince Regent could be turned to commit some evil by a man without scruples.

Her thoughts turned toward her father and Thaxted. The marquis was certainly well-informed on every aspect of her father's company. It seemed likely that matters had fallen just as Stoneleigh had described them.

She then remembered the conviviality with which they had been enjoying themselves only the night before, as if their friendship were of long standing—so at odds with her belief they were but mere acquaintances. She recalled her initial impressions of Thaxted, of her instinct to mistrust him and how he had sneered at her values at Lady Purcell's ball. In her mind's eye she could see the red lines veining his cheeks and brightening his nose, a strong indication of his mode of living. Finally, she remembered vividly his state of undress when she had returned beforetimes to her father's town house and how smoothly he had reclothed himself while in her presence. All confirmed rather than disproved her growing belief that what had begun as a falsehood she had concocted as part of the kidnapping ruse had somehow transformed into the truth.

She experienced the worst numbing sensation that Thaxted had seen her vulnerability when she had returned so completely devastated from Ashurst and at that moment had exploited her wounded heart and pride. She had become his dupe instead of simply a help to her father.

How malevolent were his purposes, then? Were they simply to kidnap Stoneleigh for a day or two as agreed upon? She had *heard* nothing to indicate otherwise.

She remembered how her father had been joking about the Turks before he realized she was present in the drawing room. She wondered if it were possible that the scheme in play, one orchestrated fully to Thaxted's tune, involved trading illegally, unbeknownst to her gullible father, in the Mediterranean.

"What do you know of the Barbary Coast," she asked Stoneleigh.

Again he was silent. The numbing sensation began spreading through her limbs and into her brain. She again felt dizzy.

How far had they travelled now? Three miles and a half? One and a half to go.

"Please, tell me," she said, staring forward and watching the sweat glisten off the flanks of the horses, steam rising from their bodies in the cool night air. "I must know everything."

"My communications indicate that Thaxted has been in contact with Deys of Tunis and Tripoli. Algiers was decimated by Lord Exmouth in '15. But the corsairs still afflict the Mediterranean with their piracy and kidnapping—but only as far as they dare. They don't want to risk a second British bombardment."

"What would Thaxted hope to gain?"

"Many things, I'm sure—power, an increase of wealth—"

"But he already has more than nearly everyone in the kingdom."

"For some, it is never enough. But I believe his motivations go deeper. He thrives on a greater passion than the mere acquisition of wealth—that of the thrill of conquest."

Charlotte shook her head, unwilling to believe what he told her was true. Yet she had no reason to doubt him. He could not gain by maligning Thaxted to her.

"When I returned home after leaving your ball last night," she said, "my father received word through his own associates as he called them that it was generally believed his business venture was a deceptive one—that he meant to set up a false company from which to draw funds and restore the Barbary Coast to its original, powerful state. Papa was horrified and believed you had set it about as a rumor to destroy him, since it was likely once the Prince learned of this rumor he would never use his influence to help my father."

Stoneleigh shook his head, his lips pursed tightly together. "Do you believe as much?" he asked.

"You told me you had vowed to ruin him. Do I have a reason to believe otherwise?"

Stoneleigh looked away from her, a severe frown between his brows. "You have told me, Charlotte, that though you arrived in Brighton with less than honorable intentions toward my heart, you soon found you did not have the necessary will to complete your designs." He looked back at her and held her gaze steadily. "I may have vowed to break Sir John, but I confess I was relieved when I saw that he was accomplishing the deed without the least assistance from me. And now, so many years later, if I were intent upon pursuing *his daughter,* what use could it have been to me to spread about a rumor which, if *she* discovered I had done so, would undoubtedly have set her heart against me forever? I would have been a complete gudgeon to have done something so bird-witted."

Charlotte knew his answer was both reasonable and true. She turned everything over in her mind several times and finally asked, "Why didn't Thaxted go to the Prince himself or exert his own influence in Parliament to gain a Charter? Why make use of Sir John?"

"Prinny is very fond of your father, and there is no love lost between the Prince and Thaxted. As for Parliament, the marquis has never had the ability to hold the affections and support of his peers. He is so universally disliked that had he pursued such a charter himself, he would never have been granted one. Never."

"Whatever my father is, though, he would never have consented to engaging in slavery. My father would not be so inhuman."

"I must bow to your better knowledge of his character," Stoneleigh responded carefully.

"You do not believe me," she cried, surprised.

"Charlotte, did you ever inquire of your father, as I suggested you do, precisely why it was I wished to ruin him?"

Charlotte swallowed hard. "He avoided my questions at every turn. He also told me that he was willing to forgive whatever hardness existed between you for my sake. I suppose I felt I would never get the answer I sought; and since he seemed so content with my growing affections for you, I believed, I hoped, all would be settled regardless of the nature of your quarrel."

Stoneleigh let out a long sigh and for a time only the steady clip-clop of the horses's hooves could be heard.

Charlotte waited, sensing the tension emanating from the man beside her. She again looked out the window at the odd shadows playing on the hedges, shrubs, and grassy stretches alongside the road. More than four miles had surely been accomplished by now. She felt she ought soon to reveal the true nature of the journey to Stoneleigh in the bald face of everything he had told her. Once arrived at the farmhouse, she thought it would be wise—particularly since Thaxted would not be present—for the three of them to discuss the possibility of the marquis's duplicity where her father and the Charter was concerned. For the moment, however, she waited.

When at last Stoneleigh spoke, he sounded relieved. "Given my feelings for you, Charlotte, I think it best you be informed of what happened four years ago that caused my heart to be set firmly against your father. About a year after your mother's death, Sir John fell into the clutches of the moneylenders for the first time, having accrued a figure near fifteen thousand by all accounts."

"He said as much to me last night," Charlotte responded. "Though the figure he recalled was not quite as high."

"It would seem by all appearances that he was kept reasonably free of excess by the stability of your mother's presence. Once her steadying influence was removed, his true nature asserted itself.

"Perhaps."

"At any rate," here he paused and took a deep breath, "he attempted to solve his difficulty by persuading my sister to elope with him. Besides being a great heiress, she is also mentally unbalanced. I have not been able to forgive him for that—it was not the act of a gentleman."

"Dear God, not Elizabeth!" she cried, shocked yet again, tears starting to her eyes. "How could he have done so? Emily told me of her—of her

292

indisposition. But my father to have—oh, Edward, I am so sorry. It is no wonder—I would not expect you to feel other than you do. I understand everything now and am most horridly ashamed."

"You have nothing to be ashamed of. We do not choose our parents."

"He is my father."

"That you happened to be related to him is a matter of chance, not of guilt. I won't hear you blame yourself. Only tell me this, Charlotte, do you now understand why my anger has burned so strongly against him?"

"Of course I do," she cried. "I only wonder now how you were able to invite me to Ashurst at all, nonetheless decide I was worthy enough for you to test in the first place."

He slipped his arm around her shoulders and caressed her face with his free hand. "Pray do not put me in mind of my folly. I only wish you had stayed a little longer and that Lady Purcell had not so *kindly* informed you of my intentions. Perhaps then, this visit to *your aunt* would not have been necessary at all. Only tell me this, why did you leave? Why didn't you stay and hear what it was I wished to say to you?"

She glanced up at him, wondering if he suspected her motives had not been entirely pure in requesting his assistance. She wanted to tell him the truth, especially when he was smiling down at her so tenderly. Instead, she answered his question, since her heart was still heavy with this particular aspect of the evening before. "I left your home because I wished to avoid receiving your famous setdown as Lady Purcell said I would. I suppose it was the final part of your examination, but I couldn't bear the thought of giving you the pleasure of delivering it."

He groaned and shut his eyes for a long moment. "Yes, my, er, *famous setdown.*"

"Precisely."

"I was harried quite persistently on that point alone last night until I was sick to death of it. I had hoped never to hear of it again, and so it seems a wonderful irony that I hear it next fall from your lips."

"Can you blame me then for leaving?"

"No," he said, looking back at her, his lips twitching. "But would you believe me if I told you I had had no intention of delivering that setdown?"

Charlotte felt bemused. Had he concocted another, more difficult test for her to pass? "What had you meant to do then," she said, "if not give me a setdown? Was there some greater trial I would next have been required to endure?" She could think of nothing worse.

His smile was one of sweet irony as he chuckled softly, all the while gently stroking her cheek. "I daresay it would have been a most wretched trial had you agreed to it, since my intention last night had been nothing less than to beg for your hand in marriage."

Thirty-nine

Charlotte was stunned, her face feeling as though a thousand tiny needles were prickling her skin all at once. She did not credit her ears and so queried, "To beg for my hand in marriage?"

"Yes," he responded quietly, running his thumb gently over her lips. "To drop to my knees at your feet, to confess my profound admiration for you, to admit that I have loved you from the moment I picked you up from the sidewalk on that first day and held you in my arms."

"Not a setdown?" she again asked, unwilling to believe what he was saying, aware in the vaguest part of her mind that four miles and more of the brief journey had undoubtedly been concluded.

"Not a setdown," he reiterated. "Will you marry me, Charlotte? Will you let me restore Henry's future to him? I am quite able to do so, if you are not yet aware of my worth. Will you serve as mistress over my estates? Will you share my future and bring me that happiness I am come to believe only you can give? I am not deserving of it—I know as much. I have deceived you and treated you cruelly, but I do indeed repent and promise to spend the remainder of my days proving my heart to you—as well as my re-formed character."

The coach began to slow, though Charlotte was scarcely aware of it. Her attention was riveted to the expression on Stoneleigh's face, however faint it was in the dark recesses of the coach, to the intensity of his eyes which reflected a hunger she seemed to respond to so readily. He leaned toward her, his breath on her cheek, "Will you forgive me?" he whispered, as the coach came to a stop.

He did not wait for a reply, but placed his lips on hers and kissed her thoroughly.

Charlotte's thoughts, concerns, wickedness disappeared with his touch, with the strength of his embrace, with the wondrous sweetness of his lips. She forgot everything save how much she loved him and wanted him and desired to become his wife. The soft warmth of his mouth as he nestled his lips against hers awoke within her deep and profound longings. She loved him, more than life itself. She was part of him and had been so, perhaps just as he had said, from the moment she had awakened outside the clock shop to find herself held securely in his arms.

She clutched at his arms hungrily with her hands, pulling on the fabric of his sleeves, then wildly slipped her own arms about his neck. She held to him tightly, returning kiss for kiss, her heart given completely. After a long moment, she drew back from him slightly, but only that she might express the depths of her sentiments for him. "Edward, I love you," she whispered. "I always shall." She heard the soft groan in his throat and received his kisses yet again, embracing him fully in return, dreading the moment he would release her.

With a start, she heard the carriage door open. Releasing Stoneleigh, the reality of her actions

296

flowed in upon her like a monstrous wave breaking heavily upon the beach.

"No!" she cried, at the sight of a large, unknown man who appeared suddenly in the doorway of the coach. "It is all a mistake! Stop I say!"

The next moment, as seconds split into halves then fourths, all of which seemed to extend into time and smash it apart, she watched Stoneleigh begin to turn around just as the man lifted a large club and brought it crashing down on the side of his head. He fell forward, slumping into her with a moan, to lie motionless on her lap.

"You've killed him!" she cried, then turned her recriminations on herself. "Oh, dear God, what have I done?"

Sir John threw the door wide and jostled the burly man next to him. "What is going forward here? What happened? Good God, man, you hit him! Charlotte, is he all right? See if you can feel his heart beating."

Charlotte shoved her hand beneath his chest, which was pressed heavily into her lap. She twisted her wrist about awkwardly until she reached the center of his chest. With a huge sigh of relief, she felt the beating of his heart. "Thank God, he's alive. Papa, whatever is the meaning of this? Did you order him to be struck over the head?"

"No," he said, as though he, too, were bewildered. "I would never have done so."

"It seemed necessary," a strong, masculine voice intruded.

Sir John whirled around and gave a start. "Thaxted! But you weren't supposed to be here."

Lord Thaxted laughed, a sound that penetrated into the small confines of the travelling coach and brought a shiver of fear racing down Charlotte's neck. She looked past her father and saw the figure of the marquis standing nearby. He wore a many-caped greatcoat and a beaver hat pressed low on his head. Behind him, grotesque and haunting in the dancing light of several blazing rushes, the ruins of an ancient stone farmhouse could be seen.

"I have waited a dozen years for just this moment," Lord Thaxted explained. "Revenge can be a wonderful thing, eh Amberley? But first, we must dispose of our quarry." He drew near to the coach and, leaning his head in, he smirked at Charlotte and her evident concern for Stoneleigh. "Do not bother your head about his safety, I don't mean to take his life, merely to send him on a little voyage."

"A voyage? On a ship?" she cried, startled. "But where?"

Thaxted laughed again. "Let us just say in a southerly direction." He then turned and ordered his henchmen to remove Stoneleigh to Amberley's coach.

"Don't come near him!" Charlotte cried. "Postillion, drive on! Return to Brighton immediately!"

When the postillion turned around and tipped his cap to her but remained astride the horse, Charlotte became convinced she was in the midst of a nightmare. "I can't do that, Miss," he said. "I take me orders from Lord Thaxted."

Two men shoved Sir John aside, one of them, faceless in the gloom, reached in and, with a pair of massive hands, pulled Stoneleigh from her lap. He was then carried to her father's conveyance—a hired post-chaise from Brighton—and summarily dumped inside.

Thaxted then turned and gave the order for the coach to be gone.

Charlotte watched the carriage pull into the lane which led to the King's Highway, the darkness of the night soon swallowing up the last vista of quickly spinning wheels. She felt a sickness sweep through her as she had never before experienced, a combination of helplessness and fear that turned her stomach over and over again.

"No," she breathed. "Papa, do something. Please help him."

She leaned her head through the open doorway of her coach and, because Sir John was standing near her vehicle, she tugged on his sleeve hoping to gain his attention. He was turned away from her, watching the sight of his hired coach departing toward Lewes.

When he finally turned toward Charlotte, she was horrified by the look in his eye, which was one of utter shock and disbelief. "They've taken him away, Charlie," he said faintly. "Why are they doing that?"

"Papa, please—speak with Thaxted. These must be his designs. He is your friend—" Here she broke off, remembering all that Stoneleigh had told her but a few minutes ago. She understood suddenly that both she and Sir John had been pawns in the larger game of Thaxted's making— and she had been the necessary lure to bring Stoneleigh within the power of his grasp.

"It is all so perfect," Thaxted began by way of explanation, directing his remarks to Charlotte. "Particularly when the entire *beau monde* knew that you had left Stoneleigh's house in high dudgeon." He sighed with satisfaction as he signaled to a nearby lackey. "The rumors will run rife, and how will you explain any of it, Miss Amberley— you who value honesty, uprightness, and kindness above all things? What were you doing meeting with Stoneleigh clandestinely? Did you lead him into a trap of some sort? And after he killed your father, naturally he had to flee the country."

"But he has killed no one!" Charlotte cried.

"Papa, tell me what to do? What is he speaking of?"

The servant who stepped forward at Thaxted's bidding held two swords. Thaxted first divested himself of his greatcoat, his hat, and his coat, before taking both swords in his hands. He then tossed one sword to Sir John, who caught it but immediately pointed it into the uneven gravel in front of him. The drive in front of the farmhouse was in considerable disrepair, grass and weeds sticking up through the gravel and small holes ready to trip the unwary.

He seemed unable to move or to speak for a long moment as he stared first in horror at the sword then slowly lifted his gaze to meet Thaxted. "I counted you friend," he began. "Do you mean to tell me you arranged everything in order to dispose of Lord Stoneleigh?"

"Not such a simpleton after all, eh?" he queried sarcastically.

"But why? What has he done to you?"

Lord Thaxted tested his sword and began stretching his muscles. Charlotte watched a veil cloak his eyes. His lips pinched together firmly as he responded, "I detest him. I always have. Everything he touches turns to gold. He was even able to win Emily's confidence. For a while I thought they would wed. It was fortunate for him that she chose her Colonel instead, for I would surely have killed him."

"You are jealous," Charlotte stated simply.

Thaxted glanced at her in mild surprise. He chuckled faintly. "Yes, I suppose I am."

"But is that reason enough to wish to ruin him or—or to slay my father?"

"Do I need another?" was his cold response.

"I won't fight you, Thaxted," Sir John said, glowering at the marquis. "Think man, have you gone mad? What purpose does any of this serve?

300

What of our agreement, the debt I owe you, the Charter, and our company by which we will both make our fortunes?"

In this one statement, Charlotte heard most of what Stoneleigh had told her confirmed—the men had been in league together for some time, but not on a simple business venture as Sir John had believed.

"The Rothschilds have learned of my scheme," Thaxted said, flexing his sword with the tip of his finger, then whipping the thin, narrow blade through the air. "Did you think we could really persuade Prinny that ours was a shipping concern hoping to trade in silks and spices?"

"But—but that's what we were going to do."

Thaxted merely laughed. "You are such a gullible sapskull. I could have bought a shipping firm of my own if I had wished for it. No, I wanted something a trifle more adventuresome. At times I think I ought to have been born a pirate and commandeered my own light corsair." He sighed before continuing. "I suppose there was a small chance I still could have succeeded—the Rothschilds or not—but unlikely. Besides, I have something of greater value now tucked away in your coach." He bowed meaningfully to Charlotte.

"My daughter?" Sir John asked, astounded. "But this is absurd, all of it! It must be a joke, only I don't find it very amusing. Thaxted, put away your sword and tell me what is really going on."

"Do you know how much I despise you, Sir John?"

"But I counted you friend—you helped me settle my debts—we made plans—"

"And the first moment you could, you lost another thousand at Donaldson's. You're nothing more than a flat among sharps. But you've served my purposes beyond expectation and now, if you've an ounce of bottom left—though I sincerely doubt it, you'll face me squarely and be done with it. Consider this the payment for your debts. At least then your precious Henry will be left with something—I certainly would not demand sixty thousand pounds from an orphan." He laughed again, before ending with, "Especially since he will very soon become my brother-in-law."

Sir John needed no further provocation. Shifting his sword from hand to hand, he took off his coat in quick, angry movements. Charlotte watched rage fill his body, beginning with the clenching of his fists and rising through the rigid flexing of his arms up his neck to flood his face. His eyes narrowed painfully, and his complexion flushed a dark red. "You bastard!" he cried, lunging at Thaxted with a powerful thrust.

Thaxted easily fended off the strong but awkward attack, his blade meeting Amberley's in a sliding rasp.

Charlotte felt at any moment she might be sick but swallowed hard and leaned her head next to the doorjamb. She watched the men move in a horrible dance, blade sliding against blade, all against the rushlights. The house beyond was blank with darkness and served only to reflect their lunging shadows high up to the second-floor windows.

Thaxted had the advantage of superior skill, and the whole time he thrust and parried only to thrust again he laughed lightly. He pinked Sir John over and over—on the cheek, on his hands, which were soon dripping with blood, and on his legs. His buff breeches were lanced in several places and blood welled up in clownish pools onto the fine, doeskin leather.

Sir John began to tire, his movements becoming more and more lumbering. Several times, he stepped into the holes pitting the gravelled drive, crying out as his ankles bore each painful twist. Always he rose quickly, fending off another thrust of Thaxted's sword.

Charlotte's heart ached with a fear like none she had ever known. She watched her father do battle unequally for his life and saw with each gradually faltering movement against the marquis's better skill, his abilities diminish. He was breathing heavily, sweat pouring from his brow.

Thaxted stopped smiling, his laughter ceased. "You will have been thought to have been killed by Stoneleigh," he reiterated, tapping away Sir John's now desperately poor thrusts. "And it will become known he fled the country to avoid hanging. How perfect."

With that, Thaxted's sword found home, driving deep into Amberley's right side. Charlotte heard him grunt and cry out before he fell heavily to the ground. Thaxted withdrew his sword slowly, a smile of great satisfaction on his face.

"You monster!" Charlotte whispered, doing everything she could to keep from being sick. "I shall have your head."

Thaxted quickly crossed the distance between them and catching her cloak at the throat pulled her forcefully to him and placed a hard kiss on her lips. She struggled against him until she felt herself flung backward onto the squabs.

With a laugh, he called for his horse. Several outriders brought him his white gelding. He quickly mounted his horse and with a single backward glance at Sir John lying on the weeds and the gravel, he lightly kicked his horse's flanks and drew near Charlotte's postilion.

Thaxted looked at Charlotte and delivered his orders, "Take her to my home in Hampshire. Give her over to my housekeeper. She will know what to do with her." To Charlotte, he said, "You will enjoy being my wife, I think." And in a cloud of spewing gravel, Thaxted and his henchmen swirled out of the drive.

The postillion kicked his horse hard, causing the tired steed to rear up slightly in his harness. The postboy cursed him twice, then gentled him. But when the wheels began to spin, Charlotte quickly leaped for the door and jumped from the coach. She landed hard, falling to her knees, but remained uninjured. She hurried to her father, where she nearly fell on top of him. He was still hunched over and moaning. "Papa, tell me how bad your wound is?"

Behind her, she heard the postillion cursing. "You 'eard the master's orders, Miss. Come wi' me."

She felt his hands hard upon her shoulders and she struggled to fling him off, but he was very strong and he was soon dragging her backward.

"I'll tie you up if I 'ave to."

"I'll not go with you!" she cried. "I'll die first. What sort of man are you to treat a lady like a beast?"

He laughed, having gotten a strong hold on her cloak, and was easily clearing the distance to her travelling coach. "A well-paid scoundrel, nothing more."

When he opened the door to the carriage, with Charlotte still struggling in a prone position, another figure suddenly appeared from behind the coach. He stepped over Charlotte and cocked a pistol in the henchman's ear. "Let her go, very gently, or I'll be more than happy to blow your ear off."

"Harry!" Charlotte cried. "Thank God you've come. But how did you get here? How did you know?"

"Stoneleigh suspected some mischief was afoot. I've followed all the way. What happened to Sir

304

John? I could see very little and worked hard to remain hidden until I knew I could be of use."

Charlotte quickly rose to her feet and explained all that had gone forward. At the same time, she hurried toward her father. Over her shoulder, she continued, "But I don't know where they've taken Stoneleigh."

"I heard one of Thaxted's men speaking. They are taking him to Lewes, where a convict ship is waiting to set sail on the morning tide for New South Wales. If we are to save your father and see to Stoneleigh, we must hurry. Do you have some part of your garment which we can use to tie this man up? He must come with us as proof of our assertions. The constable in Brighton will give us aid, I am sure."

Charlotte pulled the cord from her hood out of its casing and gave it to Harry. Afterward, as she tended to her father, she tore the ruffles from her muslin gown for bandages. She helped him recline in her lap, tears starting to her eyes at the sight of his chalky white face, damp with perspiration, and the feel of his unearthly cold skin.

"You must get to the Prince," Sir John breathed. "Only Prinny can keep the ship from sailing. Once Stoneleigh is gone, his life is forfeit. Thaxted will see to it. I know that now."

"Don't talk. Save your strength," Charlotte whispered. "We will go to the Prince." She began packing his wound with the muslin of her gown, stuffing it hard between his bloody waistcoat and the seeping cut.

Harry tied the postillion to the back of his own horse, whose reins were fixed to the carriage. After seeing Sir John and Charlotte settled into the town chariot, he mounted the leader himself and soon had the conveyance speeding back toward Brighton.

Forty

"Will he live?" the Prince asked, his round, rather florid face creased with concern. The hour was very late, nearly one o'clock. His Royal Highness was entertaining a few select guests and would be until two or three o'clock in the morning as was his habit.

Charlotte held her cherry-velvet cloak over the dark-red stains on her gown—the residue from her father's serious injuries—and responded with a lump in her throat. "The surgeon could not say, only that he would make every effort."

"Then he is in God's hands," the Prince said quietly, patting her on the shoulder. He then directed his attention to Harry. "Only what now are we to do about Stoneleigh? Lewes, you say?"

Harry nodded. "Yes. I overheard Thaxted's henchmen discussing their intentions while Sir John was battling the marquis."

"He's very clever, that one. But we ought to have enough time to reach Lewes before the tide becomes our enemy. I shall go with you."

"Oh, no, Your Royal Highness," Charlotte said, stepping forward and dropping an instinctive curtsy. "I never meant to place you in any danger when I begged for you to fulfill your promise to me. I thought perhaps your Light Dragoons might suffice to see the task accomplished."

A warm light swept over the Prince's face. He beamed proudly as he said, "I am a great swordsman. I was at Waterloo, you know."

Charlotte felt her heart give pause. She had heard the Prince truly believed he had served alongside Wellington's army. But to her knowledge he had not set foot once off English soil during the course of the entire war. Was he as mad as his father, poor King George III, who was known to stare at the floor, his white hair and beard flowing about his head wildly, as he cried out, "I am looking into hell!"

"Now why do you look at me in that manner?" he queried, then with a wink added, "If you and I know the truth, what does it matter? My heart was with them all. You are right in one thing, however, a detachment of the Tenth would serve our purposes well, but I still mean to go with you. After all, it is not often a prince may go on a real adventure."

Charlotte was surprised how quickly the Prince delivered his orders. Within a few minutes, his coach was pulled round and six mettlesome horses stamped restively in harness.

The trip to Lewes, behind His Royal Highness' fine horseflesh, was accomplished quickly and without mishap. When the captain of the ship was roused from his slumbers, he was astonished to learn he had a prisoner on board unbeknownst to him. It was not difficult to discover Stoneleigh's whereabouts and a few minutes more saw the viscount, still unconscious from the blow to his head, again cradled in Charlotte's lap.

"I think we should take him to Ashurst," she said, looking up at the Prince as he ascended the coach.

When he settled himself opposite her, he directed his commands to the footman preparing to close the door. "Ashurst," he stated firmly. "Give the horses the office to start." He then concerned himself with Stoneleigh. Once satisfied that he was well, if not conscious, he said, "That was conducted in good order, don't you think, Miss Amberley? I ought to have had a military career like my brother the Duke of York. Pity he got caught up in that wretched scandal with Mrs. Clark. Quite ruined his career. Yes, I believe military service might have suited me more than waiting about, hoping one day to become King. But enough of my woes, tell me more of Thaxted's schemes. I don't think it wise to try him for any of his crimes—couldn't abide the scandal—but what do you think of the notion of banishing him from England?"

Charlotte, who was watching Stoneleigh's silent face and stroking his cold cheek with her finger, had only barely heard the Prince. Forgetting she was speaking to His Royal Highness, she responded, "I don't care if you banish him to Hades, only make certain he can never touch any of us again."

"What an excellent idea you have there," he responded, chortling. "But I don't believe I have that much power. Hades, you say?"

Charlotte looked up at him and, seeing the twinkle in his eye, realized how bold she had been. "Oh, I am sorry, Your Royal Highness. I did not mean to seem impertinent. I spoke only the angry thoughts of my heart."

"Very understandable," he responded. "And don't worry your head about Stoneleigh, m'dear. He's as strong as they come. A day or two between his own sheets, and he'll be restored completely to health. A little cupping might do the trick, and a leech or two for good measure. I will instruct the surgeon myself, see if I won't."

* * *

Lord Stoneleigh drifted through dream after dream, climbing toward the light that was afflicting his eyes in hopes of extinguishing it. His nightmares had been a strange mixture of night and day, of swords and ships, of beasts and dragons, of Charlotte, her father, and of Harry. Vermin crawled across his legs, and he found he was bound by chains and couldn't move. His skin itched where he had been bitten by lice.

At last he was awakening, or thought he was, or perhaps it was another dream. But he felt the whisper coolness of damp grass on his face, with light everywhere. The blades moved across his cheeks, gently caressing him, and then across his lips. How soft the grass was. How cool and damp. The wetness trickled between his dry lips and tasted strangely of salt.

He found it difficult to breathe of a sudden, for there was a weight upon his chest that made a very strange gasping sound. He moved his hand to touch the object and found his fingers entwined in a woman's hair.

He awoke with a start, his head aching furiously, and realized that the woman on his chest was sobbing. "Will you ever forgive me, my love?" He recognized Charlotte's voice. Why was she so distraught? "Pray don't leave me. It was all my fault. I know I have only myself to blame, only don't leave me! Don't leave me, Edward, I beg of you."

Stoneleigh's mind was not completely clear and so he asked, "But where am I going, my darling, and why are you crying?"

"Edward!" Charlotte cried, rising from his chest and caressing his face with her hands. "Oh, my love, my love! You've come back to me!" She kissed him on his cheeks and chin and on his lips, and then he knew why he had tasted salt. She had been crying and kissing him, and her tears had wetted his lips.

"Whatever is the matter?" he asked, gazing at her fondly.

He watched her lip quiver. "Everything and nothing! You are alive, and that is all that matters. Edward, you have been unconscious for days, and it is all because I—I had you kidnapped."

Stoneleigh squeezed his eyes shut, forcing his brain to function better. He felt as if a thousand ocean waves were crashing over and over in his brain, making it nigh on impossible to concentrate. "Did someone hit me?" he asked.

"Yes, very hard. I thought you were dead. It happened at the farmhouse where I had arranged to meet my father and have you abducted."

He smiled. "I thought it might have been something like that. How very romantic, but wouldn't it have been better if your father had not been present? One does not ordinarily elope with one's papa-in-law!"

"Not eloped, simpleton," she whispered affectionately. "Kidnapped."

"I seem to remember something now—yes, your very strange and very urgent letter. I was on my guard instantly. Now I recall," he opened his eyes and drew her closer to him, petting her head. "Did Harry find you?"

"Yes, he saved me."

"Then I am content. I trust all is settled. Only when shall we fix the date, Charlotte? If you are of a mind to, I think once my head clears—perhaps in a day or two, we ought to seek a Special License and be done with it. What do you say?"

Charlotte pulled away from him slightly, smoothing the collar of his nightshirt. She looked into his eyes and said, "You must have a brain fever, dearest. You cannot possibly wish to marry me now when you must know I arranged for you to be kidnapped. I am very wicked, Edward. I—I suspect it is fortunate the whole incident occurred, for now you know precisely the sort of woman I really am."

"I do, indeed," he responded quietly. "The sort who would go to any length for those she loved. Now, no more nonsense. You will marry me, and the sooner the better."

"Oh, Edward," she sighed, again pressing her lips to his.

After a moment, when she had released him, he queried, "Where is Thaxted?"

"His Royal Highness banished him from England forever. He is gone already, I think. First to Calais and then Italy."

"The Prince knows of my abduction then?"

Charlotte explained the whole of it at that moment, beginning with the large man who struck him hard over the head, the sword-fight between her father and the marquis, and ending with the Prince's insistence upon fetching Stoneleigh himself from Lewes.

Stoneleigh ran his finger over her cheeks and chin. "Is your father all right? Is he alive?"

Charlotte smiled, "Very much so. It would appear he is very much like you—a little too stubborn to die easily."

"I am glad. It would not do to have to wait for a period of mourning before we are wed."

Charlotte pulled further away from him and took his hands in hers. She dropped to the floor on her knees that she might look him straight in the eye. "Edward, are you very certain? After all, when I think of what my father and I nearly did to you—besides Papa's terrible deed when he attempted to elope with Elizabeth—it seems the height of absurdity that you would still wish to align yourself with my family. Heavens, man! I nearly got you killed!"

"My own stupidity nearly got me killed, Charlotte, not you. I knew you were acting out of pique from my having *put you through your paces.* And I knew Thaxted meant to do me harm."

"How did you know as much?"

"Let us just say that his hatred of me was not a closely guarded secret."

Charlotte's face crumpled. "And I led you straight into his wretched trap. You don't know how dreadful it was to see that horrid man lift that club over your head! I'll never forgive myself for that!"

"Pray, don't, Charlotte," he said. "If I were so green as to have allowed myself to be hit over the head, I should have received nothing less than I deserved had I died because of it. I won't hear of your continuing to blame yourself. Enough. Besides, had I behaved from the first in a more gentlemanly fashion toward you, none of these difficulties would have arisen anyway—so, really, it is I who am to blame. I daresay instead of suffering the strangest dreams and nightmares for these several days and more, we should have been planning our future together, celebrating our betrothal, and arguing over where to enjoy a honeymoon."

"Then I am forgiven?" she queried, sniffing loudly.

"Am I?"

"A thousand times yes!" she cried and threw herself again on his chest.

He held her tightly to him for a long moment, his mind still washing about unsteadily. He moved his chin and then his shoulders. He scratched at his neck. "Why the devil do I itch, so."

"Lice," she said, drawing back from him. "They're gone now, but you are left with a few sores yet. We couldn't keep you from scratching in your sleep. I'm afraid you were kept in the hold of a ship infested with these creatures. If it is of any consolation, I have a few tender spots myself from having held you cradled on my lap when we returned from Lewes." She touched his face lovingly, tears again springing to her eyes. "Edward, I'm so glad you're alive. You've no idea!"

"You are a little fond of me then?"

"A little, perhaps."

When a scratching sounded on the door, she hurriedly explained that his house was quite full of guests. "Perhaps it shouldn't be, but His Royal Highness suggested that for the sake of reducing the possibility of scandal, you were to give a country party—though I don't know what he would have suggested next if you had died."

Stoneleigh laughed, then winced, the activity of laughing causing the waves to crash more loudly within his brain. "Whom, precisely, have I been entertaining?"

"My father, for one, though he has been quite ill. He lost a great amount of blood from his duel with Thaxted. Emily and the Colonel are here to give my presence an appearance of propriety. Selena and Maude . . . and Harry, of course."

He smiled faintly. "Of course. Is he still quite smitten with her?"

"And she with him," Charlotte responded quietly, running her finger over his chin and cheeks and brow.

"Well, it would seem that my party has all the appearance of an engagement celebration. You could not, therefore, have refused me anyway, Charlie."

Charlotte blinked. "You called me *Charlie?*"

"I have been wanting to do so ever since I first heard you addressed as such. My dearest, Charlie.

I'm so glad you found me." With a great effort, he lifted a hand and, placing it gently at the back of her neck, drew her close and kissed her.

The scratching on the door sounded again, followed by the entrance of Henry and Sir John.

"How is the patient?" the baronet asked, walking slowly into the chamber. Catching sight of Stoneleigh, he continued, "Well, by Jove, you are alive still. Thank God."

Henry came rushing forward to look at Lord Stoneleigh. "You are not as white as you were even this morning, is he, Papa?"

"White, eh?" Stoneleigh queried.

"Yes, like the chalk cliffs." Apparently satisfied with Stoneleigh's progress, he then immediately turned to Charlotte and addressed a subject nearer to his young heart. "Will you go sea-bathing with me tomorrow? Nurse is not half as much fun and never lets me jump off the top rung of the ladder. It would only require two hours getting there and two back."

"Henry, do mind your manners a little," Charlotte implored her brother. "Lord Stoneleigh has just come back from the brink of death. Isn't there something you'd like to say to him?"

"Oh, yes, sir. I do beg your pardon. Well, since you are not going to die, would you like to go sea-bathing with us tomorrow? Nurse says it is most beneficial to one's health."

Stoneleigh laughed. "If I am able, I most certainly will."

"Go away, scamp," Charlotte said. "You may visit his lordship later. And we won't be journeying back to Brighton for a few more days, so you will have to find some other form of amusement."

He showed the strongest disappointment for about five seconds, after which, a beatific expression overcame his small face. "I couldn't have gone to the sea, anyway," he cried. "Budgett in

314

the stables promised to let me muck the stalls if I were very good. And I have been very good, haven't I, Papa?"

Sir John patted the top of his head. "Yes, indeed, my son."

Henry needed no more encouragement than that and was off at a dead run, the stables his next objective.

Sir John, who was himself looking quite pale still, drew a chair forward. When he sat down, he winced and remained in a bent position. Charlotte could see he was in considerable pain.

"Papa, you ought to retire to your bed," she suggested softly.

"I wanted first to see if Stoneleigh had finally come round. Now that I see he has, I feel I must speak."

"You needn't, sir," Stoneleigh said. "With your permission, your daughter and I are to be married. Whatever difficulties have marred our previous relationship, I intend to forget the past completely. Would you be willing to begin again?"

To Charlotte's eye, her father appeared to have aged ten years in the past few days. His vigor was gone, perhaps mostly owing to the severity of his injury but in part because of the blow Thaxted's treachery and his own wrongdoings had brought upon his soul.

Sir John spoke slowly. "How do I recompense you for all the evil I have wrought? I have no defence except to say I was a blind man until the moment Thaxted drew his sword from my side. Then it seemed as if I understood everything—as if I'd received a sort of vision from heaven. Elizabeth weighs terribly on my heart. Whatever could have possessed me—she was little more than an innocent." Tears slid down his cheeks.

Charlotte glanced at Stoneleigh, wondering how he would respond to this confession of her father's indicating he had meant to take advantage of Elizabeth's weak mind. The viscount stared up at the ceiling, his face lined with pain. It was obvious the memories hurt him. "I had once wanted to destroy you, Sir John, because of my sister. But as the weeks and years rolled by, you seemed to be living out your own devastation. I won't deny that my heart still burns with anger toward you," here he drew his gaze away from the memories which had kept his eyes fixed anywhere but on the baronet's face and turned to regard Sir John. "But I will forgive you, for Charlotte's sake. We will not speak of it again."

He extended his hand and Sir John took it in his. He held it fast. "And the rest?"

"Charlotte spoke correctly in her letter to me when she said you had fallen under the influence of a bad man. He is gone. Pray let us begin from here. You have a son to raise and, lord willing, grandchildren to enjoy." He smiled faintly. "If I can rise from this sickbed soon, you may give your daughter to me in matrimony, and I will consider every wrong made right."

Charlotte watched her father struggle to keep his countenance. In the end, he merely gave Stoneleigh's hand a final squeeze and said, "Good lad, good lad," then rose slowly to leave the room.

When he was gone, Charlotte, still on her knees, laid her head next to Stoneleigh's. The windows were open and a breeze drew the thin muslin under-drapes billowing into the room, carrying with it the faint sounds of laughter.

"Who is that?" Stoneleigh queried.

"Maude and Harry. You will never guess! She has—"

"—has wisely accepted his hand in marriage."

"Yes."

He forced her to look at him. "Did you hound

her very fiercely to make so sensible and wise an alliance?"

Charlotte pouted. "No. Well, only a little. She loves him, you see."

"And what of Selena? I suppose you have designs for her?"

Charlotte found herself blushing a little. "As it happens, Alfred Knight has decided to come to Brighton for the rest of the summer.

"Alfred Knight? You mean that red-haired young man who followed her around like a puppy a year or so ago?"

"The very one."

"Both your friends are fortunate to have the benefit of your interests in their affairs."

"And you are fortunate to have had the benefit of their hurt pride."

"How is this?" he queried.

"I would never have come to Brighton otherwise," she said, "except by their insistence and my father's. Don't you think that rather odd?"

"I consider it an act of God and nothing less." He paused for a moment and then added, "Or Nemesis? Tell me, Charlotte, which is it? Are you to be a blessing to me or have you come to punish me for my pride and arrogance?"

Charlotte touched her hand gently to his cheek, then pinched him soundly. "Both," she cried.

"Vixen," he whispered, slipping his hand about her shoulder and again holding her close to his heart.

Author's Note

The seaport of Lewes exists only in my imagination. By the nineteenth century, many of the natural harbors along England's southern coast were silted up. The town of Rye, for instance, is now a full two miles from the sea though at one time it was a bustling seaport.

About the Author

Valerie King lives with her family in Glendale, Arizona. Among her many Zebra regencies are CAPTIVATED HEARTS, A LADY'S GAMBIT, LOVE MATCH and CUPID'S TOUCH. Valerie is currently working on her next Zebra regency, which will be published in June 1994. Valerie loves to hear from her readers and you may write to her c/o Zebra Books.

A Memorable Collection of Regency Romances

BY ANTHEA MALCOLM AND VALERIE KING

THE COUNTERFEIT HEART   (3425, $3.95/$4.95)
by Anthea Malcolm
Nicola Crawford was hardly surprised when her cousin's betrothed
disappeared on some mysterious quest. Anyone engaged to such an
unromantic, but handsome man was bound to run off sooner or later.
Nicola could never entrust her heart to such a conventional, but so
deucedly handsome man. . . .

THE COURTING OF PHILIPPA   (2714, $3.95/$4.95)
by Anthea Malcolm
Miss Philippa was a very successful author of romantic novels. Thus
she was chagrined to be snubbed by the handsome writer Henry
Ashton whose own books she admired. And when she learned he considered love stories completely beneath his notice, she vowed to teach
him a thing or two about the subject of love. . . .

THE WIDOW'S GAMBIT   (2357, $3.50/$4.50)
by Anthea Malcolm
The eldest of the orphaned Neville sisters needed a chaperone for a
London season. So the ever-resourceful Livia added several years to
her age, invented a deceased husband, and became the respectable
Widow Royce. She was certain she'd never regret abandoning her girl-
hood until she met dashing Nicholas Warwick. . . .

A DARING WAGER   (2558, $3.95/$4.95)
by Valerie King
Ellie Dearborne's penchant for gaming had finally led her to ruin. It
seemed like such a lark, wagering her devious cousin George that she
would obtain the snuffboxes of three of society's most dashing peers
in one month's time. She could easily succeed, too, were it not for
that exasperating Lord Ravenworth. . . .

THE WILLFUL WIDOW   (3323, $3.95/$4.95)
by Valerie King
The lovely young widow, Mrs. Henrietta Harte, was not all inclined to
pursue the sort of romantic folly the persistent King Brandish had in
mind. She had to concentrate on marrying off her penniless sisters
and managing her spendthrift mama. Surely Mr. Brandish could fit in
with her plans somehow . . .

*Available wherever paperbacks are sold, or order direct from the
Publisher. Send cover price plus 50¢ per copy for mailing and
handling to Zebra Books, Dept. 4381, 475 Park Avenue South,
New York, N.Y. 10016. Residents of New York and Tennessee
must include sales tax. DO NOT SEND CASH. For a free Zebra/
Pinnacle catalog please write to the above address.*